PRIEST

CATHLEEN COLE
FRANK JENSEN

C&J NOVELS LLC

Copyright © 2022 by Cathleen Cole

All rights reserved.

No part of this book may be reproduced in any form or by any electronic or mechanical means, including information storage and retrieval systems, without written permission from the author, except for the use of brief quotations in a book review.

Any references to historical events, real people, or real places are used fictitiously. Names, characters, and places are products of the author's imagination.

Publisher: C&J Novels LLC

Cover designed by: Kari March Designs

ASIN: B0B3R69ZGZ

This is dedicated to my family. Thank you for all your love and support.

TRIGGER WARNINGS

This book is meant for readers 18+. Some content may be unsuitable for some readers. For a full list of warnings, please visit https://www.cathleencolenovels.com/tropes-warnings Once there, swipe to find the series and book you're looking for.

CHAPTER 1

Jenny

"Ugh, I'm going to punch Hush in the face when I see him," I muttered, as I stood in front of the very last door I ever wanted to go through.

It was a gorgeous arid morning and the birds were singing. My heart was beating so hard in my chest, it felt like it was going to come crashing out. It was Hush's fault I was standing in front of his MC's clubhouse this early, and having a damn panic attack at the thought of seeing Priest again.

I'd met Priest in Texas when he and some of his brothers first came out to help the Austin MC celebrate a wedding, and then stayed to help with some trouble. I'd been instantly attracted to the man. We'd started getting to know each other and ended up spending one night together, not that anything promiscuous had happened…unfortunately.

No, Jenny. It's better that you didn't sleep with him since he texted you and told you that nothing could happen between us.

After he'd gone home to Tucson we'd exchanged texts and calls for a while and I thought something was building between us. I was already half in love with the stupid brute. Then he'd sent that text and I hadn't heard from him again. There'd been no real explanation as to why he cut ties with me and it'd hurt me deeply. I hadn't had long to overanalyze the situation however, because my life had spiraled out of control only a few weeks later.

I was close friends with the women of the Texas MC, but I hadn't been available to help them when they were going through hard times over the last year because my grams had taken a turn for the worse. She was the reason I'd moved to Austin in the first place. I'd been so busy taking care of her that I hadn't been available to help and that hurt my heart, but they hadn't minded. I got the feeling they hadn't wanted to put me in danger. The only good thing to come from Grams' sickness was I had been too busy to think about Priest.

Grams died three weeks ago and had taken a huge chunk of my heart with her. My mom hadn't been able to leave Tucson to help take care of her, so after losing Grams, I came back home. I hated to leave the friends I'd made in Austin, but I'd needed to come back and share in my grief with Mom. We were both lost without Grams.

My hair was slicked back into a ponytail, the curls cascading down my back in a waterfall. I'd always hated my curly hair and usually kept it shorter, but it'd grown out over the last six months and reached my waist now. If I didn't tame it I ended up looking like the Scottish girl from the Disney movie, only with chocolate brown hair instead of shocking red. Brown eyes, brown hair, and my curvy figure made me a pretty average woman, or so I'd always thought. Priest had been one of the few men who'd made me feel special.

I steeled my nerves and went to knock on the door. Only, my knuckles didn't rap on the wood. They were poised a few inches from the door as I tried to pull myself together. I'd only answered Hush's call because…well, it was Hush. You never passed up the opportunity to talk to him, because it happened so rarely. Plus, he was a friend and I'd walk over hot coals for the people in my life that I loved.

Today was the first day I'd showered in a week. I was convinced I could live the rest of my life out on the couch, surrounded by candy wrappers as I ate my feelings. My hands went down and smoothed over my hips. They were ample and plump and the last thing I needed was to gorge on Ho-Ho's, but a girl had to hold the crushing sadness at bay somehow.

My work had happily transferred me back to Tucson when I'd asked and hadn't batted an eye when I told them I'd needed time off. Mom was still working. She dealt with her grief by throwing herself into every project she could find. I sat at home watching sad movies and sobbing into my ice cream. Who could blame me?

That just meant my curves were a tad fuller on my five-six frame these days. The door swung open and all I could do was gasp as the biggest man I'd ever seen in person—and that was saying something because Priest was a huge man and this guy was even bigger—mowed me down.

"Fucking Christ!" he bellowed as we both went down in a tangle of limbs. He landed on top of me, forcing all the air out of my lungs when his body made contact with mine.

Lying there, smothering underneath him, while he continued to throw every cuss word in the book at me. I wondered if this was how I'd die? A bit dramatic, but he weighed a ton. The only plus side to this was he was packed with muscles. I could feel each one pressed up against me. If I had to die, there were worse ways to go.

"Jenny?"

Oh no.

I buried my face in the bare chest covered in tattoos that was hovering above me. He smelled like man and sweat, but it wasn't until I'd heard the voice coming from the doorway that my heart started racing and my blood heated.

Not now. Not like this.

"Hellfire, if you don't get off her I'm going to tear you a new asshole."

I peeked out from behind Hellfire's chest—what kind of name was that—and saw Priest glaring down at both of us. I was already short of breath, but now my lungs gave up entirely as I exhaled. He looked furious—and damn delicious—and I wasn't sure if it was because I was here, or that his MC brother was currently lying between my splayed thighs. Either way, we were in trouble.

"Aw, what the fuck?" Another guy walked up from somewhere behind us and crossed his muscular arms over his chest. The cut he wore told me he was a part of the MC, but even if that hadn't clued me in the attitude and tattoos would have. He looked a bit younger than Priest, and had tattoos that went from the backs of his fingers all the way up under the sleeves of his t-shirt. He also had them on one side of his neck and barbed wire on the side of his head where his dark hair was cut short.

His glower made me nervous and I was ashamed to admit I wouldn't want to meet him in a dark alley. "Lockout told me we weren't allowed to fuck outside the clubhouse. Who changed the rules for them?" He motioned toward us.

My jaw dropped, cheeks heating at his crude words. A crowd was beginning to form now and Hellfire was still lying on top of me. He grinned down at me and gave me a wink. I blinked up at him in confusion. He had originally started to haul his bulky body off me, but as soon as Priest had arrived, he'd stayed put. Was he trying to piss Priest off? If so, it was working.

"They're not fucking, Butcher," Priest snarled at the man.

My eyes widened. I'd never seen him look so angry before. Granted I hadn't known him for long, but he'd always been sweet to me, at least up until that last text.

His hand came down and grabbed Hellfire's shoulder, wrenching him off me. Hellfire stumbled to his feet, telling Priest none of this was his fault. I was too busy sucking oxygen back into my lungs to care.

For some reason Priest was sans shirt as well and unlike when I was observing Butcher my eyes lingered as I checked out all the packed muscle and tattoos on Priest. Most of these guys were loaded with ink. It didn't surprise me, bikers and tattoos seemed to go together. I still didn't know much about MCs, though what I did know I'd learned from the Austin Chapter and my friends.

Priest wasn't as covered in ink as some of these other guys but he had them on his arms and two on his chest. One tattoo swirled around his nipple and my mouth watered. I wanted to trace my tongue over it. Heat deepened the color in my face as the men kept arguing in front of me.

"Jesus are none of you gonna help the poor girl up?"

Hearing the southern drawl, I tilted my head backward until Hush came into view.

Priest finally made a move to help, but not before I was hauled to my feet by Hush and gripped in a bone-jarring hug.

"Hey, Girlie."

"Hi, Hush," I wheezed.

He loosened his grip enough that I could suck air into my lungs for the second time that day. I was surprised at the welcome. Hush and I had been friendly back in Texas, but not hugging friendly. He'd hardly touched anyone there. You were lucky if he spoke to you. I could always tell there was something deep and upsetting that weighed him down. It'd drawn me to him, even though he kept most people at arm's length. Something had changed with him. I had a feeling that 'something' was the gorgeous woman who was walking up behind him, smiling.

"Is she yours?" I whispered to him. "She's beautiful."

"Yeah." He let me go and turned to grin at the woman. "Jenny, this is my old lady, Seek. Seek, this is another friend from Texas, Jenny."

Before I had a chance to raise my hand Seek had pulled me into her arms for her own hug. I was jealous of her athletically trim body. She could probably bench press me if she wanted to. Then again, my thighs would probably deter her. I was what my mother termed 'pear shaped'. Big booty and big thighs. I'd grown to love them—most days.

"Hi Jenny!" Seek said while squeezing me almost as hard as her old man had. "I've really been looking forward to meeting you."

My eyes went from Seek, to Hush, to a glowering Priest who was waiting on the sidelines. He was the last person I wanted to speak to. It was so embarrassing to have to even see him again, let alone now with everyone's eyes on us. "I'm so glad to meet you, too."

"Come on," she said, looping her arm through mine. "We'll go fill you in on why we asked you to come."

I nodded and walked with her. Before we could brush past Priest—who was still blocking the entrance to the clubhouse—his fingers wrapped around my bicep, pulling us to a stop.

"Before we do that, Seek, I need a moment with Jenny." His deep voice sent shivers skating over my skin. I didn't want to cause problems, so I kept my mouth shut, but I didn't really want to talk to him. Hush had asked me here on behalf of the MC and Priest was part of that club. I knew, as soon as I had agreed to see Hush, that I'd have to deal with Priest, too. There was no way to avoid any member of the club. It wasn't easy to keep my mouth shut, but I managed by gnawing on the inside of my cheek.

I'd tried to tell myself many times since I'd met him that my reaction to him was ridiculous. He was just a man and one who hadn't wanted me after all. My body didn't give a flying shit. His hand was gripping me tightly and it made a thrill race down my spine. My body wanted him and the way my heart was pounding in my chest was a clear indication that my mind was being out voted on our feelings toward this biker. It left me a twisted mess because as much as a part of me didn't want to be alone with him, the rest of me did.

Seek gave me a curious look. "Not to be rude, Priest, but it sort of looks like she would rather not speak with you."

My eyes widened and I tried to wipe the emotion off my face. I hadn't realized that others could read the conflict in my expression.

"Seek," Hush growled, yanking her away from me and against his body. "Let him talk to the lady," he muttered, dragging her through the clubhouse door.

"Nice to see manhandling is the way you all deal with things," I said, before I realized the words had come out of my mouth.

The crowd chuckled at that, but Priest's scowl darkened. His fingers tightened on my arm and without another word he also dragged me inside.

CHAPTER 2

Priest

I never knew what a sly dick Hush could be. When he said he had a friend who could help us with Caitlyn, I should have realized what he was doing. I would've if I'd known Jenny was back in Tucson. She hadn't told me. Not that it was surprising since I'd cut ties with her about six months ago. She wasn't obligated to tell me anything about her life, yet I was still pissed.

Her skin was warm and soft and I had to fight the urge to crush her against me and kiss her. The need building up within me was making me extra jittery and angry about the situation, something I became aware of as she struggled in my hold.

"I can walk on my own, Priest. There's no need to drag me back to your cave like a Neanderthal."

Pausing, I glanced back at her. She was practically having to run to keep up. She was only about five-six and I had a full foot on her. She was trotting along behind me, trying to keep pace with my longer legs.

"Thank you," she said in a clipped tone as I slowed down.

A grin formed on my face. I loved her fiery nature. We'd only met a little over a year ago, but this woman had burrowed her way beneath my skin. I'd been ready to consider making her my old lady, even though she lived in Texas at the time. That had come to a screeching halt, though, and I'd ended things with her. I deserved the angry look she was flashing at me.

"Come on, Jenny," I muttered and took her hand instead, slowing my pace a bit more. She was always a ball of energy, but that didn't mean she had a chance of keeping up with my ground-eating stride. She followed me upstairs, not pulling her hand from mine, and let me lead her into my apartment.

We all lived on the compound. Everyone preferred it that way so we could all be close by when needed. The single guys, without families, had one bedroom, dorm style rooms. The rest of us had these apartments. All of the officers had apartments as well—except Hush who'd given up his when he left. Lockout already had a few of the prospects cleaning out his old one and he'd be moving in soon.

I shut the door then turned to find Jenny's chocolate colored eyes watching me closely. The first day I'd seen her, those eyes had drawn me in from across a crowd. Her hair had been loose and wild and I'd longed to run my fingers through it. Her hair suited her small heart-shaped face and wild, fiery temper. Something I learned later after I'd started getting to know her. Now she was a foot away from me and those eyes were disarming me again. That wild hair was tamed into a ponytail and something inside of me was screaming at me to let it loose. To give it that wild 'just fucked' look.

Despite being a private person, I'd almost called her more times than I could count to explain my last text. But to do that would undo the whole point of sending the message. Seeing her standing before me, now that things had settled down a bit for me, made me hopeful. Maybe we could pick back up where we left off.

The wary look on her face and the hurt lurking there in her gaze were telling. She wasn't going to make this easy. I wasn't sure whether I wanted to give Hush a hug of gratitude from one brother to another, or punch him in his fucking face. Probably the latter. The asshole should have told me that she was the friend he was calling, and that she was here so that I could go talk to her instead of ambushing both of us this way.

"Look, Jenny. I'm sorry for the way I left things between us."

"It's fine."

Every man on earth knew what that meant. Shit was *not* fine. It was anything *but* fine and the hurt-filled expression on her face deepened. It tugged at my heart and I hated that I'd put it there. I'd planned to tell her what was going on. She would've understood, but I'd been sworn to secrecy. It was stupid, and juvenile, but my ex-wife had pleaded with me to keep her secret.

We may have divorced years ago, but it'd been amicable—eventually—and Wendy was a good woman, so I hadn't explained. I'd just let Jenny go because, at the time, I was being pulled in too many directions and she was the only thing I didn't have a concrete commitment to. Was it a dick move? Absolutely. Did I regret it now? Fuck yes.

The awkward silence spread between us. "What brought you back to Tucson?" It wasn't what I should be asking. I should be telling her why I'd cut things off—Wendy's secret be damned—but she just seemed so damn uncomfortable and I hated that I was the cause of it.

Tears welled in Jenny's eyes and panic had me reaching for her. She stepped back and shook her head, rubbing the back of her hand over her eyes. She refused to look at me.

I felt like a pile of dog shit. This was not going the way I'd planned. If the whole Silverbells mystery hadn't popped up a few weeks ago, I would have been on my way back to Texas, to talk to Jenny and make things right. It'd always been my intention to get her back. Not that I'd had her in the first place, but I wanted to change that.

"What-"

"Sorry," she said softly. "I moved back a week ago because my grams died."

"Shit." I scraped a hand over the rough stubble of my short hair. Keeping it neat and trimmed down was a habit left over from my military days and I still preferred it. Long hair was too much work.

Jenny had told me she'd moved to Texas in the first place to be with her ailing grandmother. My question had put more misery and sadness in her eyes and I wanted to kick myself. "I'm so sorry, Jenny."

She didn't fight it this time when I tugged her into my arms. She melted against me and I had to bite back the groan building inside my chest. Her body was full and felt perfect resting against me. Before everything had taken a turn for the worse I'd been biding my time before I could get between those rounded thighs. The need hadn't gone anywhere. If anything it'd built during our time apart.

Right now it was about comforting her though. My hand smoothed over her as I rubbed it up and down her back. As soon as I'd pulled her in for the hug she'd started crying. Her face was pressed into my chest, her tears wetting my skin. It reminded me that I hadn't put my shirt or cut back on after Hell and I had gone a few rounds of boxing in the gym.

I was sweaty and had inadvertently brought up a recent trauma for her, yet she was snuggling in closer to me. My heart sped up, urging me to protect her from everything in this world. The need to fix all her problems and claim her as mine was riding me hard. If I made one wrong move it'd put me right back in the damn dog house, however, so I held her close and let her sob it out.

After a few minutes she settled down and pulled away from me, wiping her face again while sniffling. I had to fight down the urge to yank her back against me. That wasn't going to win me any points at the moment so I resisted it.

"Sorry," she mumbled, cheeks flushing with embarrassment. "It's been hard..."

"I'm sure. I know how close you were with Gail." I'd met her grandmother once and we'd hit it off right away. It'd surprised me that the spunky old lady hadn't cared that her granddaughter was getting involved with a biker. If it had bothered her she'd never made it known.

"Why did you bring me up here, Priest?" she asked with a sigh. It wasn't irritation, but an overflow of emotion that caused the question.

The release of tears had probably felt good, but seeing me was clearly bringing those emotions to the breaking point.

I crossed my arms over my chest to keep from touching her. If I did, I would kiss her and that would likely just get me slapped. "I wanted to apologize to you."

"I appreciate that. Don't worry, I'm still willing to help with whatever I can for the club, despite what happened between us."

"That's not what I'm worried about, Jenny." We knew she was trustworthy, thanks to her involvement with the Texas Chapter. Even if she refused to help us, we wouldn't hold it against her. "I just want to make sure you're okay and explain what happened-"

A knock on the door interrupted me. A growl of frustration building in my chest, I turned and yanked the door open. I instantly swallowed my irritation because Caitlyn was standing there, silent as the day we'd first brought her home. We'd found her out in the Silverbell area where she and her mother had gone missing.

Seek had called us out to search after the cops had given up. Seek being in Search and Rescue, and having two badass canines meant we'd ended up finding the girl and her mother. Unfortunately, her mom was dead at the hands of some unknown group of men. We'd found them before they'd had a chance to harm Caitlyn, much to our relief.

"Hey, Sweetheart," I said, squatting down so I wasn't towering over the little girl.

She gave me a hesitant smile, her eyes moving past me to land on Jenny. I could feel the stunned silence behind me and cringed. I hadn't even gotten to clear up what'd happened between us and now I had to explain this.

Caitlyn had latched onto me as soon as we'd found her. She'd somehow sensed that I could be trusted and would protect her. She refused to speak—a child therapist we'd taken her to said the trauma she'd endured was keeping her mute—but she obviously felt safe with me. I was damn good with kids and they seemed to sense that. They always gravitated my way. I didn't mind at all. Caitlyn was a sweet girl who'd been dealt a shitty hand.

"Caitlyn, this is my friend Jenny." I glanced over my shoulder at Jenny. "This is Caitlyn. The reason Hush asked you to come here today." I stood and held out my hand for the girl. She took it, and I told Jenny, "We'll drop her back off with Sylvia and I'll take you to the meeting. Lockout and Riptide are probably getting impatient anyway."

Irritation was boiling over inside of me because everything seemed to be conspiring against me. Instead of me going to Jenny and showing her that I wanted her back, she'd shown up first. Now she'd likely question whether I even wanted her or if it was just convenient. My ex had taught me a lot about women—and most of it not in a good way—so if Jenny was anything like Wendy my assessment would be spot on. There wasn't much I could do about it now. I'd used up all the time I had and I wasn't willing to piss off Lockout by making him wait longer than I already had.

"It's nice to meet you, Caitlyn," Jenny told her with a friendly smile.

Caitlyn gave her a shy smile as we walked toward a room we kept upstairs for the kids to play in. Sylvia opened the door just as we approached and the worry melted off her face.

"Sorry, Priest. I didn't even see her slip out."

"That's alright, Syl. Appreciate you watching her while we have this meeting." I introduced Sylvia and Jenny then let the sweet butt take the girl back inside the room. Caitlyn paused in the doorway, looking back at me. "Don't worry, Kid. I'll come find you as soon as this meeting is over. Deal?"

She nodded solemnly and followed Sylvia inside. As soon as the door shut Jenny launched into a tirade of questions.

Chuckling, I held up my hands to ward off the assault. "It'll be better to answer everything downstairs. Come on." I waited until we hit the stairs before telling her, "I didn't get a chance to finish our talk. I plan on doing that."

She shot me a challenging look, but didn't respond. I was just glad the sadness had departed long enough for her curiosity to get the better of her. Anything to get that look out of her eyes.

CHAPTER 3

Jenny

My curiosity was killing me as Priest led me into a room where the officers of the club, and Seek were waiting. I really wanted to know what he was going to tell me before we were interrupted. I'd fallen asleep every night for almost six months wondering why he'd suddenly pulled away. As much as I wanted to know, I was sort of afraid, too. If he told me something like I was too plain Jane to be an old lady it would break my heart.

Then Caitlyn had interrupted and now I had even more questions. Who was she? Why was she here? It was obvious she wasn't speaking to anyone since she hadn't uttered a single word, but she'd looked at Priest with such trust and hero worship it was hard not to see she felt safe with him. That made me slip a little further down that cliff I was teetering on.

Trying to find my balance around Priest was damn near impossible. One wrong move around him and I was going to tumble head over heels in love with him and that would be a death sentence to my heart and most likely my ego. He'd told me he planned to finish telling me what'd happened months ago when he broke it off, but that didn't mean that he wanted me. I couldn't allow myself to get my hopes up, it was just too dangerous. I needed to guard my heart around the man or I'd lose it and never get it back.

"What the hell took you so long?" Priest's vice president asked, glaring at him.

A muscle flexed in Priest's jaw and the sudden urge to lean up on my tiptoes and scrape my teeth over it nearly overwhelmed me. This was why he was so dangerous. He made me feel and act in ways that weren't typical of me. I wasn't a virgin, but I didn't have what anyone would call a lot of experience with men. They tended to go for the lithe beautiful women and that wasn't a descriptor anyone would use for me.

I'd had one boyfriend after high school and though we'd parted ways after a year, we'd done so on friendly terms. All the other men in my life had just been friends.

"Sorry, Rip. Lock." Priest nodded at his president.

Lockout was sitting there with a bemused look on his face as he watched Priest and me move together to sit down. I'd only met him once, but Priest had told me quite a bit about some of his MC brothers, so it sort of felt like I knew them even though I doubted they knew a thing about me. Lockout was sort of intimidating. Which was funny to think, because Priest was the one who towered over everyone—except the man from earlier, Hellfire—and had a perpetually pissed off look on his face most of the time.

"You get everything resolved?" Lockout asked with an arched brow.

Before Priest could answer, Butcher opened the door and motioned for Lockout. Thank God, because I didn't exactly want to hash out what Priest and I had—and hadn't—spoken about upstairs in front of everyone. Although with how impatient everyone was looking, I doubt they cared about the details.

"Be back in a minute," Lockout said, standing and following Butcher outside.

My hands were in my lap, twisting together as I fought not to bounce my leg. It was a nervous habit. A strong hand clamped down over my knee and squeezed. I glanced over at Priest and smiled. He knew I was fighting the urge and that was his way of helping.

We'd been bordering on dating before he'd ended things so we were left now in that awkward in-between stage of things where we didn't know every deep-seated fear, hope, and dream, but we knew just enough to have our own inside jokes. And feelings of longing. Did I mention those? Because they were persistently tapping me on the shoulder right now, as though to remind me they existed. As if I could forget, especially with his giant hand gripping my leg. I could feel a heat building, starting from my thigh and working its way upward to pool between them.

I wanted him to take me in his arms and kiss me. To tell me he'd made a mistake and he wanted me to belong to him. Stupid. It was dumb of me to want that so badly since he had essentially broken up with me, but I did.

Lockout came back in the room and all the quiet conversations the others had been having stopped. Everyone focused on him as he sat at the head of the table. His hazel eyes focused on me as he began. He explained about Seek being Search and Rescue—which I thought was so cool and I couldn't wait to pick her brain about that later—and what had been happening out in The Silverbells. He went on to explain how they'd found Caitlyn.

I couldn't contain the gasp that slipped past my lips when he said that they'd found her crouched over her mother's dead body while the men who'd kidnapped them and killed Sherry dug a grave for her out in the desert. My hand covered my mouth to keep any more outbursts contained. I adored children. I wanted a whole brood of them someday—put these child-rearing hips to use—but until that day, I settled for working with them.

Working for CPS was oftentimes heart wrenching, but when I was able to help even just one child in need it made all the troubling cases worth it. It was also how I'd met my friends and the MC over in

Texas. One of their old ladies—Julie—ended up working for us for college credits.

"Is that why she's not talking?" I asked, my eyes straying over to Priest.

He had a grim look on his face as he nodded. "I took her to a local therapist, she said all we could do was wait for Caitlyn to feel safe enough to talk to one of us. Caitlyn's been seeing her a few times a week."

I reached over and covered his hand with mine. His skin was warm and it eased something within me even though I'd been trying to comfort him. There was worry in his eyes and I wanted to erase it. He flipped his hand over and squeezed mine, his long fingers entangling with my fingers. The silence around us sank in and embarrassment rushed over me as I realized everyone was staring at us. Most of the guys wore amused expressions—I didn't even want to contemplate why—and Seek was looking at us with hearts in her eyes.

Priest's hand clamped down on mine as I tried to pull away. He snared it and kept holding it while the conversation started up again. I shot him a glare, but eventually had to ignore him, so I could focus on what the others were saying.

"We contacted Caitlyn's Aunt Sharon, but she lives on the East Coast and is disabled. She said she can't take care of her niece. Aside from her, the girl has no other family, other than her father," Hush told me.

"Who we suspect is a part of this whole thing," Riptide finished for him.

"Why?" I asked.

"According to the sister, Sherry was on the run from her husband. She had an elaborate plan to check in with her sister daily in case he found her and Caitlyn," Priest answered.

"You don't take precautions like that if the guy's not a dirtbag." The guy who spoke looked a lot younger than all the other men sitting around the table. I'd guess close to my own age of twenty-six, maybe a few years younger even. I frowned, reading his name patch. His name was Ricochet. Priest had explained to me once that each ranking member of the MC was retired or ex-military. There were older guys like Priest and Hush, but some of the others looked too young to be retired. Ricochet's dark blonde hair and bright blue eyes made him look even younger. Or maybe it was the sorrow that lurked in his eyes. It made me wonder what his story was.

"So you're looking into the father?" I asked.

"Yeah, and we're going to find out what's really going on out in The Silverbells," Seek said, eyes glinting with determination.

"Well, I'll be happy to help," I said, perking up a little. Maybe helping them with this would get my mind off losing Grams.

"No way," Priest growled next to me.

I looked over at him in shock and disappointment. Was he so adamant about getting me out of his life that he was going to reject my help with something the MC had asked me to come in on?

His eyes narrowed as he searched my face. He must have seen the confusion because he explained. "We didn't ask you here to put you in danger, Jenny. I don't want you anywhere near The Silverbells."

"Seek is helping," I pointed out.

"She was the one who brought it to our attention and we needed her dogs to help find Sherry and Caitlyn," Hush clarified. He shot Seek a warning glare. "But now she's not gettin' involved in this mess."

"What!" Seek snapped, glaring at Hush.

I winced since I'd just inadvertently started that fight for my new friend. *Serves him right for cutting her out though.*

"I was the one who started this whole thing, Hush. I brought *you* in. You're not cutting me out now." She crossed her arms over her chest and glared at her boyfriend.

Lockout cleared his throat and everyone looked at him. "This isn't up for debate, Seek. You asked the MC for help and we agreed. We're going to take care of this, but we're not putting either of you in harm's way while we figure it out."

We could all but hear her grinding her teeth in irritation. I didn't blame her, there were things we could help with…probably. I tried to stamp down my own aggravation. "So what do you need me for then?"

It came out far more aggressive than I meant. Priest squeezed my hand hard, warning me to watch my attitude.

I gave Lockout an apologetic smile. This was their club, their world. They were asking me for a favor, but I had no authority here. No woman did, it was their organization to run as they chose.

"We were hoping you could help us with Caitlyn," he answered, ignoring my surliness from before.

"I want to adopt her," Priest told me.

My jaw dropped so far it almost hit the table. "Adopt her? What makes you think that CPS is going to let a young, unmarried guy like you, with no kids, adopt a child?" I wasn't asking to be mean; it was just unlikely. Usually they wanted these kids to go to families with both a mother and father present and usually other children when possible. A safe, steady home.

"That's why Hush called you," he said, biting back his irritation at my questions. Though his restraint said that he already knew that those were problems.

"He makes the most sense out of all of us," Riptide said with a shrug.

My gaze flicked back to Priest as I tried to figure out why he would be best suited to adopt a child. I mean out of all these—mostly single—men I guess he'd do as well as any.

"I don't-"

"He's one of the few of us with kids around her age," said a voice from behind me, cutting me off.

I hadn't realized Butcher had snuck back into the room. There was another man standing next to him that I didn't recognize. A look at his cut told me his name was Toxic. He looked very much like all the rest. Older, dark hair, gorgeous, and danger emanating from every pore of his being.

Kids around Caitlyn's age.

My eyes widened in shock as Butcher's words penetrated my surprise and my heart sank. Toxic shook his head then smacked Butcher upside the head.

"What the fuck," Butcher snarled at him.

"You deserve that and I saved you from Priest doing worse," Toxic told him, then went to take his seat.

Butcher rubbed his head and shot us a baleful look. "How was I supposed to know he hadn't told her about his kids?"

"You have children?" I asked Priest in a strangled tone. The realization was just sinking in that I hadn't known him as well as I thought I had. Months of 'getting to know each other' had almost culminated in us dating and he hadn't told me anything important about himself. It made me remember back to when I'd been telling him about myself and he'd obviously been holding back from really letting me get to know him. Hurt settled over me.

Priest sighed. "I was going to tell you. I just…" He broke off and shot a glare at Butcher before meeting my gaze again. "We'll talk about this later."

"No need," I snapped, yanking my hand from his. "It's none of my business." My heart cracked down the center once again. This man was already responsible for more bruising on the organ than I should have allowed.

Hush muttered a curse under his breath and gave Butcher his own dark look, though I wasn't sure why he was mad at the man. This was Priest's fault, not Butcher's.

"Look, Jenny. We need your help makin' sure that Caitlyn stays with us. If she goes into foster care she'll be in danger. If what we suspect about her father is true and he gets to her, she's as good as dead," Hush explained.

"Have you reported this to CPS yet?" They all gave me stares that said I was crazy. "Right. Of course not. Okay. I was on leave, but I'll let them know I'm coming back to work tomorrow." I looked at Priest. "We'll set up a time for you to bring her in after I have a chance to start a file on her and notify my bosses. I'll figure out a way to make sure I end up as her permanent case manager. That gives me time to start thinking the rest of this through."

When I'd gone to Texas I'd been an assistant to one of their most prominent case managers. Too bad he'd been a dirty, evil bastard who had almost cost the lives of two of the Austin Chapter's babies and my friend and co-worker Julie. After he disappeared—much to the shock of the agency—they'd promoted me.

"Great. Thank you, Jenny," Lockout told me. He glanced over at Priest, then Hush. "I'll leave it up to you two to explain to your women further that when it suits the club to have them help we're grateful, but otherwise this is our business."

My eyes narrowed, but I didn't bother to say anything else. I understood, even if I didn't like being left out. Who was I kidding? I wasn't even an old lady, just a friend they'd asked for help with a little girl who'd found herself homeless. Clearly Lockout was confused in thinking I was Priest's 'woman'.

Seek had more cause to be angry than me and if the scowl on her face was any indication, she was furious. She too kept her mouth shut, but that could be because Hush had his hand wrapped around the nape of her neck. He was silently telling her not to speak, though none of us missed the gesture. Judging by the look on her face, she was going to be having words with him once they were alone. I didn't envy Hush at that moment.

Lockout stood up and leaned over the table, catching my gaze. "Seriously. We appreciate the favor, we'll owe you one. If you ever need any help in the future, anything, we're here for you."

"Thank you." I meant it. It was kind of nice knowing that if I had any trouble I could come to this powerful group of men with my problems and it would be handled. That's exactly what he meant too, any trouble, of any kind, they would be there.

The meeting room cleared out quickly and despite her rage, Seek stopped to give me a hug goodbye. "We need to get together one of these days. Get lunch."

"I'd love that," I told her with a happy grin.

Soon it was just Priest and I left and I turned toward him. "Well, I'll get out of your hair now."

"Jenny, wait-"

I didn't bother. The hurt was churning in my chest. He hadn't told me he had kids. I could understand not wanting me to meet them until we were official, but to not even tell me something as important as that? In all the time we'd been talking? What else hadn't he told me? Clearly a lot.

The fact that we'd lived states away should have made it easy for him to tell me something like that. It wasn't like I could pop over, unannounced, to meet his kids. It was the reason we hadn't started a relationship sooner and had only barely begun talking about one by the time he sent that text. I walked out of the room and through the clubhouse's lounging area, where the bar was.

His arm wrapped around my waist just as I reached the door, yanking me back against a hard chest. "You're not leaving until I explain." He must have jogged to keep up with me, because I'd gotten a head start on him and had practically bolted out of the building.

Who are you kidding, with those stumpy little legs compared to his? He might have only walked.

"There's nothing to explain, Priest," I said, spinning in his hold. As soon as I faced him, I shoved his chest as hard as I could.

He let his arms drop to his sides, but not because I'd pushed him. I had no hope of breaking his hold. He was too strong. He let me go because I wanted him to.

"I'll see you in a few days." With that I ran out the door. I couldn't bear to look back at him. I was too angry and hurt to deal with him right now. Too raw from my recent loss to be able to sort through what I was feeling.

CHAPTER 4

Priest

My head dropped back with a groan as Jenny ran out the door. This was one huge cluster fuck. "Shit."

"Good going, Butcher," Ricochet said with a shake of his head.

Butcher looked over from the bar and glared at me. "How was I supposed to know this asshole was keeping things from his old lady? Fuck all of you," he growled, snagging the beer Pixie held out for him and stomping out of the room.

Riptide chuckled as we all watched him go. "What are you going to do about that?" he asked, motioning to where Jenny had raced from the clubhouse like a haboob—a dirt devil—sweeping over the desert.

It was fitting because like one of those devils she was wreaking havoc with my fucking emotions. Seeing her again was like a punch to the gut and after all my plans to apologize to her and explain myself, now she wanted nothing to do with me. How had I managed to fuck things up this badly so quickly?

I sighed and shrugged. "I'll figure something out."

Hush came back downstairs, looking as miserable as I felt. "You deserve that," he said, pointing at me. "Shouldn't have jerked the girl around in the first place."

"I didn't fucking jerk her around, asshole. I had shit to deal with and couldn't do it all at once." I knew he was just getting back at me for fucking with him when he was trying to deny being interested in his old lady.

Hush's expression softened. "Yeah. Sorry, man. The guys told me about Wendy."

It didn't surprise me. There weren't many secrets amongst our brothers. That's why Butcher had called Jenny my old lady. Everyone knew I wanted her, even though I'd broken things off. Of course, in Butcher's world, the only difference between wanting and having was a matter of minutes. *And sometimes some screaming.* When I'd told Wendy I would keep her secret she knew that included everyone but my MC brothers. If she hadn't wanted them to know she would have said so explicitly, that's how it works. Lockout or Riptide must have spread the news. I didn't care. I didn't have secrets from these men.

"How pissed is Seek?"

He palmed his face and rubbed his hand back over his hair, rolling his eyes and looking irritated. "Extremely, but she'll get over it."

"That why you're down here with us, Old Man?" Rip asked with a grin.

"Fuck off."

"Kicked you out, didn't she? I bet you get sick of sleeping down here before she backs off The Silverbells mystery," Toxic wagered, with a malicious grin. "I like your woman. She's got brass balls."

Seek and her dogs spent most nights at the clubhouse at this point and we were all happy to have them around, Hush most of all. She was already treating our home like hers and that included kicking her man to the couch if he pissed her off. Just so happened there were couches down here if the women needed more space to be pissed off in and didn't want them in the apartment. I'd feel sorry for Hush if he hadn't fucked me over by ruining my plans with Jenny.

Hush shook his head and flipped us all off. Before long more of our brothers joined us. I left them to drink and went upstairs to find Caitlyn. It was best I didn't disappoint two females in one day. I could make things right with Jenny, eventually. I couldn't bear the thought of disappointing that little girl.

* * *

I didn't wait for Jenny to call me. There were things I needed to get done yesterday so she'd gotten a reprieve from me, but she wasn't getting away that easily. I'd given in before and let her go. I wasn't doing it again.

Walking into the CPS building, I glanced around and spotted her inside an office. She was sitting with her elbow on the desk, chin propped in her hand, as she stared at the computer screen in front of her.

"Hi, can I help you?"

I glanced over and my brows shot up. The woman was probably five-nine, blonde, with a stacked body that was squeezed into a tight skirt and tighter blazer. She didn't have anything on under it and my eyes dipped down to where the top button strained, trying to contain her tits. When my eyes flicked back up to hers I read the knowing in them. A sultry look was pasted on her face. She liked that I'd checked her out, though it'd been more reflex than anything else. Seemed my interest was more in small, curvy, curly-haired brunettes these days.

Her hand went to my bicep as she continued speaking. "I'm sure I can help you with *whatever* you need."

I didn't miss the clear invitation. I just wasn't interested. "Looking for Jenny Jacobs."

The woman's lips turned down into a frown. "You don't want her. I can help you-"

Stepping out of her reach, forcing her to take her hand off me, I shook my head. "No, I don't want *you*." I left her there with her mouth hanging open.

I didn't make it two more steps before another woman stepped into my path. "Hi, I heard you say you needed to speak with Jenny."

There was a friendly smile on her face and she was wearing something that seemed more in line with working here. "I can take you to her."

My lips twitched in amusement since Jenny's office was directly across from where we were standing, but I followed after the woman. I waited while she knocked on Jenny's door then shoved it open.

Jenny's eyes widened when she saw me, then darted over to the other woman.

"There's someone here to see you," the woman said, an amused tone to her words. I caught her wiggling her brows at Jenny and bit back a smile.

"Thanks, Darlene," Jenny replied, narrowing her eyes at the woman.

Darlene patted my shoulder. "She'll take good care of you." With that she turned and walked away.

Shutting the door, I walked over and pulled the blinds closed, blocking us out from the rest of the building.

"Why are-" She frowned as she watched what I was doing and changed her question. "What're you doing?"

"I'd rather do this in private," I told her, turning to face her.

A suspicious look crept over her face. "Do what?"

My grin was slow, like my gait, as I walked toward her. She stood up behind her desk, looking like a scared little woodland creature who was about to flee. I wanted her to run, then I'd get to chase. Never mind the chaos it would cause in the office, it would be fun. Her sharp tone brought me back to reality.

"Don't." Her beautiful eyes widened in surprise as she said it. She didn't trust me, and that was fine. I'd given her reason not to. Now she'd just have to learn to do so again. No time like the present. She edged around her desk as I kept coming and tried to run to the door.

Catching her around the waist, I yanked her against my body and did what I'd wanted to do yesterday. Her lips were soft beneath mine and she stilled as I fitted our mouths together. She was a sweet little handful and I ran my hands down and cupped her ass. As much as I wanted to feel it in my hands, I'd really only done it so she'd part her lips.

Her gasp gave me the opportunity to plunge my tongue into her mouth and thrust it against hers. I moved my hands up to her face, cupping her cheeks as I backed her against the wall. She was pliant, stunned into obedience, as I moved her into the position I wanted.

It wasn't until her back hit the wall that she seemed to snap back into reality. Her hands fisted in my shirt and for a brief moment I thought she was going to throw caution to the wind and kiss me back the way I wanted her to. Instead, she pushed against my chest and turned her head away, breaking our lips apart.

I let her go and stepped back, watching her retreat from me, even though it was the last thing I wanted to do. We were both breathing hard and I had to reach down and adjust my dick to keep it from tenting out my jeans.

Her eyes followed the movement and her cheeks flushed a pretty pink. I loved when she did that. It made me want to see what all I could do to her that would cause her to blush.

"You can't just do that, Priest," she said, breaking the silence.

"Apparently I can?" I gave her a predatory grin.

She tossed her hands up in exasperation. "You dumped me. Left me with one brief text and no explanation. You don't get to pick up where we left off because all of a sudden you've decided to."

She wasn't wrong. What I'd done hadn't been fair to her, but I planned on making that up to her.

"Get out."

My brows shot up at the anger in her tone. She was scowling at me, hands on her hips, one foot tapping. It was as though her body needed to release the stress and energy stored there. She seemed to have an overabundance of energy and was always on the move.

"No." As much as I wanted this to be over, for us to just be a couple, I was loving the fight inside her. The fact that she wasn't a pushover, was standing her ground, just made me want her more. She was going to make me work for it, and deep down that thrilled me.

Her eyes narrowed and she huffed out a frustrated breath. She picked up a file folder from her desk and walked back over to me, slapping it against my chest.

I bit back a grin. She was pissed at me, but it was sort of cute. I wasn't stupid enough to say that out loud of course. Grabbing the file, I opened it. "What's this?"

"Fill that out and get it back to me. I need the information for Caitlyn's case file."

Scanning the documents, I nodded absently to her as I read. Name. Address. Income. History. All pretty standard stuff. I knew they'd run a background check on me and thanks to my military achievements I knew I'd pass with flying colors. There wasn't a single black mark on my record—and if there had been Riptide would make it disappear—so there wasn't anything for them to latch onto. Other than being in the club and living at the clubhouse, there weren't any red flags.

There was an easy enough answer to those problems however. The Oro Valley house was in my name, so I'd put that down as my address. Jenny would be able to explain why I was living at the clubhouse. As far as CPS knew it would be a temporary residence until I 'found' another place.

As for the club itself no one knew what we were. As far as the community knew we were just motorcycle enthusiasts who got together occasionally to ride. We kept it that way on purpose. The only people who knew what we really did were either family, close friends, or people we'd helped and not a single person would rat us out to the cops, or to CPS.

"Go to lunch with me." It came out as more of a demand than a request. It may not have been the right approach, I realized as her expression darkened. Oh well, she was just going to have to get used to me. I wasn't the kind of man who used pretty words and flowers to get my way.

"I have work to do," she insisted. There was a flicker of desire that showed on her face before she chased it away.

It gave me hope. That and the way she'd responded to my kiss. She was hurt and angry, but there was still a chance. She still wanted me.

Deciding not to push my luck, I opened the door to her office. "This isn't over, Jenny."

She didn't say anything as I walked out. Eyes followed me across the building as I left, but I ignored them. I was already forming a plan on how to win her back.

CHAPTER 5

Jenny

I sat down at my desk after Priest left and let my head drop into my hands. It hadn't been easy for me to refuse him, especially not after that kiss. I'd fallen asleep just about every night with scenarios exactly like what had just happened playing through my mind and weaving themselves into my dreams. I'd wanted more than anything to have him come back and say that he wanted me. Now that it was happening, though? I didn't trust it. Didn't trust him to not play me for a fool.

I wanted to trust him. It was hard not to drop my guard and just dive back in with him. I had to be reasonable though. He'd dropped me so suddenly before; I just couldn't risk it.

"It's for the best," I whispered to myself.

"Jenny!"

Jerking, I looked up and let out a sigh as I watched Darlene come into my office and shut the door.

"Who was *that*?" she asked, eyes wide and a grin on her lips.

"A father trying to adopt one of our kids," I told her. I refused to say more even though she was motioning for me too.

She gave me a dubious look. "He seemed like more than that. Girl, if a man stared at me the way he had you…" She fanned herself. "I'd combust on the spot."

"He wasn't-" I sighed and decided not to argue with her. "We're not allowed to date co-workers or clients," I reminded her.

She snorted. "What the boss doesn't know won't hurt her," she quipped. "If I were you I'd snatch him up in a heartbeat. I mean, he just flatly ignored Boobs and Stuff up at the front desk. She's pissed, too. A man with that kind of narrow-minded obsession is one you want to keep around."

It was a small comfort to know he took no interest in our very own office flirt. Priest had come in wearing jeans and a t-shirt—thankfully he'd taken his cut off so I didn't have to explain that—but he looked damn good in them. A muscular man in jeans and a well-fitted t-shirt was far sexier than a guy in a suit. I had a feeling most of the women working in this office would snatch him up if they could.

That didn't mean it was a good idea for me to put my trust in him again. My phone buzzed on the desk and Darlene got up.

"I'll leave you to it, but seriously…think about it." She wiggled her brows at me. "I know I will be."

My jaw dropped open and then I laughed. "Go away you horn dog. I have work to do."

Darlene and I had been work friends before I'd moved away to Texas. I was glad we were picking up where we'd left off. We'd never gotten close enough that we'd spent time together outside of work, but we enjoyed each other's company while we were here.

I'd grown up here in Tucson, but the few friends I'd made in high school had moved away. I was what my mom liked to refer to as an extroverted introvert. It wasn't hard for me to make acquaintances and have a good time if I happened to be in a social setting, but I much preferred to be at home when given the choice. That made it hard to make a lot of friends. Not to mention finding a new group of people to hang out with as an adult wasn't easy. Where was I supposed to find them? The grocery store?

A picture of me walking up to a woman in the produce section and striking up a conversation about melons made me shake my head. The gym? It wasn't exactly a place I frequented anyway, going just to find new people to meet wasn't ideal.

When Julie had come to work for my office in Texas it had been so easy to befriend her. I'd taken her to lunch and eventually her friends had become mine. I'd tried taking a few people here to lunch before and it'd been a disaster. One I wasn't eager to repeat.

I picked up my phone and frowned. It was a text from Priest. This man was going to drive me insane. He was dangling forbidden fruit in front of me and I desperately wanted to give in to temptation.

Ignoring his text asking what time I got off work, I forced myself to focus on my job. All I had to do was stay professional and keep my distance from him when I could and maybe he'd get the hint.

The day passed slowly and every time I found my mind wandering it landed back on the sexy biker and his kiss. By the time I shut down my computer and walked out the door my nerves were a jumbled mess.

The heat hit me as soon as I stepped outside and I hurried toward the back of the parking lot toward my car. It was nearing mid-September, but the fall in Tucson wasn't the same as everywhere else. It would stay warm until mid-November and then would cool off into more tepid temperatures for the winter. My heart skipped a beat when I saw Priest leaning up against my car, waiting for me. For just a moment I was so excited my heart jumped in my chest. I quickly remembered I was angry at him and suppressed the urge, forcing a frown onto my face instead.

I stopped by the vehicle parked next to mine. "I don't think Leann will appreciate you leaning on her car," I told him with a wicked grin.

He returned it and there was a dare in his gaze. "Probably not. Why don't you give me a ride?" He pointed to the car—which was not mine—and arched a brow. He was calling my bluff.

Rolling my eyes, I walked over toward him. "How do you know which car is mine?"

"Had Rip check the security footage from the other day." He didn't miss a beat.

"Okay. Why are you here? Again."

He handed over the file folder I'd given him that morning. I opened it and scanned the documents. They were all filled out. My lips twitched when I saw his handwriting. Every letter was capitalized and he'd written in small neat letters. I'd worked with veterans before and they all wrote this way. When I'd asked one he said the military insisted on it so they could read people's handwriting.

"Thank you for getting it back to me so quickly. I'll go through it all in the morning." I paused, waiting for him to move. When he didn't I gave him a pointed look. "Excuse me."

He stepped forward, invading my space, and the breath caught in my chest. His hand went to my hip, gripping it, and heat pooled low in my belly. "Go to dinner with me." That low, husky voice was doing things to my insides. Pleasant, wonderful things.

It wasn't really a question, but there was a hint of a request there in his words, as small as it may be. He was a man who was used to getting what he wanted. He was trying to make me believe he wanted me.

As much as I wished I could say yes, I'd fallen for his charms before. Shaking my head, I stepped around him, grateful when he let me go. He turned and watched as I got into my car and drove off.

Glancing back in my rearview, I saw him still standing there as I pulled out onto the main road and headed toward home. My hip still felt heated from where his hand had been.

By the time I got home and changed into my comfortable pajamas he'd already texted again.

Priest: You looked beautiful today.

I sighed and left my phone to charge in my bedroom while I went into the living room to have dinner with Mom.

"You're quiet," she said halfway through dinner.

"Sorry," I told her with a smile.

"What's wrong?" she asked, not buying my fake upbeat tone.

I set my fork down and focused on her. "Would you give someone who hurt you a second chance?"

She looked taken aback for a moment, but then considered my question. "It depends on how bad they hurt me."

This was why I loved her so much. We were more than just mother and daughter. We were friends and she always told me the truth. "I had a guy I was sort of seeing and he ended up breaking up with me over text. No explanation, just that it wasn't going to work."

"When was this?" she asked with a frown.

"In Texas. Anyway, now he wants to get back together."

"With him in Texas and you here?" she asked, doubt heavy in the words. "Long distance is tough-"

"No, he lives here in Tucson."

Confusion clouded her expression as she tried to put together the timeline without all of the information. "He'd been over visiting some friends in Texas when we met," I told her. "Never mind all that. What would you do?"

The look on her face made me laugh. She blinked quickly—dramatically—a few times as she absorbed all the information. "Well, without knowing details I'd say give him a chance to explain."

"I found out once I got home that he hadn't been completely forthcoming with me about everything before…" He hadn't told me he had kids. Or an ex-wife. I'd found out about the wife as I'd skimmed through the papers he'd dropped off with me. He'd listed her as the mother and she had his last name.

"Give him a chance to explain," Mom suggested. "Worst case scenario he has a bullshit excuse and you cut him out of your life. Best case, you realize you can live with whatever the excuse is and see where it goes. He had his reasons, men always do. Whether it was good or bad, listen to him, and decide."

That was logical. I just hoped my heart realized this wasn't grounds to forgive him immediately and start pinning all my hopes and dreams on him.

You don't make the decisions here, I mentally warned it. The way it fluttered back told me that probably wasn't true.

"Thanks, Mom."

"Welcome, Baby."

I forced myself to leave my phone in my bedroom while we finished dinner and cleaned up. As soon as Mom went to bed, I walked back to my room and laid on my bed. Grabbing my phone, I checked it and sure enough he'd kept texting.

Priest: Give me a chance to explain. Go to dinner with me tomorrow.

I texted him back, telling him I'd go to dinner with him and that I was going to bed. Hope filled my chest when I read his goodnight text. It probably wasn't the best idea to go along with this, but it really was what I wanted. I needed to know why he'd cut ties with me before. Even if I didn't like what I heard, at least I'd finally know.

CHAPTER 6

Priest

"You look fine."

Caitlyn glared at me in outraged indignation—in the way only a girl could—and crossed her arms over her chest. She went back to the closet in her room and grabbed a different dress.

"Fine. Put it on, but hurry up or we're going to be late," I told her, shaking my head. Amazing how decidedly... female she was. Even though she wasn't talking yet, between the glares and eye rolls I was in familiar territory, and knew exactly what she was telling me.

It took another twenty minutes to get her out the door. I borrowed one of the cage rides, buckling a booster seat in the back. She was still too small to let her ride loose. I kept extra of all my kids' stuff here at the clubhouse for when they came to visit, so Caitlyn was all set up with everything she could need. Eventually I would get her her own things, especially clothes. I knew it was important to a kid to not be perpetually borrowing from others. But compared to our other problems, that was further down on the list and she wasn't complaining. I knew from my other girls that Caitlyn didn't need to be speaking to protest about something like that.

Getting her situated, I climbed into the front of the pickup and drove across town to the CPS office where Jenny was working. As soon as we stepped into the building I spotted the riotous curls inside an office across the way. I suppressed a smile; much like Jenny's personality, there was no containing those curls. "Come on, Cait."

I couldn't wait for today to be over. Then I'd be able to focus on Jenny at our dinner tonight. She deserved my attention and my explanations. Kit was all set to watch over Caitlyn while I was out on my date.

My eyes were locked on Jenny, my heart giving a heavy thud as I approached. She looked beautiful, sitting there, frowning down at something on her desk. She'd texted me this morning to bring Caitlyn in at nine. I was appreciative that she was making this a priority and getting things done so quickly.

Her head popped up as soon as we got to the door. It didn't surprise me. One thing I'd learned about Jenny as soon as I met her was that she didn't sit still well. She was always racing from one thing to the next, and if she was forced to sit her leg would bounce hard enough to shake anything near her.

"Hi." Her tone was completely detached and professional, beautiful chocolate eyes wary as she looked at me. Irritation threaded through me at her brush off. She softened it then and smiled at Caitlyn. "Hi there, Sweetie."

Caitlyn gave her a small smile and stepped into the office when I urged her forward. Her small hand was clutching mine in a death grip, but otherwise she didn't show her fear. I was proud of the way she was handling all this. She was being incredibly courageous.

It was the reason I'd decided to fight for this adoption. I would gladly watch over any orphaned kid in her position. Some of our brothers had kids and would also take an orphan in without hesitation, but I wanted to be the one to care for her. Caitlyn, despite her silence, was a fighter. I'd known it from the moment we rescued her.

That much trauma would make most adults go catatonic. Yet here she was, with the loudest silent personality you could imagine. I'd be damned if I let anyone else take her. I'd die before I allowed anyone to harm her. This girl would grow up to shine right alongside my other kids. I was going to make sure of it.

I got her settled before taking the chair next to her. "Morning, Jenny."

It was impossible to miss the light flush that rose on Jenny's neck. I purposely lowered my voice a bit. "What do you need from me?"

Her plump lips parted in surprise and I had to fight off the wicked smile that wanted to emerge at her shock. I'd worded it that way on purpose. She thought she was going to give me the cold shoulder and keep her professionalism. She was wrong. I didn't have her address here in town—though I could get it—and it wasn't time to take things that far. Especially not since she'd agreed to dinner.

"Can you please fill out this form?" she asked, voice a little breathless. She hitched in a breath when our fingers brushed as I took the paper from her.

This wasn't necessarily going to be easy, but I was grateful that I could read the interest in her body language. It was a good thing, because she was sure as shit trying to keep me at arm's length any time her mind cleared enough to realize what I was doing. I'd been surprised she'd agreed to go out with me tonight. Happy about it, but I knew she was fighting the attraction between us.

Jenny spoke quietly with Caitlyn while I filled in the information —or to the girl since she still wouldn't talk. It didn't matter how much I assured her she was safe with our family, she wouldn't speak. The therapist said she would in her own time and I'd have to be patient.

I'd been a sniper in the Army's Ranger Battalion. If there was one thing I knew, it was waiting patiently until I had the right shot. I once waited three days on a rooftop, covered in linen to hide myself, just to shoot one asshole. In retrospect, that was easy compared to this, but I had the patience. I'd have to utilize that legendary control with both these females. I could handle that.

"You want to live with Priest and the others?"

I glanced over at Jenny's question and watched as Caitlyn's head bobbed up and down. Relief was quick and sharp. I didn't want anything happening to her and I knew my brothers and I could protect her.

There were some who might think it was odd for a single man to want to adopt her, but I knew she'd fit in perfectly with my three girls. Lockout had given me the largest apartment in preparation of what was to come. I didn't know when I'd have full custody of my children, but I had a feeling it would be soon.

In any other circumstance I'd be fucking thrilled at getting full custody. Right now, for their sake, I would push that off as long as possible.

Regret and sadness filled my chest. Wendy and I had been volatile together. We'd lasted ten years, but they hadn't always been good. Despite all the arguments and fighting, she'd stood by me deployment after deployment. She had always been faithful, and since the divorce she had asked nothing of me other than this, and I was honoring her wishes now. That was all I could do. Our divorce was the best thing that happened to us—second only to our girls—and we'd managed to co-parent and end up friends somewhere along the way. We'd managed that much for the girls' sake. I'd put them through enough with the deployments, the least I could do was be friendly with their mother.

I handed the paperwork back to Jenny, letting my eyes roam over her as she read through everything, making sure it was correct. She pulled the other documents I'd filled out yesterday out of the folder as well.

She hadn't slicked her hair back into a ponytail today and it hung down past the edge of the desk. I loved it like this, all wild and free. The curls weren't frizzy, but smooth ringlets, there were just so many of them it caused her hair to go everywhere. If I didn't know better I'd guess it was a perm, but it was natural. Her inky black lashes were lowered as she looked down, contrasting against her silky smooth pale skin. There was a smattering of freckles over the bridge of her nose and they feathered out onto her cheeks.

The urge to strip her bare and see where else she had freckles had a stranglehold on me. I swallowed hard and tried to pull my mind away from what those delicious fucking thighs might look like bared. Or, even better, of what her thick ass would look like in a pair of swimsuit bottoms. The kind that didn't cover nearly enough cheek. I licked my lips and shifted in my seat so I could subtly adjust my growing dick. This wasn't the time, place, or company for these thoughts. Didn't mean I could stop them, though.

"Everything looks like it's in order," she said, looking up, then past me. She was speaking a little louder than she had before.

My lips twitched in amusement. The fact that she wasn't shying away from helping me—helping the club—was amazing, but an actress she was not. I didn't want her to get in trouble with her work, so I'd play along however I had to. As long as it didn't include giving her up.

"You have every right to still be pissed at me. Thank you for agreeing to come to dinner tonight."

Her eyes darted back to mine, then she glanced meaningfully at the little girl next to me.

"She's going to be living in the clubhouse. She'll hear a lot worse than that."

Her lips turned down into a frown and I wanted to wipe it off her face with my lips. Replace it with ecstasy. "That's going to be the hard part," she told me, lowering her voice again, and also effectively changing the subject. "Getting my managers to sign off on a single dad —living in an MC clubhouse—adopting her."

I sat back in my chair, thoughts of our naked bodies rubbing together leaving my head. "Maybe we could grease some palms."

Her brows pinched together. "God, I hope that wouldn't work."

She was so adorably naive. I loved it. I never wanted her to change, but it *would* work. It always did.

The look on my face must have convinced her because she sighed in disappointment. "Let's leave that as a last ditch option. I have another plan."

"What?"

She spun her chair around and away from the desk and plucked a paper off the fax machine sitting on a table behind her. She rolled back forward and handed it to me.

I smiled as I read the contents of the letter. It was from Caitlyn's Aunt Sharon. It pleaded to allow Caitlyn to live with her dear friend as she was unable to take care of her niece herself. Jenny had contacted Sharon—though I didn't know when—and after speaking with her convinced her to write this, the devious little vixen.

"Will it work?" I asked her.

She picked up my paperwork again and smiled. "That along with my recommendation?" She looked down at what I'd written and smiled. "You're damn right it'll work, Mr. Mitchell. Grant Mitchell," she said, as though rolling my name around on her tongue.

"How long do you think it'll take to get custody of her?"

She pursed her lips as she thought about it. "I'll be honest. It usually takes quite a while, but I'm hoping that with her mother..." she paused and looked over at the little girl who was watching her with solemn eyes and changed course. "I'm hoping that with her Aunt Sharon willing to sign over her rights as Caitlyn's last living relative—that they know of—we'll be able to push this through a lot quicker. My bosses are going to want her to be able to settle into your home securely, rather than being kept in limbo. Especially considering her inability to speak. She needs a stable environment and her Aunt knows that is you. That'll go a long way to smoothing everything out."

I took a deep breath, glad that we had Jenny on our side. She was already making this process easier and I'd always be grateful to her for that. Reaching over, I squeezed Caitlyn's little shoulder, comforting her. Her eyes moved over to me and she gave me a brief smile. I focused back on Jenny as she began speaking again.

"It would also help if you had full custody, or at least joint custody of your kids. Perhaps you can have your...ex," I couldn't help but note the anger in her voice, not at Wendy, but at me, "also write a letter."

I hesitated before answering, "I, um, I can work out something like that. I'll have full custody soon."

Her head perked up in curiosity. "Really? When? What changed?"

I couldn't do this now, and especially not in front of Caitlyn. It was just too much. "Something changed. A lot changed. Anyway, you think all this together will work? Caitlyn will get to stay with me?"

"I think you have a really good shot." She looked down at Caitlyn and all her anger drained away. She looked back at me, smiling hugely before remembering she was angry with me. "I'm going to fight as hard as I can to make this happen, Grant."

I liked the way she said my name, though I didn't hear it much anymore. Like most of my brothers, I went solely by my road name since retiring from the Army. I'd gone in young—at eighteen—and worked my way through the ranks until I'd gotten that coveted spot in a Ranger Unit. It'd always been my goal. I'd only retired two years ago at thirty-eight.

Hit my twenty years and called it a day. I'd seen more than enough to last me a lifetime. Spent so much time away from my family that I'd almost lost it. Not my brothers, they'd always be there for me. I'd joined the MC when I hit twenty-five. The Army knew, they just thought we were a band of military men who liked to ride bikes. They had no clue what we did over the years. We'd been together since before we retired—and some of them were medically or honorably discharged—and we stuck together now. Nothing would tear us apart.

It hadn't been the same for me and Wendy. She'd taken my girls from me and left. It'd taken over a year before I could convince her that we could work together to raise them. Finally, she'd begun letting me see them again. That year without my kids was one of the darkest of my life. I'd never choose to go back to that.

"I'll still have to play this by the book," Jenny warned, snapping me back into focus. "I'll file this with my managers once we get back."

"Get back?"

"From the home check," she said in a tone that told me she'd just gone over this while I was zoned out.

"Sure. No problem. Now?"

She sighed. "Yes, Priest. Now."

We walked outside toward the truck and she tilted her head. "Who's is that?"

"Belongs to the club."

She frowned, then shot a look around. "You're going to need to prove you have reliable transportation that belongs to you. Not the club. And not your bike. Something that you can take Caitlyn back and forth in."

"No problem." Buying my own truck was a waste with the cage rides always available at the clubhouse, but it was a small price to pay to secure Caitlyn's safety. I could probably get Lockout to sign over the title of one of the trucks or SUVs to me. "You may as well ride with us," I told her, putting a hand on her shoulder to stop her from going to her car.

"You'd have to bring me back. That makes no sense-"

"Ride with us. You can talk more with Caitlyn." Caitlyn, picking up on my vibe, reached out a hand and grabbed Jenny's, then proceeded to give her the doe eyes. I owed that little girl for that alone. Giving her a wink, then letting my face smooth out into an innocent expression when Jenny stared at me suspiciously, I fought not to laugh. I knew bringing Caitlyn into it would get her. I wasn't above using my daughter—I already thought of Caitlyn as mine, we just had to make it through the formalities—to convince this woman to spend time with me.

"Fine," she said with a glower at me, then a sweet smile for the little girl holding her hand.

She stepped aside as I settled Caitlyn into the booster seat. She scribbled something down on her clipboard.

"Seriously, Jenny?"

"I told you. I have to do this by the book. Anything you do right, I'm noting it. If there's something wrong I'll have you fix it," she told me. She waited until I shut the door so our voices would be muffled. Still she lowered hers before continuing. "I have eyes, Priest. That little girl is already in love with you. More importantly, she feels safe with you. *That* is why I agreed to help the MC so quickly. If it wasn't the best thing for her, I wouldn't be doing this, no matter how nicely you asked."

"Lucky for me it is then."

"Lucky for you," she echoed, tapping her pen against my chest.

I grinned and opened the door for her. I'd dressed the part today, was wearing a pair of slacks and a button down shirt with a collar. Felt like a prison. I longed for my jeans and cut. Soon enough I'd be back to being me and I'd be hard at work pursuing the woman climbing into my truck. Once we got this inspection out of the way, she was all mine.

CHAPTER 7

Jenny

We hadn't gotten more than a few miles down the road when his cell phone rang. It was connected to the Bluetooth in the truck so the ringtone blared through the quiet cab and made me jump.

He cursed under his breath as he looked over at the screen. "Sorry. Have to take this." His finger jabbed a button on the steering wheel. "Hey Wendy-"

"Dad?" A trembling voice came over the speakers and Priest tensed up visibly.

"Gabby? What's wrong, Angel? Where's Mom?"

Fear gripped my heart at the worry in his voice and the helplessness in hers. It was hard to determine her age just by voice alone. I still knew nothing about his kids and that was a bitter pill to swallow. I was being unreasonable, he wasn't obligated to tell me anything. I just wanted him to. Wanted him to let me in. To let me help him through whatever this was that was making him so tense.

No. You wanted him to before you found all this out. Now you want him to leave you alone. Even with the reminder from my inner voice the desire to know him inside and out stirred in my chest.

"Dad, Mom passed out. I don't know what to do."

"Okay, Angel. I'm on my way right now. Just sit tight. Where are your sisters?"

"They're here. They're fine."

"Okay, good. Listen, we've been here before. Put a pillow under her head, make sure she's breathing alright. Is there any blood? Did she fall?"

"Yeah, I think she fell. She's on the floor in the living room. I don't know if she's breathing." The girl's voice hitched on a sob and my heart broke apart in my chest.

"Alright, you did good, Gabby. Okay? I'll be there in a few minutes. Just hang on."

I clicked off my seatbelt and turned in my seat. Caitlyn's eyes were wide and her skin was pale. "Hey, Sweetie. Everything's okay. Have you met Priest's other daughters yet?"

She nodded her head, answering my question, her eyes flicking over to the man who'd jammed his foot on the gas pedal. The truck lurched forward. Despite her fear, I wasn't about to tell him to slow down. Not when his other daughters were alone and scared and their mother was injured. A thousand questions raced through my mind, but now wasn't the time to ask them.

I reached back and brushed a lock of her hair away from her face. The feel of my fingers on her skin had her leaning into the touch. She was trusting despite what she'd gone through. Or maybe she just knew no one would ever harm her while Priest was nearby. He was her protector. I couldn't blame her, I felt safe with him, too. At least physically. Emotionally was another story.

Turning back around, I clicked my belt back on then reached over and laid my hand on his bicep. The massive muscles there bunched under my palm.

"I can't slow down." Anguish raced over his face.

"Not asking you to. How far are we?"

"Five minutes." It came out through gritted teeth.

We made it in three. The truck's tires squealed as we flew into a driveway in a nice subdivision out in Oro Valley. It was beautiful and quiet, with a gorgeous view of the Catalina Mountains.

Expensive.

I wondered if he helped his ex-wife pay the mortgage. Not that it was any of my business. I could ask for the adoption paperwork and check his financials—and might have to in the future as this moved forward—but for now I wasn't going to use the process to find out about him. If he'd wanted to tell me any of this, he would have during one of his trips to Texas. Or over the phone. Instead, he hadn't mentioned any of it. Not a wife. Or kids. Or anything remotely personal.

Whether it was fair or not I was still angry that he'd withheld so much from me when we were originally getting to know each other. He'd said earlier that I had the right to be pissed at him. That was part of it. The other part was fear. I was scared he was going to make me fall in love with him and then drop me the moment things got sticky for him. It seemed to be his pattern.

"Go," I told him, shoving down the anger and hurt. This wasn't the time to be focusing on any of that. "I'll get her."

He ran inside, leaving me with Caitlyn. I got out of the truck and unbuckled her. Her hand slipped into mine and I couldn't help but smile. Her mom must have drilled it into her head to hold an adult's hand. She was six, so it wasn't always necessary. Maybe it just made her feel connected. Either that or it made her feel safe. Which meant I made her feel safe. My heart clenched and I fought the urge to gather her into a hug.

The warmth filling me vanished as we walked into the house. His three girls huddled together, arms wrapped around each other while watching their dad tend to their mom.

He was on his knees next to her unconscious form. I led Caitlyn over to the other girls. "Hi," I said with a warm smile, trying to keep them calm. The oldest gave me a brief look of curiosity through watery eyes. "I'm Jenny. I'm a friend of your dad's. Can you watch Caitlyn while I go help?"

"Yeah." When she spoke I recognized her voice.

"Thanks, Gabby."

I hurried over to Priest. There was no time to react to the condition of the woman lying on the floor. Her scarf had fallen off her head, revealing hair loss that could have only come from chemo. She was skin and bones. I didn't need to be a medical professional to know she had some kind of cancer. Sadness for her girls—and for Priest—battered at the calm exterior shell I'd erected around myself. More questions arose, even as the answers were staring me in the face.

"What can I do?" I asked him as I knelt down by her other side.

"Call an ambulance," he said, his gaze tracking over her body as he tried to find the pulse at her neck.

I pulled my cell phone out of my back pocket and dialed 911. "Hello, I need an ambulance at…"

He grunted out the address as he began doing chest compressions. The cracking sound of ribs made bile rise in my throat. I choked out the address to the dispatcher. My eyes went to the girls. They looked frozen, terrified, and so unbearably sad.

"Gabby," I called out, ignoring the operator for a moment. "Take the others into your room, okay?"

Her eyes were wide, tears tracking down her face, but she nodded. She ushered the other girls from the room and I was grateful she didn't argue. His kids were sweet and the last thing they needed was to watch their father try to resuscitate their mother. I finished giving any information I could to the dispatcher.

I stayed on the phone while he worked diligently to make sure Wendy's body stayed alive until the ambulance got there. There was a flurry of activity as the paramedics loaded her on a stretcher, one continuing CPR.

"I'll stay with the girls if you want to go with her," I told him softly.

His tortured eyes met mine. He wanted to go be there for her, but he was dying to go to his kids. I'd never seen this side of him before and it drew me in even more. Whatever shallow jerk I'd tried to make him into was being proven wrong. He had depth to him, and it was hard not to want more.

"Thanks, Jenny," he said, voice deep and low. "Take care of them."

"I promise," I told him. "Go."

He nodded, hesitating for a brief moment before walking out the front door, following the others to the waiting ambulance.

I shut the door and leaned back against it. My body was shaking. I needed to get myself under control before I could help those girls. Dealing with a sick patient wasn't anything new to me. It was the CPR that had gotten to me.

It brought me right back to the afternoon when I'd come home from the grocery store. I hadn't wanted to leave Grams, but it was either go to the store or starve. I'd found her on the floor in the kitchen, not unlike Wendy lying in the living room. I'd done CPR, but there was no bringing her back.

Tears welled in my eyes, but I knuckled them away. There was no time to sit here feeling sorry for myself. I shoved away from the door, then took a deep breath before going into the room marked 'Gabby'.

She was sitting on the bed, her sisters gathered in close, reading them a story. This was why I loved kids so much. Their innocent, sweet natures. Gabby must have been terrified herself, but she'd called her dad and now sat comforting the others.

"Hey."

They all looked up, a mix of fear and hope on their faces. Even Caitlyn had it. I wondered if she was remembering her own mom's death? I couldn't begin to understand how awful that must have been for her.

I went and sat down on the edge of the bed. "They took your mom to the hospital. Your dad went with her. Hope you don't mind being stuck with me as a babysitter in the meantime." I smiled brightly. One of the younger girls let a shy smile peep through the worry.

"Who are you?"

"I'm Jenny. A friend of your dad and Caitlyn here." It didn't surprise me that she didn't remember my introduction. There'd been a lot happening, and all of it fast, when we'd first gotten here.

Gabby looked over at Caitlyn—who nodded enthusiastically—to confirm she knew me. Some of the wariness slid off her face. "I'm Gabby. That's Taylor and Cassie."

I gave them a little wave. "How old are you girls?"

Cassie popped a thumb out of her mouth. "Five."

"Taylor's six and I'm nine," Gabby finished telling me.

"Is Mama going to be okay?" Taylor asked, voice quiet and withdrawn.

"Oh Sweetie, I hope so." I couldn't bring myself to outright lie to her. "They're going to do everything they can for her at the hospital, okay?"

She nodded and looked down at her lap. Gabby leaned back and went back to reading the story to us. I looked around at each of the girls and hoped there would be good news for them.

* * *

It was nearing midnight when the front door to Wendy's home opened. I gasped and held up the broom in my hands like it was a baseball bat. I could have sworn I'd locked it.

"Whoa there, it's just me." Priest held up his hands.

I sagged in relief, the broom dropping from its position. "Sorry. Just a bit jumpy."

"That's alright. Where are the girls?" He looked exhausted. Even so, he filled the room. He just had this presence about him that drew the eye. Huge and dangerous. But right now he was a worn out father worried about his daughters. The dichotomy of it all tugged at those places inside of me that wanted him. Not the naughty places that couldn't seem to quit thinking dirty thoughts. The soul deep spots that saw the man and yearned for all he could give.

Stupid. Stupid. Stupid. I was just begging to have my heart shredded. "I fed them some dinner and they passed out not long after. That was about eight." I eyed the clock. I hadn't realized how quickly time had flown.

Priest nodded and walked back into the hallway to go check on his girls. I gave him privacy. Even though I wanted to run to him, throw my arms around him, and ask him how Wendy was, I couldn't. His priority was to those sweet little girls. I had to give him space for them first. I could wait.

Needing to keep busy like I had been for the last four hours, I went back to sweeping. I'd already dusted, cleaned the bathrooms, vacuumed, and washed the sheets and comforter in Wendy's bedroom. I'd have done the girls' too, but they were using them. In between all that, I'd been cooking up every scrap of food Wendy had in the house. I was sticking it all in the freezer for when she came home.

A quick peek into the hall showed him moving toward the bedroom and looking in. I wasn't sure if he was going to wake the girls or just check in on them. I went back to cleaning.

It didn't matter if the man I was half in love with belonged to Wendy. Not when she was sick and had just gone to the hospital. I'd make her homecoming as easy as possible because that's the way my mom and Grams had raised me. If Wendy was who he wanted, I'd get out of their way. My heart gave a wrenching throb.

I paused in the act of sweeping. *If* she came home. The thought made the panic rise up within me so I doubled my speed while sweeping. Strong hands clamped down on my arms from behind, stilling my movements.

"Hey, hey, what are you doing?" Priest spun me so he could look at my face.

"Cleaning. Cooking. Making myself useful," I muttered. Trying to jerk out of his hold, so I could go back to work, I shrugged when he held firm. "I need to do something."

He let me go and watched quietly as I swept the dirt in the kitchen into a dustpan. I set a mop bucket under the sink faucet and started filling the bucket with hot water. Searching under the sink, I grabbed a cleaning agent and dumped some into the water, watching it create suds.

"Sorry about missing dinner tonight."

As if that was important right now. Sure I wanted to know what he needed to tell me, but that could wait. No one could have foreseen all this happening. I didn't want to talk about it, so I changed the topic.

"Is Wendy…" I couldn't bring myself to ask the rest of the question. There was no reading the expression on Priest's face, it was closed up tight behind a blank mask.

"She's alive, but in rough shape," he told me, then fell silent again.

I didn't pry, even though it all but killed me not to ask him anything. Instead, I went back to cleaning. My mom's house was so clean you could eat your dinner off the floor. It was only after I cleaned it from top to bottom each day, during my time off work, that I'd resorted to watching movies and eating junk food. Both helped ease the grief.

A hand flashed past my face and he jerked the nozzle until the water turned off. "What's going on Jenny?"

"Nothing." I wasn't about to tell him that if I stopped for too long that thoughts of my grams would creep in. Or that I was worried he still wanted to be with Wendy. He didn't need that right now. The man was already carrying a huge burden on his shoulders. He didn't need mine.

"If there was nothing wrong you wouldn't be flying around my ex's house like the Tasmanian Devil." His mouth was set in a grim line.

Ex. I knew they weren't together anymore, but the title eased some of the burden in my heart, which only created more shame. I shouldn't be wanting Priest to assure me that he wasn't interested in Wendy anymore. Not while she was lying in the hospital fighting for her life. It made me feel lower than pond scum, but I couldn't seem to help it. The relief that flared inside my chest was white hot.

When I didn't respond, he grabbed me again and this time jerked me against his body. He didn't kiss me, just held me close, his huge hand smoothing over my hair. I wasn't sure if he was hugging me because I needed it, or he did.

"I'm fine," I mumbled against his chest. When had I turned my face into his shirt? Why was I breathing in the spicy scent of his cologne like it was the only thing keeping the air moving in and out of my lungs?

"Okay, but just let me hold you a minute."

How could a girl say no to that? So I stood there, with his strong arms around me, letting myself enjoy this one last time before I had to let him go. I had to remember that it didn't matter that he and Wendy were separated. As much as I wanted him I was more afraid of getting my heart broken again. Why was it so difficult to remember that when I was around him?

CHAPTER 8

Priest

She felt so right in my arms. Fucking perfect. Like she'd always been meant to be there. I'd never regret the years I spent with Wendy. How could I when she gave me three out of four of my perfect daughters and had been a friend in the process? The bad times between us were in the past and I didn't hold it against her, the same way she didn't for me. But Wendy wasn't my wife anymore. She wasn't the woman I wanted.

That role belonged to Jenny. I couldn't get her out of my head. She'd been stuck in there ever since I'd seen her at my friend's wedding. Even after I'd broken things off with her she'd remained.

My eyes ached with exhaustion. The girls were all asleep in Gabby's bed, curled together as though none of them wanted to be alone. I didn't blame them. Even Caitlyn was part of the pack now.

"Come on, Taz," I told Jenny, taking the mop she was still holding and setting it aside. "Let's get some sleep."

"Taz?" She blinked up at me with a frown puckering between her brows.

"Tasmanian Devil," I answered. I liked it. It fit her well.

She didn't respond to that, just shook her head. "I figured I'd take the truck home. I can come pick you up in the morning."

"No way in hell I'm letting you drive home at midnight. You'll sleep here." I propelled her forward with a hand at the small of her back.

She must have been as tired as I was because it wasn't until we stepped into Wendy's room that she tried to bolt. "I can't sleep in here."

"*We're* sleeping in here," I corrected her. "It's fine."

"This is her room. Her bed," she said, giving me a frustrated look. "It's rude."

I chuckled, but didn't bother to mention that I paid for the house, the bed set, the mattress. Everything in this house I'd bought for my ex and my kids. I'd done so happily in order to allow my daughters the most time they could get with their mother. Everything I did was for my daughters. I wasn't going to let their last year with their mother be a constant fight over money and basic amenities. I'd have bought them a palace if I had the money.

With this happening, I was glad they'd gotten the extra time over the last year. Wendy's disease had progressed quickly. In fact, with how sick she'd been we hadn't sent the girls back to school when it'd started. All so they could spend uninterrupted time with their mom. I stripped off my shirt, then the uncomfortable slacks. My lips twitched as Jenny's eyes widened and stayed glued on my chest. I was only in my boxer briefs.

Flicking on the bedside lamp, I moved back over and turned off the overhead light before climbing into bed. Even my fucking bones were weary. I wasn't an overly emotional guy, but having my oldest call and tell me that her mom had passed out, then hearing what I had at the hospital was enough to drain me.

"Take off your clothes and come to bed, Taz." The nickname felt right on my tongue. I planned on using it from now on. Just another way to tether Jenny to me until I could take the time to fix things with her. If everything could just take a breath and give me a few damn minutes to adjust, it'd be nice.

Her eyes narrowed. "I'm *not* taking off my clothes."

The way she tucked her arms around herself made me grin. "Just the shirt and pants. They won't be comfortable to sleep in." When she made no move to undress, I sighed. "Seriously. Take them off and come to bed or *I'll* take them off and put you to bed." It came out as more of a threat than I'd meant, but it got her ass into gear.

She glared at me, but started unbuttoning her shirt. She made a half-hearted attempt to turn away from me, but stopped mid turn. Maybe she wanted me to watch, or maybe she knew I was going to anyway. My eyes followed her lithe fingers as they released the buttons and she dropped the shirt onto a chair nearby. She hesitated, standing before me in her slacks and a lacy black bra.

Fuck. My tongue was glued to the roof of my mouth. She had such pretty tits. They weren't huge, but were just the right size, and were being pushed up by the cups of the bra. I wanted to trail my tongue over those mounds. To feel how smooth and soft her skin was.

"What are you waiting for?"

"I can sleep in my pants," she replied, a slightly desperate look in her eyes.

I shook my head, eyes roaming over her. "May as well be comfortable, Baby," I told her.

She glared at me, but finally unbuttoned the slacks. The little booty shake she gave to get them off her hips had me biting back a groan of appreciation. She turned and folded the slacks before setting them on top of her shirt.

My dick was so hard it ached at seeing her in her panties. They didn't quite cover her thick ass, giving me the slightest tantalizing look at her cheeks. I wanted to cup that sexy ass in my hands while I rammed my cock so hard inside of her she screamed my name.

Swallowing thickly, I held up the covers for her. Nerves and worry flitted across her face and I could only hope they kept her from noticing my raging hard-on. Otherwise she was going to run screaming from the bedroom. I knew she wasn't ready for me to touch her. I had a lot of explaining to do before I could gain her trust back. She was being force fed the last year of my chaotic life in one evening. It was a lot for anyone to take in.

She crawled beneath the comforter and scooted over as far toward her edge of the bed as she could. She rolled onto her side, giving me her back.

I turned off the lamp and laid back down. It was too soon to push things, so I stayed put and didn't crowd my way against her back even though I wanted to more than I wanted my next breath. If I were to throw my arm over her and press my hard dick against her ass, I really would have a full on Tasmanian Devil on my hands. *Might be worth it...*

We were lying in the darkness and it struck me that this was the perfect opportunity to start clearing the air. Fuck. I knew there wasn't going to be time in the morning once the girls woke up.

"Wendy has cancer. Breast cancer." My voice was low in the quiet of the room, as though talking too loud would pierce the peace that had settled around us.

"Oh Priest. I'm so sorry."

The size of this woman's heart was unbelievable. So many women would be pissed to be here, in the home of the woman I'd once been married to. Jenny had taken one look at Wendy's situation and started cleaning and cooking for a woman she didn't even know. She was going to make a great mother. A great wife. The perfect old lady.

My dick twitched at the thought of Jenny carrying my babies. I wanted as many kids as I could produce and I wanted them with my little tornado. I just needed to get her to forgive me first.

"I should've told you what was happening instead of sending that text," I told her, meaning every word. "Wendy was back in chemo and was so sick she was having a hard time taking care of the girls. So they were living with me, and I was taking her to her appointments. Then all that shit kicked off in Texas and I was getting pulled in every direction all at once. I didn't have the time to devote to you then. I kept thinking that once things settled down I'd have the time. Except that things never settled down."

She'd rolled over and though it was dark in the room, I could see the outline of her body. I could feel her watching me. "Why didn't you just tell me?"

"I should have told you about Wendy and the girls, but she didn't want anyone knowing she was sick. It embarrassed her." I sort of understood it. I wouldn't want others to know if I was sick either. "As for the club stuff, I couldn't tell you."

"I understand."

There wasn't any sarcasm in her voice. She really did get it. "Does that mean you forgive me, Taz?"

She was silent for a few long moments. I held my breath, waiting. "Yeah, Priest. I forgive you." There was a mix of hope and desperation in her voice.

My grin was slow and predatory. I was across the tiny space in the bed before she could say anything else and my mouth was on hers. Groaning at the feel of her, I swiped my tongue over the seam of her lips, asking for entrance. She gasped in surprise at my sudden move and I used the opening to sweep my tongue into her mouth.

Her moan was deep in her chest and I echoed it. Shifting my body, I moved until I was lying between her thighs. It'd been too long since I'd gotten to kiss her and having her half naked in bed was too tempting to resist.

Cupping her tit, I flicked my thumb over her nipple. It beaded up beneath the lace and I trailed kisses down over her neck. My mouth closed over her lace covered nipple and I sucked hard. Her hips bucked hard against me, rubbing her pussy over my hard cock. I groaned in response.

"Priest," she gasped. Her hands went to my head, but instead of holding me close, she was pushing against me.

I growled in irritation at being stopped when I'd been waiting so long to feel her sexy curves against mine, to taste her. "What?" I lifted my head. We were close enough that I could see the shadows of her features.

"We can't…"

I dropped my head down onto her chest and fought to control my breathing. My cock twitched again, as though to remind me of what it wanted. Like I didn't know. Rolling off her, I stared up at the ceiling.

"I'm sorry. I just... I understand why you did what you did, Priest. But you hurt me."

My eyes closed as I heard the sadness in her voice. "I'll make it up to you, Taz."

"I don't think that's a good idea," she said, hesitation threading through her words.

She didn't really mean it. I knew it, but still aggravation flashed over me. I rolled again, covering her body with mine again. Her throat was smooth under my hand as I encircled it. She swallowed hard and I felt the movement against my palm.

"I don't expect you to forgive me right away, Taz. But you need to realize something."

"What?" she whispered.

She wasn't struggling against my hold. I'd bet every fucking dollar I had that if I dipped my fingers beneath those lace panties she'd be soaked for me. I didn't touch her though. She wasn't ready and I wasn't going to push her too fast.

"You're mine. I'll give you the time you need to come to grips with that, but you're not getting away a second time."

"You-"

I tightened my grip on her throat and she stopped talking. "Let's get some sleep." I shifted onto my side, tucking her up against my chest. Her sexy ass was pressed against my hard dick and I heard her quick inhalation of breath.

We laid there together in silence and I thought she'd dropped off into sleep when she spoke quietly. "What's going to happen to Wendy?"

"She's dying," I told her, not bothering to sugar coat my words the way I'd have to with my kids. I knew I could lay the burden on Jenny and she'd help hold it, at least for a few hours while I slept. "They're putting her into hospice once she gets out of the hospital. The doctors gave her three to four weeks."

"God," Jenny breathed, reaching down and squeezing the arm I had wrapped around her waist. "I'm so sorry. Your poor girls."

That was the tragedy of all of this. My girls were going to suffer the loss of their mother at far too young an age. I buried my face into the riotous curls of her hair and inhaled her peaches and cream scent. She always smelled so fucking good. I let my thoughts drop away and just enjoyed holding her in my arms as sleep claimed me.

CHAPTER 9

Jenny

Sunlight woke me the next morning and I stretched. I tried to roll onto my back, but something heavy kept me pinned in place. The fog of sleepiness faded quickly and I remembered where I was. Who I was with.

I peeked over my shoulder and saw Priest behind me, his body plastered to mine. His face was relaxed in sleep, so I studied him for a moment. It was the first time I'd gotten to see him unguarded, just relaxed and natural. That face had been tormenting my dreams—and my heart—for months now.

The way he kissed me last night was going to replay in my mind every night for sure. I sort of regretted stopping him. A wicked thought entered my mind. Facing forward, I arched my back, grinding my ass back against him.

My eyes widened when his dick responded immediately. It pressed against my flesh, heavy and thick. I bit my lip to keep from laughing. Part of my amusement was because he'd responded so quickly, but the other half was nervousness. He felt fucking huge. It wasn't surprising because he was such a big guy to begin with. Still, it was a little worrisome. Suddenly I wasn't so upset we hadn't had sex.

Besides, I really needed the space to sit down and think about everything he'd told me. Unwrap my emotions, which were tangled up more than a fishing line in the reeds. I felt so raw and confused after yesterday. And I really didn't want to jerk him around. I needed to figure myself out so I wasn't unfair to him.

Seeing his ex almost die. Watching his children trying to process it and hardly being able to help. Having him finally explain what happened between us and then holding me all night long. It was all just too much for me to absorb in the moment.

"If you don't stop grinding that sweet ass against me, I'm going to fuck you."

I froze, unaware that I had in fact continued to rock back against him while I was overanalyzing the last twenty-four hours.

His arm tightened around me and he thrust his hips lazily. I felt his length slide along my butt and I had to swallow back a moan. Why did he have to be so sexy? It made it really hard to stay mad at him. That wasn't completely accurate. It wasn't just his looks for me. The way he was with his daughters and the way he always seemed to be helping those he cared about turned my heart to mush. It would have been so much easier if he were a cheater or a liar. I could walk away from that. No, my man had to be family oriented and fiercely defensive.

Oh fuck, did I just call him mine?

"I have to go to the bathroom," I squeaked out, and scrambled out of his arms.

His laughter followed me as I shut the door to the ensuite bathroom. It was deep and husky from sleep and it slipped along my skin, causing heat to flash over me like a wildfire. Or maybe that was from us dry humping each other like teenagers. Either way, I was a damp mess.

Leaning against the counter, I stared into the mirror and shook my head at my reflection. "What are you doing, Jenny?"

I honestly didn't know. I wanted him. Badly. But I was so afraid of opening up to him again and getting hurt. If I got closer to him and he cut me out again it would destroy me. I just knew it. He was it for me. So was it better to take the risk and be with him, knowing he could shatter my entire existence with a few words or actions? Or should I withdraw and keep that distance between us? Guarding my heart meant he'd never reach it and therefore couldn't break it.

Sounds of the bedroom door opening and little girls piling into the room filtered through the door. Damn. I was in my bra and panties. I didn't want them to see me like this.

Slipping into the robe that was hanging on the back of the door, I said a silent apology to Wendy for using her stuff. It didn't take long for Priest to wrangle the girls out of the room. I slipped out of the bathroom and found my phone on the nightstand.

I tapped out a quick text before I got dressed. My clothes were wrinkled beyond repair. I looked at the clock and sighed. I was going to have to call in sick. It'd been such a late night and emotionally packed day yesterday that we'd all slept in until nearly ten a.m.

Looking around, I made sure I hadn't forgotten anything, then made the bed. Finally, there was nothing left to do but face Priest with a conflicted heart and mind.

He looked up from the stove as I walked into the kitchen. He had on the slacks from yesterday, but hadn't put the shirt back on. All that tanned, smooth muscle was on display. Not to mention his tattoos. I longed to run my hands over the ink on his skin. Taste it with my tongue.

My phone dinging made me jump and pulled me out of my trance. Priest was watching me with knowing eyes. The heat between us simmered in the air. It smelled like we were burning up. My eyes dropped to the pancakes—which were, in fact, what was burning—then gave him a hesitant smile.

"My mom is here to pick me up," I told him. Shock played over his features. "Better get those before you set off the smoke detector."

He cursed under his breath and started scooping small pancakes out of the pan. While he was busy, I turned to the four girls watching me from the table.

"It was so nice to meet you all," I told his three daughters. I gave Caitlyn a wink. "I'll see you later, okay?"

She smiled and nodded. They all waved goodbye as I hurried out of the house. I ignored the cursing coming from Priest, just as I tuned out him calling my name.

I was getting in my mom's car as he stepped into the doorway to the house.

"Who's that?" The awe in my mom's voice had me glancing over. Her eyes were wide as she stared at Priest. He was a sight, only half dressed, scowling at us.

I couldn't help it, I started laughing. My mom was sitting here ogling the man who I'd just spent the night with. The one who claimed I was his.

"The one you told me to give a chance to," I told her.

She pulled out of the driveway, careful not to hit Priest's truck, which was parked very crooked. "Man doesn't know how to park, that's for sure." I couldn't find a short way to explain to her the hurry he'd been in. Or how exhausted he probably was when he returned from the hospital.

As we drove home, I filled her in on what'd happened. My dad had never really been around, so it'd always just been me and my mom. We were best friends. I would do anything for her. Give anything to make sure she was happy and healthy and I knew she'd do the same.

"Honey," she told me, glancing over at me with a serious look on her face. "That man has it bad for you," she informed me.

I rolled my eyes. "Mom. You saw him for all of twenty seconds."

"Yeah, and I saw the look on his face as you went bolting out of his house."

"I didn't bolt," I muttered, crossing my arms over my chest. "And it's his ex-wife's house."

It was her turn to roll her eyes. We had so many of the same mannerisms and identical attitudes. "You seriously don't think he bought that house for his kids?" When I shrugged, she shook her head. "Trust me. His name is on the mortgage for that place. Guaranteed."

"Dad never did that for me," I pointed out.

"That man is not your father," she argued.

"You're acting like you know him," I said in exasperation. "I don't even know him and I'm the one he said he wanted. Besides, I know that he's not like Dad."

I wasn't embarrassed to tell her about the things Priest said to me. She wasn't going to judge me, besides, I was a fully grown woman.

"Look, Honey. I get it. He hurt you." She flashed me a dark look. "And don't think I won't be having words with him about that someday soon." Before I could tell her she wasn't going to be meeting him—most likely—she continued on. "You don't trust him because of what he's done. Makes sense. You don't believe me when I say he's hooked on you."

"Because you don't know him," I stressed.

"Exactly. So what you need to do is really simple."

"It is?" I asked.

"Find someone who does know him and talk to them." She grinned at me, happy to have solved my problem.

I didn't have the heart to tell her I didn't have anyone I could ask about him. His MC brothers weren't going to talk to me, and that would be embarrassing, even if they would. I doubted even Hush would…

Tilting my head as an idea formed, I pulled my cell phone out. I tapped out a text, smiling when Hush responded almost immediately. I saved the phone number he sent me then wrote another text.

Hey! It's Jenny. Want to get lunch with me today?

I smiled when I read the reply a few minutes later. We were just pulling into our driveway as I made the plans. I had just enough time to shower and head over to the restaurant.

Leaning over, I kissed my mother's cheek. "Thanks, Mom."

"You're welcome, Baby," she said, patting my arm.

I rushed out of the car and into the house. Maybe my new friend could help me figure out the mystery that was Priest.

CHAPTER 10

Jenny

"Jenny! Over here!"

I skirted around tables and made my way to where Seek was sitting. A frown pulled at my brows as I realized she wasn't alone. Oh no. How was I supposed to pump her for information if there were other women here?

Seek jumped up as I approached and pulled me into a hug. "Jenny, this is Kit, Susie, Daisha, and Tory. I thought maybe you'd like to meet the other old ladies in the club," she said as she introduced us.

"They're old ladies," the gorgeous dark-haired woman said with a husky laugh. "I'm just the sister of one of the members." This was Kit. Seek had tossed a lot of names at me, but I was good with details.

"Who's your brother?" I asked after I said hi to all the others.

"Smokehouse," she said with a roll of her gorgeous blue-gray eyes.

"Oh, I remember him," I said with a grin. He'd nearly started a fight at my friend's wedding. It'd been a bit of a misunderstanding, but had gotten cleared up. *Quickly, and with a lot of fists.*

Kit's brows shot up. She gave Seek a questioning look. "I thought you said she was Priest's?"

"She is."

"Then why does she know my slutty brother?"

My eyes widened when I realized she thought I'd slept with Smokehouse. He was a charmer, so it didn't surprise me that he had a reputation with the ladies. My response came pouring out so fast I couldn't filter at all. "God no! Gross. I didn't have sex with *him*," I said it a bit too loud and three older ladies glared at us from the next table. "Or anyone else." The last part was a weak whisper as my face flushed.

Daisha, Susie, and Tory all burst into giggles. Their heads had been swinging back and forth like they were watching a tennis match while they listened to our conversation.

"That's good," Susie said. "It'd take the whole club to pull Priest off Smoke if the idiot had fucked with his old lady."

Temporarily side tracked by the thought of Priest and Smokehouse fighting I blurted out, "They would fight each other over a woman? Like, brothers from this chapter would fight?" For all I knew that was typical for the Austin Chapter as well. It was the women I'd known better than the men after all.

Kit gave me an indulgent smile. "Honey, if the cable so much as goes out and, absent of anyone else to hit? Yeah, they'll fight each other. Sometimes out of sheer boredom."

My head was spinning. I hadn't spent a lot of time around the MC in Austin so a lot of this was still very new to me. "Okay…" I needed to get back on topic. Where to begin explaining? I motioned to Kit. "I met your brother in Texas about a year and a half ago or so. At a wedding."

Seek explained to the others that I'd been living in Austin and had been friends with the MC there. Once she finished, I looked at the other women. "I don't know where all of you are getting the idea that I'm Priest's old lady. He broke up with me months ago."

They all exchanged knowing looks. "We heard," Kit finally said. "But we also know he was planning on heading back to Texas to clear the air and bring you back."

I blinked in shock, my mouth momentarily unable to form words. He'd been coming back for me? I'd come to the conclusion that he was only claiming he wanted me because I was conveniently dropped on his doorstep. Now to hear he'd been planning to come back...

"Why can't he ever tell me *anything*?" I growled in frustration.

That set them all off in laughter this time. "Welcome to the club," Daisha said with a wink.

"Yeah, the MC, the old ladies club, and the group of us who can't understand men at all," Tory said in a droll tone.

"Especially not these men," Seek added. "It took months before Hush stopped jerking me around and made me his old lady. I mean, I understand why now, but do you think he told me why at the time?"

"No," everyone chorused together.

"I've come to the conclusion that they can only speak so many words a day, so by the time they need to tell you something important they've already hit their limit, so it's up to you to guess your way through grunts and groping," Daisha said.

That was Priest right down to the last grope. It lightened my heart to have a group of women who legitimately understood what I was going through. It made me feel an instant bond with them. I sighed and gave them all serious looks. "I don't really know any of you yet, but I could use your help."

"Ooo," Kit said, shifting in her seat and eyeing me because she knew I was about to tell her something good. "Lay it on us."

"I don't want you guys to think I'm gossiping-"

"Pleeeease, gossip," Susie begged. The others nodded.

I told them about everything that happened yesterday. Once I opened my mouth, it just spilled out. I probably shouldn't be telling them about Wendy, but judging by the looks on their faces they already knew about her cancer.

"That's so sad," Tory said.

"Wendy is a nice enough lady," Daisha added.

"And no one deserves what she's going through," Susie followed up with.

"But she never really belonged," Kit said. "I'm not trying to be mean. She just never wanted to be a part of the lifestyle. Priest wanted to be in the MC and she just sort of…"

"Tolerated it," Susie supplied.

Daisha continued, "As you're well aware, this MC does more than ride bikes on Saturdays. These men especially, they need a bit…more…in their lives. They never really left the military lifestyle, that part of it anyways."

I knew she was referring to their vigilante activities. I knew all about it since I'd seen them help the Austin Chapter out when they needed it. The fighting, the adventure, and helping others was ingrained in them. I didn't mind that. Sure there were some who wouldn't understand how I could condone it, but each of these guys had their own moral code. I've seen it in action, and I've seen how they love their families. Who am I to judge them? I wasn't a saint either.

"Wendy knew Priest needed the club and this lifestyle, but she wanted a family man. Not that Priest isn't. She wanted a banker, who'd be home by a certain time and never get into trouble with the law. Ultimately she just put up with it, until she didn't," Tory explained.

"Exactly. Which is fine, but with all of us living on the compound it made things awkward," Kit continued. "Then there was what she did when they divorced. It's sort of hard to forgive her for that, even though Priest has."

"What did she do?" I asked, curiosity clawing at me.

"That's his story-" Kit started.

"Took those sweet girls away from him and wouldn't let them see each other…" Susie said, trailing off when she realized Kit wasn't going to tell me that. "Oops."

"We should tell her everything," Seek suggested. "Not that I know much." She gave me a sheepish grin. "When you asked if you could talk to me about him I figured not only could you meet the others, but they'd know more than me. Two birds, one stone."

I laughed. "Thank you. I appreciate it."

Kit caught my attention again. "Priest is a pretty private guy. I know he looks all surly and grumpy a lot of the time, but he has a heart of gold."

"Big as Texas," Daisha said with a nod.

"He's a good guy," Kit continued. "He was torn up about sending you that text-"

"How did you know about that?" I asked.

"Priest and Kit are friends," Susie answered. "She's one of the few women around he talks to. He hardly ever talks to any of the sweet butts."

"Except Sylvia," Tory reminded her.

"Yeah, but Syl is different. She's happy just having a place to belong and work. She's not searching for a biker to make her an old lady, at least not the guys in the club now," Daisha commented.

"We're friends," Kit reiterated, getting the conversation back on track. "I've known the guy for too many years for us not to be. Anyway, he never wanted to hurt you. He was just overwhelmed with taking care of his ex and his kids, and trying to make sure that everyone in his life was okay. That's a common theme for him."

Seek glanced over at me. "Is the Wendy thing an issue?"

I looked at her in shock. It was like they could read my mind.. "You mean am I jealous of her?" There was a tiny piece of me that was as awful as it was to admit.

"I would be," Tory piped up.

We all fell silent as the waiter put down two glasses in front of each of us. The orange liquid could have just been orange juice, but the fact that it was in champagne glasses gave it away for what it truly was.

"Yum! I love mimosas," Susie said with a grin. "I haven't gotten to drink in far too long." She shot me a pained look. "Can't drink while breastfeeding. But I pumped enough this morning to make sure this is out of my system before I go back to being the milk cow."

Everyone laughed and I just shook my head. She didn't look like she had a young baby. At least not from what I could see while she was sitting down.

"Drink up," Seek said with a laugh. We all picked up our glasses and said cheers.

"I don't think I'm jealous of Wendy," I told them. "At least not for the most part." It was pretty obvious that Priest and she were over. Or as much as it could be between co-parents. Then I remembered what he'd told me last night. Wendy was going into hospice and wasn't expected to live past a month.

Sourness spread in my stomach for even having the faintest negative feelings toward her. I took a large swallow from my mimosa to take the edge off the guilt.

"Don't let her stop you from getting together with Priest," Kit told me. They obviously hadn't heard the news yet. Priest was probably spending the time with his kids. It could be days before the others would find out, but I wasn't going to tell them. It wasn't my place.

"That's not it," I replied, hesitating. If Kit was as close to him as she said, I didn't want to piss her off talking about this.

As though she could read my mind she reassured me, "I'm not going to tell him anything we talk about here."

"Those men can gossip with the best of us," Tory said with a happy smile, "but we don't tell them anything an old lady tells us in confidence." They'd given me a quick rundown on who their men were. I was realizing I wanted to know more about these women and I hoped we could all be good friends, even if I didn't date Priest.

"I'm not sure I can give him another chance," I told them. It was embarrassing, but I admitted, "He really hurt me the way he went about it before. And then to find out he'd hid so much from me when I was opening up to him about my life… How can I trust him?"

They all fell quiet as I spoke. The others looked to Kit to explain. She gave me a sympathetic look. "I understand. All I can say, once again, is that Priest is super private. He doesn't tell just anyone about his life. And I know he should've been more open with you, but he obviously hadn't gotten there yet. I know he would have if Wendy hadn't taken a turn for the worse." She drained the first glass and plopped her elbows on the table, and her chin in her hands while she spoke. "I can promise you one thing, Jenny. If you give him another chance, he's not going anywhere. He'll make you his old lady. He'll bring you into his family, both with his kids and the club, and he won't let you go."

"He let Wendy go," I said softly. It was as though talking too loudly would break the hope that was building up from somewhere deep inside. Her words were everything I wanted.

Kit shook her head, her dark hair reflecting the light. "It was never going to last with Wendy. We all knew that from the moment we met her. Never told him that, of course, but those of us who know him, and love him, knew it. You?" Her eyes sparkled as she said the thing I longed to hear the most. "You're different. He's never going to be able to let you go, Jenny."

God. I wanted that so badly. Was I letting myself get talked into this because it was such a deep-seated need burning within me? I wasn't sure, but I somehow knew these women wouldn't lie to me. Kit believed every word she spoke.

I didn't mention to them that he was already claiming that I was his. A thrill raced through me at the thought of belonging to him. Of him being mine and always being there for me. I still had some thinking to do, but Mom had been right. Talking with these women, who knew Priest well, had eased some of my fears.

CHAPTER 11

Priest

It'd taken a week to move all my daughters' things into my four-bedroom apartment in the clubhouse. I'd double Cassie and Taylor up, giving Gabby and Caitlyn their own rooms, with one left for me. That would get us by for quite a while before the girls would be cramped for space.

Most of our time was eaten up by them visiting with their mother, first in the hospital, and then spending time with her in her home. I'd paid top dollar to have nurses provide her around the clock care. It was what she deserved at the end of her life. What I was paid by the MC and from my retirement was more than enough. I wasn't hurting for money.

Wendy was wasting away in front of us and my fucking heart was breaking for my girls. Even Caitlyn seemed distraught, but I had a feeling it had to do more with the other girls being so upset, than the loss of Wendy herself. I was proud of my girls; they were making their mother's last days as good as could be. They were all smiles and cuddles while spending time with her. They kept up a strong face, but at night I was the one rocking them to sleep while they sobbed. I was the one chasing away the nightmares.

No one questioned me as to why we weren't living in the Oro Valley house. I needed to be here at the clubhouse and the girls needed to be with me.

"Priest."

I paused in the act of carrying the last box full of Gabby's things up the stairs. Lockout watched with solemn eyes for a minute before he jerked his head, indicating I needed to follow him.

Cursing, I handed the box over to Riptide. He, Hush, Hellfire, and Toxic were helping me move. "Can you keep an eye on the kids, Rip?"

"Sure thing, Bro."

I grinned, but quickly headed down the stairs and caught up with Lockout. He brought me into the meeting room and shut the door. I watched him with wary eyes.

"Quit looking at me like that. I just wanted to fucking check in on you. It's been a rough year for you, Brother." Lockout scowled at me.

I returned the expression. "So? I'm fine."

We'd known each other for so long, I didn't mind speaking to him like this, but I didn't want his pity.

"Ah quit being a fucking asshole." Lockout sat down in a chair and I followed suit. "We're friends," he confirmed. "I'm allowed to be worried about you."

"You're sounding like a woman, Prez," I told him, a shit-eating grin splitting my face.

He flipped me off, grinning back. Then it slipped off his face. "In all seriousness. Everything alright? You need a bigger place?"

"The apartment's fine. Plenty of space for us all."

"I was surprised you didn't opt to stay at the house. At least for now."

I shook my head. "The girls need the break from seeing her wither away. I'd keep them away from it all if it wouldn't be so unfair to both the girls and Wendy. It's hurting all of them, but the second option would be worse." He nodded in understanding. "Besides. I need to be here. This place grounds me."

"Yeah, I get that. But we're doing fine right now. Honestly, with everyone still digging into what the fuck is going on out in the desert and trying to track down Caitlyn's father we're at a standstill anyway."

"Is that why you haven't given me any work over the last week?" I asked, a scowl settling on my face again. "I'm still your Road Captain, Lock. You can't cut me out-"

"I'm not cutting you out of shit, Priest." He sat forward, pinning me with a glare. The silence was thick in the room as we locked eyes. Finally, he sat back again, relaxing. "There's not much to do right now. And what there is, the others can handle. You have enough going on with the girls, Wendy, and moving." He gave me a sly look. "If you have any free time I'm going to expect you to be making up with your old lady."

My lips twitched. Lockout was a pushy bastard and after seeing how happy our Texas Chapter was with their wives and kids I had a feeling he was getting ideas. Either that or he just wanted to see us happy.

"I'm working on that," I told him.

He arched a brow. "How long has it been?"

"A week," I muttered. Shit had kind of imploded on me again. I wasn't ignoring Jenny, or cutting her out, this time. I'd texted and called each night this week. She'd responded to a couple of the texts, telling me what progress there'd been with Caitlyn's paperwork. I wanted to hear that news, but she refused to let me draw her into any conversations involving only the two of us. I would have driven to her, forced the conversation, but at the moment I was too overwhelmed. Again.

Each time we'd texted she'd asked how my girls were. If I hadn't wanted her before, I sure as fuck did now. This woman was perfect. A goddamn saint in tornado form. That she was so genuinely worried about my daughters just made the feelings I had for her deeper.

"Better work faster, Brother," Lockout told me with a grin. "What else do you need from me?"

"A fucking assignment would be nice."

He shook his head. "You're a stubborn dick, you know that? I'll give you an assignment when I have something for you to do."

"I could help track down Caitlyn's piece of shit father."

"Why? Your time is better spent with your kids right now."

He wasn't wrong. It was fucking killing me to sit and watch them have to live through the misery of their mother dying, but I couldn't abandon them. I wouldn't leave them to face that by themselves. I was their rock to lean on, the wall that protected them, and no matter how difficult, I'd always be by their sides. "Yeah, alright. But once things get going with The Silverbells, I want in. You're not leaving me home."

"I won't. You'll be there. I fucking need your skills and you know it."

Grinning, I nodded in agreement. I was, by far, his best shooter, and that was saying something with this crowd. I was the only trained sniper in our club and Lockout never went into a fight without me.

"Get out," Lockout told me, his lips tipping upward.

"See you later, Prez."

I hadn't made it more than two steps out of the room when Hush found me. "Hey, my old lady wants to know if we can babysit tonight."

My brows shot up. "You want to babysit my kids?"

"That's right. It'll give us some practice."

It wasn't possible for my eyebrows to inch up any higher. "Shit. Is Seek-"

"No, not yet, but not for lack of tryin'," he said with a wicked grin. "Won't be long now."

I laughed and slapped him on the shoulder. "Good for you, you surly bastard."

"You're one to talk."

"You sure you can handle all four?" I asked, hesitating. A night off meant I could go find Jenny, but I didn't want my girls to need me and not be there. Wendy had treatments scheduled for today and tomorrow, so we'd been finishing up the move and the girls had a few days off from seeing her. It was perfect timing.

"We'll all pitch in," Lockout said from behind me. "We'll set up a game night."

I chuckled, picturing all the guys playing cards with my daughters. "Alright. They'll have fun. Keep an eye on Taylor. She cheats," I warned them. Not that they didn't know already, the girls had been having game nights with my brothers for years, though the poker was relatively new.

"So does Butcher. She fits right in," Lockout told me.

"Yes, but in terms of maturity and general deviousness she's older than Butcher, so make sure he doesn't throw a tantrum," I told him with a grin.

"We'll go pick the girls up from your apartment right now," Hush said. "You're officially free until after ten a.m. tomorrow mornin'."

"Why ten?"

"I don't want to be gettin' up at the ass crack of dawn," Hush grumped, giving me his back and heading upstairs.

I followed him up and explained to my girls about the game night and sleep over with Uncle Hush and Aunt Seek. Excitement shone on their faces and it helped ease some of the guilt about the last week. My kids loved their 'uncles' and being here at the clubhouse. It would soon feel like home to them again.

Grabbing my keys, I hugged each girl and told them I'd be back later on. I caught Hush's eye. "They've been having some nightmares. If you need me-"

"It'll be fine, but if we do, I'll call. Promise."

"Thanks, Brother."

We shook hands and then I went downstairs. I made a beeline for the door, almost plowing over Pixie as she came into the building. My mind was already on the back of my bike. I couldn't wait to ride. I also couldn't wait to see the look on Jenny's face. It was time to finish our conversation from the other night.

I'd had Dash find Jenny's address. He may be a great hulking beast of a man, but he was a whizz with the computer shit. Not nearly to the level as Rat—one of the Austin Chapter's members—but still damn good. He and Riptide were busy looking into The Silverbells and Caitlyn's father. If they weren't successful Lockout would probably call up the Texas guys and ask for help. He was hesitant to bring them in on anything. They'd gotten out of the one-percenter lifestyle and didn't need to be caught doing anything illegal. Both Dash and Riptide had been commo guys—the communications techies for their special force squads. Tech was their forte. I was sure they'd find a lead.

It didn't take long to get to Jenny's place, or rather, her mom's. I cut the engine on my bike and stared at the house. It looked nice, well kept. Swinging a leg over, I got off and headed up the walkway.

A dog barked from the next door neighbor's yard as I knocked on the door. It was after five and still the sun blazed. It was September, so most of the monsoons were over, but it wouldn't start cooling down until November. I was used to it, a desert rat through and through. I'd been born in Tucson and planned to stay here until I died.

The door opened and I watched as the smile slipped off Jenny's face as she realized who was standing there. That was a punch to the nuts. I wanted to be the cause of her smile, not the wary look in her eyes.

"Hey there, Taz."

"Priest. What are you doing here?"

I deserved it, I guess. And she was going to make me work for this, but in the end I'd win. I always did. And she was my reward.

CHAPTER 12

Jenny

Priest was the last person I'd expected to see at the door when I opened it. I knew at some point he was going to show back up. And to be fair, he'd kept in contact over the last week, so it wasn't like he'd disappeared like before. I just hadn't been ready for him this soon. Especially not looking like the hot mess I currently was. I was in jean shorts and an old raggedy t-shirt that I've never been able to throw out, while I cleaned.

I was still sifting through and processing everything the girls had told me. I'd had another talk with Mom and asked her what she thought about her daughter dating a biker. She had only said as long as she got grand babies she didn't care. I'd mentioned the four who came with Priest, a small head start as far as she was concerned. I knew she was already hearing the wedding march song. I swore I woke up one morning to her measuring me for a dress. She claimed she was bringing me breakfast in bed, but the distinct lack of breakfast, and the soft tape measure in her hand, had called her bluff.

Priest's eyes narrowed at my question, but he didn't look pissed. He seemed to be contemplating how best to deal with me. I wasn't trying to be a pain in the ass, I was just so conflicted. Nothing he'd done so far had reassured me that my heart was safe with him.

That realization struck like lightning. That was what I was waiting on. A declaration saying I was his. A wild kiss in the darkness. Even explaining what had happened before wasn't enough. I needed him to prove to me he was going to put me first. Not before his daughters. Or even his club necessarily. Fine, I didn't need to be first, but I did need to be a priority. I needed to know he wouldn't drop me at a moment's notice just because the club, or anyone else who was more important pulled at him. I needed to be included.

"Can I come inside?"

That was a dangerous game. My mom wasn't even home to be a buffer between us. Still, I wasn't going to make him stand on the porch in the heat. That was a bit more rude than I was willing to be. I stepped back, my answer to his question.

He gave me a heated look as he came inside. He already thought he'd won. That irritated me a little. This wasn't a game to me. There was no winning and losing when it came to my feelings for the jerk. There was just happiness or utter devastation.

"Why are you here?" I asked again.

"I came to see you."

"Yeah, I got that, but why?"

He moved forward, his huge body backing me into the wall next to the door. When I went to duck out of the way, his hand shot forward. I was left staring at a muscular, veiny forearm. Why was that so sexy? It really shouldn't be.

It would be sexier still if it was wrapped around me.

"What are you doing?" It came out as a whisper.

"I told you the other day, Taz. You're mine. You don't seem to believe me when I say it."

"Can you blame me?" I snapped, a hand going to his chest as I tried to shove him away. I needed space. To think. To breathe. Sucking in a shuddering breath, my nipples scraped against his chest. My silent plea for space was ignored and if anything he leaned in closer. My body was already screaming for relief. Only from his hands and mouth, not from his distance.

I closed my eyes in a failing attempt to get myself under control. Anytime he came near this was how my body reacted to him. It made it damn hard to remember why I was hesitant to trust him again. I opened my eyes and tried again.

"No. I fucked up. I realize that. But I'm telling you now. It's not going to happen again."

The urge to tell him 'I'll believe it when I see it' was so strong the words nearly spilled from my lips. I managed to bite them back at the last second. Issuing a challenge to a man like this was a dangerous move and I wasn't stupid.

"Okay." Funny, that one word was filled with more attitude than even I thought possible.

His jaw flexed as he ground his teeth together. His voice came out as a low growl. "I know you don't trust me, Taz, but you're going to have to get over that."

There was no holding back the harsh laugh. It forced its way up from my gut and it was full of bitterness. "Sure. I'll go ahead and jump right on that, Priest. And stop calling me that."

"Taz?"

"Yes," I gritted out. "It's insulting."

Genuine surprise flickered in his gorgeous brown eyes. "It's not meant to be insulting."

"You named me that when I was running around cleaning in panic mode," I told him wryly. "How else am I supposed to take it?"

One side of his mouth kicked up in a smirk. "Take it as a loving nickname. The cleaning may have inspired it, but you're always charging around in the middle of one task or another." He leaned in closer until his lips brushed my ear. My eyes fluttered closed. "Maybe I've been wondering what it'd be like to have all that energy focused on me. What you'd be like writhing beneath me as I fuck you. Will you still be my little tornado then?"

I couldn't breathe. No matter how much I willed my lungs to suck in air, they weren't cooperating. Hearing Priest say such dirty, delicious things to me had robbed me of all sanity. I was a woman with needs and it just so happened that the object of all my desires was currently pressed up against me, whispering filthy things into my ear. There's only so much a girl could take.

Turning my head toward his, I trailed my lips over the rough stubble of his five o'clock shadow. I'd never seen him with a beard, but he almost always had this stubble and I loved it. It rasped against my skin, shooting sparks all the way down to my toes. I was playing with fire, but I was so tired of overanalyzing the situation. I just wanted to *feel*.

Our mouths met and I sank into his kiss with a sigh. His tongue traced the seam of my lips and I opened for him. I knew this was going to make it that much harder if things didn't go anywhere between us, but at least I'd have this one memory afterward.

His hands slid into the hair at my temples and clamped down, holding my head still. I wasn't sure if he thought I was going to change my mind, but it was clear he wasn't letting me go anywhere.

The decision was made. My mind made up. I wanted him too badly to deny myself at least one time with him. If he truly meant what he'd said about wanting me to be his, I was on board. A week of agonizing came down to one simple fact: if I didn't give him another chance I could be missing out on everything I'd ever wanted.

If I walked away from him with a broken heart, at least I'd tried. I'd figure out a way to live on without him. For now, I was going to bask in the pleasurable sensations he was creating within my body.

"Where's your room?" he rumbled against my lips.

"Down the hall, second door on the right," I answered breathlessly.

He released his hold on my hair, but before I could lead the way, his hands went to my hips. I gasped when they kept going and slipped around and covered my ass, lifting me into the air. Instinctively my legs went around his hips to help hold myself against him.

He'd lifted me like I weighed no more than a bag of feathers. Granted, he was a huge guy, but I wasn't a tiny woman. The world spun as he turned and started down the hall.

His hands were still gripping my ass, fingers digging into my flesh. He groaned and leaned forward, his mouth latching onto my neck.

My head dropped back as he raked his teeth over my sensitive skin. It'd been far too long since I'd felt a man's mouth on me. Even so, I was pretty sure Priest's felt better than any who'd come before him.

I grunted as we hit the wall. He wasn't paying attention to where we were going and had taken the turn too soon. Muttering curses under his breath his lips broke contact with my skin long enough for him to find the doorway.

He kicked the door shut behind us and I let out a laugh as he dropped me back on my bed. I scrambled backward just enough to give him space to crawl on top of me and still half his body hung off the mattress.

We were kissing again as he laid his hard body on top of mine. I relished his weight shoving me down into the bed. The feel of his heavy muscles pressed against my body.

He bit my bottom lip, then wasted no time working his way lower. The sound of rending fabric made me gasp. He'd just taken my shirt in both hands and ripped it down the middle.

"Priest!"

He didn't bother to look up, instead he'd buried his face between my breasts. His hand delved under my back and with a flick he unhooked my bra.

I didn't have the breath to scold him about ruining one of my favorite shirts because he jerked my bra off and those wide, calloused hands were cupping my breasts.

His thumb swiped over my nipple and I bit my lip, trying to hold back the pleas that were building in my chest. Desire darkened his eyes from a deep brown to almost black. He gave me a wicked grin before he dropped his head.

My back arched, shoving my breast more firmly toward him. He sucked hard on the nipple in his mouth, causing me to cry out. Somewhere in the back of my mind, I was grateful my mom wasn't here. Judging by the fact that he had me moaning and whimpering within the first few minutes there was no way I'd be able to stay quiet. Thank God she wasn't going to be here to hear this.

"These are fucking perfect," Priest muttered against my skin, dragging his lips over to my other breast and licking that lonely tip.

"They're small," I panted.

His eyes flashed up and met mine. He lifted his head slightly, his bottom lip hovering just above my aching peak. "I'm the one doing the fucking judging here, Taz. They're perfect," he insisted, then went back to showing me how much he liked them.

My breasts had always been super sensitive. Every pull and draw from his mouth shot pleasure straight from my nipples to my clit, making it throb in time with his suckling.

I wrapped my legs around his waist and ground my pussy against him. It didn't matter that we both had our jeans on, I had to have friction against my needy pussy.

"Bad girl," he said with a nip to my rib cage. He sat up until he was on his knees between my splayed thighs. With one hand he reached behind him and dragged his shirt over his head.

My eyes greedily took in every inch of his exposed skin. When his shirt was finally off, I sat up and gave into the temptation and licked the tattoo curling around his left nipple.

His huge hand cupped the back of my head, holding me there while I flicked the tip of my tongue over him. His groan vibrated beneath my lips.

My gasp was sharp when he fisted his hand in my hair and dragged my head back, away from his skin. I fought back the pout, but my lower lip stuck out.

"You'll have your chance another time, Taz. It's *my* turn to taste *you*."

He dragged me down to the bed, the bite of my hair pulling against my scalp only making me hotter, wetter.

"You're going to lay there like my good girl and take what I give you."

My eyes widened at his words, and my lips parted. Hearing him call me that sent delicious shivers down my spine. I liked it. Liked that I could please him. And I wanted to please him badly.

His hands pulled my jean shorts off my body, taking my panties with them. A momentary flash of embarrassment washed over me. What if he didn't like my body? What if my ass jiggled too much? This was the worst part of sleeping with someone for the first time.

Priest's eyes raked hungrily over me, leaving no spot left unexamined. Heat threatened to drown me in the molten lava pit of my desire. The look on his face assured me he liked what he was seeing.

"I've been waiting so long to see this gorgeous body. There's one part of you I've been fucking coming to the thought of though," he told me, voice low and husky.

"What-" He'd been thinking about me while he…did that?

His hands went to my hips and flexed. My world spun as he flipped me on the bed.

"Fuuuuck me." His hands went directly to my ass, gripping my cheeks.

My face heated with embarrassment. My thighs and butt had always been my insecure spots.

"This is so incredibly sexy."

I gasped as I felt him tug my cheeks apart. There was zero reason for him to be staring at my asshole. I turned as much as I could with him straddling the back of my thighs and slapped at him. "Stop that."

"No way," he growled. "This perfect little ass is all mine, Taz. Don't you fucking forget it."

He was back to kneading instead of holding me open, so I didn't swat at him again. Air brushed over my back as he leaned down and I yelped when his teeth closed over my flesh. He'd just bitten me on the butt.

"What's wrong with you?" I asked him, shooting a glare over my shoulder.

"I have a thing for juicy asses and thick thighs," he growled back. "Fucking sue me."

He shifted off me and suddenly I was, once again, on my back staring up at the ceiling. My pussy clenched as a tremor of ecstasy raced over me. I loved that he was able to toss me around, putting me wherever he pleased. It was so hot.

Without bothering to take his own jeans off, he dove between my legs. The loud moan that burst from between my lips would have embarrassed me if I wasn't already drowning in pleasure.

He gave me a long, slow lick from my opening to my clit. "Delicious."

I couldn't respond because after that one word he'd gone to work, devouring me like I was an ice cream cone on a hot summer's day. His tongue was circling my clit, edging me closer and closer to that precipice.

It'd been so long since I'd had an orgasm and suddenly I was worried about the speed at which this one was barreling down on me. It was going to break me, I just knew it.

"Priest," I whimpered.

He hummed in his throat, one hand going to my hip to pin me against the bed while his other delved between my legs.

Oh God.

He plunged a long, thick finger inside me and started rubbing my G spot. There was no holding back while he showered attention on my clit, filled me with his finger, and rubbed that spot.

My orgasm slammed into me like a runaway train. I didn't bother to try to stifle my scream. I arched up into him as my mind fractured into blissful pieces.

Pussy clenching around his finger, I heard his chuckle as though it were far off.

"That's it, Baby. I fucking love hearing you scream. Next time you'll be screaming my name, though."

I didn't bother to respond to him, wouldn't have been able to even if I wanted to. I was floating, the aftermath of tingles making me feel loose and relaxed. It wasn't hard to enjoy the moment.

His hand grasped my chin and I gazed up at him. "There you are. I want to watch those pretty eyes cloud over while I fuck you."

My eyes widened as I felt him settle between my legs, his dick sliding through the wetness of my pussy. He paused before shoving inside, looking down at me. I hadn't even been aware of him taking off his boots or jeans, I was so busy riding the high he'd given me.

He thrust forward and lowered his head to catch my gasp in his mouth. He kissed me hard as he picked up the pace. The sounds echoing off the walls of my childhood bedroom were filthy and so hot I clenched around his thick cock.

I hadn't even gotten to see it yet, though judging by the feel of him stretching me wide, he was packing a monster. Considering how big of a man he was, I wasn't all that surprised. It seemed like there was no end to it, it just kept going deeper.

His lips released mine and he started tonguing my nipples as he picked up the pace. My thoughts fragmented and all I could focus on now was chasing the next orgasm.

"I want you to come all over my cock, Taz." He pushed up on his arms, his intense gaze catching mine. The muscle in his jaw flexed as he gritted the demand out from between clenched teeth.

"I'm going to make you come over and over again, until you wonder if you're going to die from pleasure," he promised me. "But not this time. Your tight little pussy has me ready to bust inside you already. So come for me, Baby. Now."

Our bodies slapped together as he pounded into me. Between his dirty words and the sensations building within me, I couldn't resist. I obeyed his command and fell apart underneath him again. He'd been right before, I screamed his name as the waves of bliss battered me.

He dropped his head and growled in my ear as he followed me over. I felt his cock twitch, deep inside me, and then the wash of his cum filling me.

It took me a few minutes, while I was boneless with pleasure, before I realized the implications of that. "Priest," I yelped.

He grunted, rolling his heavy weight off me, and taking me with him. I ended up sprawled against his chest. Shoving up, I stared down at him in disbelief.

"Did you use a condom?"

He pried one eye open. "No."

My jaw dropped. "What? I'm not on birth control, Priest!"

A slow smile spread over his face as his eyes dropped closed again. "Good. I hope you give me a baby, Taz."

I smacked his chest, which had both his eyes opening as he glowered at me. "I can't just give you a baby, asshole!"

"Why not? You're mine."

That made me freeze, even though I was still angry at him. He sighed when he saw the indecision on my face.

"I wouldn't have slept with you if I wasn't planning to keep you forever. I want you to be my old lady, Taz. You're already mine." His arms tightened around me. "Make it official."

"We hardly know each other, Priest."

"I'm looking forward to getting to know everything about you. I just want my claim on you while I do so." His eyes searched my face, asking me silently to agree.

It was crazy. It was sexy. It was exactly what I wanted. I was done running from him. "Okay."

His eyes narrowed. "Okay, what, Taz?"

"I'll be your old lady." I laughed when he flipped me again, pinning me beneath his huge body. He wiped the grin off my face when he kissed me.

By the time we came back up for air, I was ready to go again. How was it possible that he could have my body thrumming in anticipation after having just given me two orgasms?

His hands slid over my body and I was tempted to let him have his way again, but it reminded me of our earlier argument. He'd derailed it by asking me to be his. "You really want another baby?"

"Fuck yeah," he rumbled in my ear as he sucked on the lobe. He nibbled on it, shooting sparks down my spine. "I want as many as you can give me."

"What about…everything?"

"We'll deal with it, Taz. One thing at a time."

"Fine, but I'm going on birth control for now." His head snapped up and he scowled at me. "Just until things calm down a bit." I tilted my head and gave him back my own glare. "If you have any STDs I'm going to kick your ass."

He chuckled and shook his head. "Haven't had sex in years, Baby. I'm clean."

"Years?" I asked doubtfully. How was it possible a sexy guy like him didn't have women lining up to be in his bed?

"You don't believe me. One thing you'll learn about me, Taz, is I don't lie. I may not tell people much about my life, but I don't lie when I do. I've been too busy and not interested in random pussy."

That made the tightness in my chest loosen and I sighed in contentment as he rolled us onto our sides and pulled me in close to his body.

CHAPTER 13

Priest

I hadn't meant to fall asleep, but it'd been a week of nearly sleepless nights. Add in a round of intense cardio with Taz and that massive orgasm and I'd dropped off almost immediately.

The dinging of a phone woke me, I cracked open an eye. I didn't know how much time had passed, but Jenny was still lying in my arms. She'd picked up her phone and was texting. I wasn't sure where she'd found it since I was pretty sure mine was over on the floor somewhere. The ringer was on, so I'd know if Lockout or one of the others were calling about my kids, or the club.

"Everything okay?" My voice sounded like I'd been gargling gravel and I was groggy as hell.

Her body jerked in my arms and she shot me an apologetic look over her shoulder. "I'm sorry that woke you. Yeah, everything's fine. It's just my mom. She's stuck late at work."

I made a sound low in my chest in answer and ran my lips over the soft skin of her shoulder. Enjoying the small breath she dragged in at the action, I did it again.

She was still texting, but my eyes were starting to drop closed again. "Shit. Can't seem to stay awake," I muttered.

She set the phone aside and rolled in my arms. I managed to pry my eyes open so I could look down at her pretty face. The grin that stretched over my face was inevitable. Her hair was everywhere, curls going in all directions.

"What?"

"I knew your hair would look like this after I fucked you." I smoothed my hand over the wayward curls, loving that they bounced right back into position afterward.

She gave me a mocking glare—the little tilt to her lips giving away that she wasn't really mad. "Are you making fun of my hair?"

"Never. I fucking love it." I tilted my head and studied her. "I want curly haired babies," I decided.

Her eyes widened again. "You keep throwing me off when you say stuff like that," she admitted. "This is all so…sudden."

"Story of my life," I said with a chuckle. My fingers trailed up and down her arm. I didn't want to ever stop touching her. "That's not to say that I'm impulsive to the point of detriment. I think about what it is I want. Weigh all the pros and cons, but I typically come to my decision quickly."

"And you've decided you want me?" She nibbled her bottom lip and my eyes focused there as I imagined her mouth wrapping around my dick. It kicked underneath the covers as I started to get hard.

"I'm not trying to be a typical girl," she said with a laugh, "but…why me?"

I went back to running my fingers through her curls, pushing them away from her face. "Oh, I don't know. You're fucking gorgeous? Sexy. Sweet as can be. You love kids. And since the first day I met you, you've been there in the back of my mind."

Her eyes widened and I decided there was something to this whole thing of telling a woman how much you like them. I hadn't been great about that in the past. I rolled until I had her underneath me, staring down into her beautiful eyes. "I can't stop thinking about you, Taz. I need to know what you're doing each day. How you're feeling. I want to see your smile light up when I walk through the door."

Pink was flooding her cheeks, making her freckles stand out more and I gave in to temptation. Lowering my head, I brushed my lips over them.

"Priest," she said breathlessly when I finally stopped.

"Hmmm?"

"That sort of sounds like you love me."

My grin was cocky and wicked. I wouldn't have asked her to be my old lady if I didn't already know that. I certainly wouldn't try putting a baby in her if I wasn't going to spend the rest of my life with her. It didn't mean I was going to give her those words just yet. It wasn't about playing games, but making sure I knew for sure before I admitted it. I had more than myself to think about here. She and the girls had to bond to each other as well.

She covered her face with her hands when I didn't answer. Her voice was muffled, but I was close enough to hear her. "I don't need you to tell me that yet, but… I think I might love you, Priest."

I swear my fucking heart stopped when she said it. Grabbing her wrists, I dragged her hands away from her face. "Why's that a problem?"

"I don't know you," she huffed. "How can I possibly be in love with you?"

Arching a brow, I grinned down at her. I liked my ego to be stroked as much as the next man, but she wasn't ready to list off the reasons why. There'd be plenty of time for that later. I glanced over at the clock on the nightstand. It was still relatively early, only six p.m.

"Want to come somewhere with me?" I asked her.

Her eyebrows shot up, but she nodded. Staring down at the eager expression on her face, I debated on just staying here. I'd happily spend the rest of the night seeing how many orgasms I could wring from her body.

As if she could read my thoughts on my face, she pushed against my chest. "Let me get dressed."

I rolled off her and watched as she got up, still naked, and gathered her clothes up from the floor. I'd tossed them aside in my hurry to rid her of them.

She tossed my jeans, briefs, and shirt at me. My cut she picked up and hung on the back of the chair that sat at a desk in the corner. She gave me the cutest fucking smile before she disappeared into the ensuite bathroom.

Sitting up, I rested my forearms on my knees as I stared at my cut for a minute. She didn't know it, but with that one move she knocked me on my ass. The MC was important to me. I couldn't love another woman who hated my involvement with them like Wendy had. I'd hoped—since Jenny had been cool with the Austin Chapter—that she wouldn't mind the lifestyle. Seeing her treat my cut with respect, by hanging it up instead of leaving it on the floor, I knew that this would work out between us.

Tonight would be a great test of that.

It didn't take us long to get dressed and we walked outside. I went over to my bike and pulled a helmet out of the saddle bag. Climbing on, I motioned her over and tightened the strap beneath her chin.

"Will you teach me?" she asked, excitement flaring in her eyes.

"To ride? Like, not just on the back, but for your own bike?"

She nodded, giving the bike a wistful look. I knew at that moment it wasn't going to take me long to tell this woman I loved her. I'd already seen how she was with my kids. Add in the moment with my cut and her excitement over my bike? Fuck. I was a goner.

"Sure, I'll teach you. Not today though, this bike is too big for a beginner." I waited while she climbed on behind me, enjoying the feel of her body pressing to mine as she looped her arms around my waist.

The ride over was quick, but I tensed up as I pulled into the clubhouse parking lot. I helped her off my bike and watched her expression closely as I followed her.

"Does Lockout need to see us?" she asked, curiosity shining in her eyes.

There wasn't any anger or sign of irritation on her face. This was what I'd be doing until I knew for sure she was going to fit into this lifestyle, test her. Not shit test her or play games, but show her what my life was and see how she responded. She couldn't really agree to it without experiencing it first. I didn't want to compare Jenny and Wendy to each other, but I'd learned from my ex that I needed to find a woman who didn't mind low-key nights at home with the kids. Or that a club barbecue was going to be date night. Or that I'd have to leave our bed in the early morning hours after a phone call from my president.

"No. I just thought maybe you'd like to get in on this." Shoving open the door to the clubhouse, I grinned when I saw what my brothers and kids were up to. I'd figured this was going to be the case.

They all looked over, guilt morphing their smiles into frowns. Except Butcher and Toxic. Butcher was...well, something else, and there was a reason Toxic had his name.

"Daddy!" All four of my girls ran over and I dropped down to a squat so I could hug them.

"You girls remember Jenny, right?"

There were nods and shy waves passed around. "Did you come to play?" Gabby asked. She lowered her voice. "I've already won fifty bucks off Uncle Riptide."

"Your daughter is a cheater," Riptide called out as he shuffled cards. "Deals from the bottom of the deck."

I looked down and gave Gabby a conspiratorial wink. "No you're just shitty at cards, Rip."

He grumbled then nodded in hello at Jenny. "Am I dealing you two in?"

Jenny's eyes met mine and she nodded enthusiastically. It was genuine, too. I was damn good at reading people. She wasn't just trying to placate me in order to worm her way into my life so she could change everything. She was truly glad to be here. It went a long way toward easing the tension that had been building inside of me since we pulled in.

Lockout got up and went to get more chairs. Jenny took his seat next to Seek. The girls started chatting about something while I sat between Taylor and Caitlyn.

I didn't miss the smile that Jenny gave me as I sat between my daughters. It didn't seem to bother her in the least. I picked up the cards that were sitting in front of me.

"Here's your chips, Jenny," Hush told her, sliding them across the table.

"Taz," I corrected him.

"What?" he asked.

"Her name. It's Taz."

"Well fuck me," Toxic said with a grin. He ignored all the glares and pointed looks at the little girls. "Does that mean you finally made her your old lady?"

"That's right."

"Congratulations, Brother," Lockout said, coming up from behind us. He set the chairs down and clapped a hand on my shoulder. "And to you, Taz," he said and tugged her out of her chair to give her a hug.

Butcher leaned across Seek and whispered to Taz with a grin on his face, "Looks like you were walking a little funny, and not from the bike." He winked as Seek slapped him back to his side of the table. Taz blushed and I made a mental note to choke Butcher out later. He'd pay for that comment during our weekly sparring match.

Lockout ignored him and clamped a hand on my shoulder. "I'm happy for you, both of you." It was his way of showing the crew that he accepted the match. Most of us check in with Lockout before officially making a woman our old lady. As I'd learned, the wrong woman could end up making a lot of trouble for our club. Hell, if they made too much trouble a member could get booted. You had to be careful who you chose. Lucky for me, Jenny was passing every test so far. Time would prove to us all that she was the woman I knew her to be.

Cheers and congratulations were passed around the table until Butcher finally slammed a fist down on the wooden surface. "We've covered this enough. Congrats to you both. Now can we get fucking going? This one," he said, pointing at Cassie, "has thirty bucks of mine." He narrowed his eyes on my little girl and snarled, "And I want it back."

Jenny's jaw dropped and I saw her gearing up to rip Butcher a new one. Before she could say anything, Cassie let out a loud giggle, then stuck her tongue out at Butcher. "You're gonna have to win a round to get it back, Uncle Butcher," she taunted, completely unfazed and unafraid of the man sitting across from her.

Jenny joined in on the laughter and Butcher grumbled a few 'threats' at my daughter before he grinned at her. He looked over at me. "This one is vicious. I like her."

I leaned around Taylor and whispered to Jenny. "Don't worry. The girls have grown up around these men. They know how to put them in their place."

"I see that," she said with a quiet laugh.

"Enough talking!" Butcher called. "You're up, Taz." He pointed from her to the deck.

CHAPTER 14

Jenny

It was impossible not to have fun with this group of people. Everyone was laughing and slinging insults at each other while we played. I couldn't help but smile as I watched Priest bring over pretzels that were long and stick shaped. He and the girls popped one in their mouths, pretending they were cigars as they played.

I was sure there would be people who'd be horrified that these guys were gambling with kids this young, but from where I sat? Those girls were having the best night of their lives. Considering what was going on with their mother, I was so happy to see them smiling and laughing. Also, they were damn good at poker. It was obvious this is what game night for them was and somewhere along the line they'd weaseled their 'uncles' into playing for cash.

Gabby had a pile of green in front of her and her sisters hadn't fared too badly either. Caitlyn was still learning the ropes, but Gabby would lean over and whisper advice to her during each hand.

Although she still wasn't talking, occasionally you would see her smirk or grin. Her new family was drawing her out of her shell.

My heart clenched every time I saw it. They'd clearly accepted Caitlyn into their fold already. A small piece of me wondered if it would be that easy for me? I hoped so, but would also understand if they had a hard time accepting that their dad had a new woman in his life.

Toxic had spilled the beans earlier, but the girls hadn't really reacted, so I wasn't sure if they knew what it all meant. It didn't matter, I wanted to become a part of this family, so I'd take whatever trials came my way and hopefully by the end we'd all get what we wanted.

The night passed quickly and I was actually disappointed when Priest called out that it was time for the girls to be put to bed. I wasn't the only one. Butcher almost threw a full on tantrum, worse than the girls ever could have.

Hush nudged Priest and motioned to the girls. "I know we're babysittin', but if you want to come help get them to sleep, we don't mind."

Priest's eyes found mine and I nodded in encouragement. "I'll wait here," I told him with a smile. It wasn't my place to be helping with bedtime yet, even though my heart longed to go up those stairs with them.

I watched him herd his kids upstairs, then looked around as the men started cleaning up the mess from poker night. I grabbed the bag of pretzels and brought them back to the kitchen. When I came back into the living area, Riptide smiled at me.

"You don't have to help clean, Taz," he told me. It was strange how quickly they'd all gone from calling me Jenny to the nickname Priest had given me. Then again, they were used to nicknames.

"Bro," Butcher complained. "If she wants to help clean, let her. Less for us to do," he muttered as he grabbed the folding chairs.

Riptide just shook his head, but didn't say anything when I grabbed a towel from the bar, wetted it, and wiped off the folding tables before they broke them down and brought them back to the storage area.

After everything was put away Lockout stopped and leaned on the bar. "I'm glad you're here," he told me. The others had all drifted away, calling goodnight to me as they went.

"Thanks, Lockout," I replied.

His eyes strayed over to the stairs. "He's going through a rough time, but having you around is going to help. Goodnight, Taz." With that he left me alone to wait for Priest.

I sat down at the bar and smiled. It was nice to know I was accepted by Priest's brothers and their old ladies. That took a lot of pressure off my shoulders. Now all I had to do is make sure that his daughters didn't think I was the wicked step-mother.

Jumping when the door behind me opened, I glanced over my shoulder. The two women stopped short when they saw me sitting there. The smaller of the two narrowed her eyes at me, but didn't say anything. She just ran a hand through her short blonde hair and went behind the bar.

The second woman gave me a quick smile then hurried past. They started restocking the small bar area quietly and efficiently. I didn't need anyone around to tell me that these were two of the sweet butts, or club bunnies, as the guys in Austin called them.

"Hi," I finally said after a few minutes. I didn't want them to think I was completely stuck up. These women hung around the club, hoping one of the men would make them an old lady. If that ever happened I didn't want them to think I'd treated them badly.

"Hi," the brunette said with a grin. "Would you like a drink?"

"Oh, no thank you. I'm Jen…Taz." I went with Priest's nickname. If he was going to use that while I was at the club, then I would too. I didn't mind it so much now that I didn't think he was making fun of me.

"I'm Scarlett. That's Pixie," she said with a wave over to her companion.

"It's nice to meet you both."

Pixie just gave me a sullen look, but didn't say a word. She kept wiping off the bar.

Mentally, I shrugged. I didn't need to be friends with her if she wasn't willing. That was fine by me. I just didn't want to be rude to anyone in the club. I knew that could cause problems for Priest and that wasn't what I wanted.

Before Scarlett or I had a chance to talk more Priest came back downstairs. He came over and stroked his hand over my hair. He seemed to really like it, which made me happy because it'd always been a pain in the ass to deal with. Now I didn't mind the over the top hair care regime I had to be dedicated to. Not if he liked it.

"Hey. I'm yours for the rest of the night," Priest told me.

My chest warmed at the look in his eyes. The fact that this man wanted me was still a shock, but I wasn't stupid enough to talk him out of it. At least, not anymore.

"We can go out. Go back to your place. Or…we can go up to my place." There was nothing implied there, he was genuine. I knew what each of the options meant, but he was leaving it entirely up to me. Given that fact, there really was only one option I cared for.

I bit my lip, shooting a glance at the women behind the bar. Scarlett was grinning, but Pixie was glowering down at the glass she was wiping out. "Let's go upstairs," I told him, trying not to blush since the others were listening.

"Sounds good to me. Have a good night girls," Priest called out to the others as he led me over toward the stairs.

They both returned his greeting and I heard Scarlett giggling as we went. "Scarlett is nice," I said as we walked up the stairs and down the hallway.

Priest looked down at me in surprise. "You know her name?"

"I introduced myself," I replied, with a shrug.

His smile slowly moved over his face as he stared down at me in disbelief.

"What?"

"Most old ladies wouldn't bother, that's all." There was a far away look in his eyes now and I wondered if he was remembering back to the way his ex had dealt with club life.

"There's no reason for me to be rude," I informed him. "Though I don't think Pixie and I will be friends anytime soon."

He snorted and opened a door, allowing me to step through first. "She's been in a mood since she started a fight with Seek, got her ass handed to her, then almost got kicked off the property."

My eyes widened and I looked back at him. "Seriously? Who'd want to fight Seek? She's like twice the size of Pixie."

"Pix has a thing for Hush," he said, his hand going to the small of my back as he directed me farther into his apartment. "Pissed her off when she realized Hush had found himself a woman. Not that he ever gave Pixie the time of day. She just held out hope he would."

In a way I understood how Pixie felt. I'd moped around Grams' house waiting on my own biker to call or text and tell me he'd made a mistake. Eventually, I'd let the hope go, thinking it wasn't realistic to think he still wanted me. That's why everything that's been happening with him over the last couple weeks felt like a dream.

His arms wrapped around me from behind and his lips trailed over my neck. A shiver of desire raced over me. "The guys are having a party later tonight. It'll probably get loud," he murmured in my ear.

"Oh. You can go if you want."

He grasped my chin in his strong fingers and forced me to look back at him. "You think I'd rather go down there than be up here with you? I was hoping we'd make our own party."

The low rumble of his voice had my nipples hardening. This man always seemed to make me melt whenever I was near him. I turned in his arms and leaned up so I could brush my lips over his.

"I like the sound of that." He'd already mentioned that Hush and Seek were babysitting the kids tonight, so we had the apartment to ourselves.

He growled deep in his chest and suddenly I was airborne. I gasped, but he had a firm hold on me as he picked me up and started toward his bedroom. The apartment flashed by and I tried to take in everything I could. "This place is bigger than I thought it'd be."

"Yeah, Lockout gave me one of the bigger spaces 'cause of my family."

That was all he said before he kicked the door to the bedroom closed behind us and, for the second time that day, dropped me onto a bed. His was much bigger than mine. It would need to be for him to sleep comfortably in it. He was so tall his feet had hung off my bed.

I watched him with heavy lidded eyes as he stripped out of his cut and t-shirt. My tongue was glued to the roof of my mouth seeing all his muscles on display. He was so gorgeous I almost expected to wake up to find out this was all a dream.

He flicked open the button on the top of his jeans and toed his boots off. I bit my lip as he shoved his jeans down and off, leaving him in only his boxer briefs.

All I could do was lay there and devour him with my eyes. I didn't take off any of my clothes. I sort of liked it when he did that, even though he ended up ripping them. Sex with him was going to become expensive, but so worth it.

He crawled across the bed like a predator stalking its prey and my belly fluttered with excitement. I gripped the sheets, stopping my impulse to run. I didn't actually want to get away; it was just hard not to bolt under his intense scrutiny. His lips were warm and firm against mine and I relished the way his body covered mine.

I moaned into his mouth, arching against him. I couldn't seem to get enough of the feel of our bodies pressed together.

Something chirped nearby, but I was too wrapped up in the haze Priest seemed to create within me whenever he touched me.

Chirp, chirp.

He swore and pulled away from me. "Sorry, Taz. I have to get that."

Get what?

I blinked in confusion, heat leaching away from my body now that he wasn't on top of me. Watching as Priest grabbed his pants, I lifted up onto my elbows.

He pulled out his cell. "Yeah?" He waited a beat, then spoke. "It's late-" He shook his head, his eyes fixing on me. I could see the apology in them, but there was something else. "Yeah. Okay. We'll be there."

He disconnected the call and came to sit on the edge of the bed. His shoulders hunched as he rested his forearms on his thighs.

"Is everything okay?"

"Wendy wants to see the girls."

I looked over at the clock. It was nearly ten o'clock at night. "She can't wait until tomorrow?"

"No." The way he said the word I knew something was going on, but I didn't ask. He'd gone from happy and carefree to looking like he was carrying the weight of the world on his shoulders in the span of a minute.

"What can I do to help?" I asked, sitting up and scooting over to him. I rubbed the smooth skin of his back, enjoying the feel, but mostly needing to offer him comfort.

Wordlessly he turned and dragged me onto his lap. He buried his face into my hair as I wrapped my arms around him. We sat that way for a few minutes, in silence.

Finally, he raised his head, the fierce look of a warrior on his face. "I'll go get the girls."

I scrambled off his lap and watched as he got dressed again. I was still fully clothed, so I just waited to see what he needed from me. "My mom can come pick me up if you want," I offered since I didn't have my car here.

He shook his head, but didn't meet my eyes. "Would you come with us?"

Surprise flashed through me, but I nodded. "Of course."

"Thanks," he murmured.

I knew asking me to come was for himself. He'd have to be strong for his girls. Deal with whatever was about to come. But I could do that for him.

CHAPTER 15

Priest

It didn't take long to get my girls up and into the truck. I glanced into the rearview mirror and saw their wide eyes and worried expressions. They knew that night time drives weren't normal, therefore it must be a bad thing. I fucking hated this. I didn't want to be dragging them all around Tucson this late at night.

There'd been something in Wendy's tone, though. Something she hadn't wanted to say over the phone. So in the end, I'd woken them—Caitlyn insisted, silently, on coming with us—and here we were driving to the house.

I'd paid for at home care for Wendy. It was the option that had given my girls the most time with her. Seeing their mom at home, although bed ridden, was still infinitely better than at a hospital. I parked in the driveway and Jenny and I helped the girls climb out. As one unit we went into the house.

We were quiet about it. I didn't want to wake up the night care nurse. Not until I found out what was going on.

"My babies," Wendy called out softly as we came into her bedroom.

"I'll be out here," Jenny whispered to me, pausing by the door. Caitlyn went over and took her hand, wanting to wait as well.

I nodded and brushed a kiss over each of their foreheads before going into the room and shutting the door.

Wendy looked like hell. She'd lost even more weight since she'd left the hospital and her cheeks were gaunt and pale. The girls climbed onto her bed and she cuddled them close.

Despite the problems we'd had, Wendy had been a good mother to our girls. They were her world and I knew this wasn't easy on any of them. It was fucking killing me, to see my daughters' hearts breaking this way.

I gave them space, leaning up against the wall near the door. I watched, a silent guardian, as Wendy hugged, kissed, and whispered to them. These were her goodbyes. Had she gotten news from the doctor? She didn't look well, but didn't seem like she was fading either.

The last thing I was going to do was interrupt my children's last moments with her to ask. There were tears. They even threatened to spill from my own eyes as I watched my daughters sob in their mother's arms. I blinked them back, determined to be the rock they needed.

"I love you all so much," Wendy whispered. "Go on now."

The girls cried and flung themselves against her. Her eyes met mine and she silently begged for me to intervene. One by one, I picked up my daughters and carried them from the bed. Opening the door, I handed them over to Jenny.

She squatted down and they fell into her arms, sobbing. Jenny's worried eyes met mine and my heart kicked in my chest when I realized she was crying too. The fact that she'd shed tears for Wendy, for my girls, just showed what a huge heart she had, and why I could never let her go again.

Turning my head, I saw Wendy watching Jenny and our girls from the bed. There was a speculative look on her face. I couldn't begin to know what she was thinking at that moment.

"May I speak to her?" she asked me.

My brows shot up and I frowned. I didn't get a chance to voice my thoughts before she spoke again.

"I'll behave," she promised with a tired smile.

Stepping out into the hall, I spoke quietly to Jenny. "She wants to talk to you."

Jenny's curls bounced as her head snapped up in surprise. Her eyes darted from me to Wendy, but she nodded. I squatted down and gathered my girls close, letting them lean into me as they cried. For their sake I needed to hurry this along, whatever it was.

Watching as Jenny stepped into the room and walked over toward the bed, I smoothed my hand over Gabby's back. It shuddered under my palm and though she wasn't making a sound, I knew she was sobbing. She tried so hard to hold it together for her sisters. I wished she didn't feel she had to be that strong. She took after me in nearly every way.

The girls settled down and I could just barely hear the conversation between the two women.

"Priest and the girls told me that I have you to thank for watching them while I was in the hospital." Wendy stopped and a wry smile passed over her lips. "And for the clean house and food in my freezer."

"Oh. I like to keep busy," Jenny said with a tentative smile. "I hope you don't mind that I made myself at home."

Wendy blew out an audible breath, as though something were paining her. When the words finally came I knew it was them that caused the reaction, not the illness coursing through her body. "I don't mind. I wanted to thank you." She paused again, building up her nerve for something.

I watched them like a hawk. It didn't matter how sick Wendy was, I wouldn't allow her to say anything bad to Jenny. In the order of my priorities, Wendy was at the bottom of the list. I took care of her for my girls.

"May I ask you for a favor?"

Jenny's wide eyes flicked over to me. I shrugged and waited, along with her, to see what my ex-wife wanted from her. Jenny made an encouraging noise, so Wendy went on.

Wendy's eyes moved over and settled on the little girls in my arms. She kept them there as she spoke to Jenny. A single tear tracked down her face. My heart turned to stone. Seeing the only tear that Wendy had cried through this entire ordeal confirmed my suspicions. I knew why she'd called us over here.

"I see the way he looks at you," Wendy told her. Jenny didn't seem to know what to say, so she remained silent. "They need a mother. Will you help him watch over them?" Wendy's eyes finally locked onto Jenny, as she waited to see what Jenny would say.

Jenny's jaw dropped and it looked like she tried to speak only to have nothing come out. She cleared her throat and tried again. "I'm not sure that's my choice to make," she said quietly, looking over at me again. Her cheeks flushed and she dragged her gaze away.

Wendy smirked at her. "Trust me. I've known him almost my entire life." She paused as though it was just hitting her that this was the end of that life. Sadness seemed to creep over her. "He's going to keep you, Jenny." Her hand gripped Jenny's wrist as desperation moved in. "And I need to know that my girls will grow up with a mother to help take care of them." She swallowed hard. "As much as I want to be the one to do that, I can't. So, I'm asking you."

Both Jenny and I knew how hard it was for her to be asking this favor. Jenny's other hand came over the top of Wendy's in a reassuring grip. "I'll be their mother. I'll love them as fiercely as if they were my own," she promised.

The breath exploded out of me. I hadn't realized I'd been holding it. Hearing those words from Jenny set both Wendy and me at ease.

Wendy let go of her arm and settled back against the pillows again. "Thank you."

Jenny nodded, reaching out to squeeze Wendy's hand again before she left her side. I passed the girls, who'd calmed down by the time the exchange was over, over to Jenny. She started to usher them out toward the living room.

I quietly thanked her, waiting for her nod of acknowledgement, then shut the door, barricading myself inside with Wendy. I turned and studied her. The machines she was hooked up to were beeping and clicking.

She sniffled into a tissue and I gave her a chance to compose herself. When she finally looked up, I saw the resignation in her eyes. My heart sank. This was hard on her, and was going to be so much more difficult for my daughters. It made my chest ache for them.

"Grant."

I went over and sat on the edge of her bed. My hand covered hers and I marveled at how bony it had become. I swallowed hard as she began talking.

"I can't do this." Tears filled her eyes. "I hurt so badly, Grant. I can't keep going." A sob tore from her throat. "But I can't end it on my own." She swallowed hard, squeezing my hand and her voice came out as a whisper. "I'm too much of a coward."

My eyes closed briefly and I rubbed my thumb over the back of her hand. Somehow I'd known tonight would be her last night, but it hadn't occurred to me when she'd called what she would ask me to do.

When I opened my eyes again she was watching me with a pleading look. "It's not fair to ask this of you, but…can you help me? Please?"

Jesus. I'd done some shitty things in my life. Some that were considered heroic. I'd killed a lot of people, but I'd always managed to convince myself that they deserved it. Could I end the life of my ex-wife? The mother of my children?

One look into her eyes told me how serious she was. The desperation there conveyed more about the pain she was in, and how badly she needed it to end, than words ever could. This was well past begging. This was nearly a demand. So, could I do this?

Yes. Because she was in pain and begging me to. The real question was, could I do it without losing myself? Could I keep this from my girls without it tearing me apart. They wouldn't understand. I'd never be able to tell them the truth. For just a moment I hated Wendy for putting this on me, for what the price would be. That feeling faded quickly though. If I were in her position… I would ask someone, too.

It just so happened I had more people in my life than she did. Which meant this was up to me.

"Alright. Give me a minute." I'd locked the bedroom door, but there wasn't anyone pounding or begging to get back inside. I knew Jenny was taking care of my girls.

Pulling out my cell, I hit a number and waited while it rang.

"Hey. Where are you?" Lockout asked.

"Wendy's."

"I see." His tone was grim. He knew me being here in the middle of the night wasn't a good thing.

I took a deep breath. "Lock. There's something I need to do. I thought I had Cade's number, but I don't."

The silence on the other end of the line was deafening. Finally, he spoke. "If you're calling the Austin MC for something, I'm going to need to know why, Priest."

My eyes shifted to Wendy, but I nodded. Not that he could see me. "I'm ending it for her. I need to know how."

"Fuck. Yeah, alright. I'll text it to you. What can I do?"

"Nothing for now. Thanks, though."

We hung up and I sighed as I made the next call.

"Cade here."

"Cade, it's Priest."

The Texas Chapter president must have heard the agony in my tone. "Everything alright, Priest?"

"No, not in the least. I don't have time to explain right now. I need to talk to Ming." Ming was one of their member's wife, and a doctor.

"Alright, give me a minute and I'll give her my phone." He didn't talk while he went to go find her and I appreciated that. That was the thing about the club, both chapters. The men knew when to ask questions, and when to act. Answers could come later.

Rubbing a hand over my forehead, I waited. It felt like an eternity passed before another voice came over the line. "Priest?"

"Ming, hey. I'm sorry to call so late."

"That's okay, we were actually having a movie night and just finished up not that long ago. What can I help you with?"

Sucking in a breath, I went over and sat next to Wendy. Her eyes were closed, but I knew she was listening. I explained Wendy's prognosis. "She wants me to help her, but I need to do it in a way where she won't feel anything and it will look natural. I have four kids and I can't go to jail for this. They don't need to lose both parents."

"Do you have any medications there with you?" I appreciated her no nonsense approach. I could hear the sadness in her voice, but she didn't waste time telling me how sorry she was. Her willingness to help me was comforting enough.

I stood and walked over to where the nurse had them locked up in a cabinet. Pulling my wallet out of my back pocket, I opened it and pulled out a small tool. It took me a few minutes to pick the lock, a testament to how this was affecting me.

Listing off the medications inside the cabinet, I listened as she told me which to use, how much, and what would happen once I did. There was a faint buzzing in my ears, but I forced myself to focus.

"Give her the shot under her tongue. By the time the nurse finds her, she'll be gone and they won't be able to detect the drug on the toxicology report. If they even run one."

"Thank you, Ming. I…I don't know how I can ever repay you for this."

"You're welcome. And we still owe you for your help with getting the club out of all that trouble before. Listen, I've seen what her future looks like. You're doing her a kindness." She paused, then kept going. "It's not going to be easy for you. Do you have someone to talk with?"

"Yeah. I'm squared away there. Listen, I'd better do this before that nurse comes in for a check. Thank you again."

"Of course. And seriously, don't try to take this burden alone."

I hung up the phone and carefully loaded a syringe with the medication Ming had suggested. I put it back, making sure the bottle was where it had been prior. Closing and locking the cabinet back up, I went back over and sat near Wendy again.

Her eyes opened and she studied me. "You're a good man, Grant. I'm so sorry that I couldn't be the woman you needed."

My lips twitched and I patted her hand. "I'm convinced the only reason we were meant to come together was for those girls out there," I told her. "And for that, I'll always be grateful to you."

Her smile was soft, but tinged with a hint of pain. "You're a great father. The only reason I'm able to let go is knowing that you'd die to protect our girls."

"Yeah. I would."

"But more likely, you'd kill an army first." She chuckled, then coughed.

Tears dripped down her cheeks as she continued. "I'm really sorry to ask this of you. I know it's awful, but I can't lie here withering away in agonizing pain for who knows how long. I don't want my girls to remember me like this."

I'd been about to ask her if she was sure, but that was all I needed to hear to know. "This will stop your heart."

"Will you stay with me?"

I nodded. It was a bad idea, Ming had warned me to leave after the injection. But the fear in Wendy's eyes, that was a look I had seen far too many times in combat. I wasn't going to leave her. I would stay here through this.

"Thank you."

"Okay. Give me five minutes? I'll be right back."

She nodded again and let her eyes close. I left the syringe on the nightstand and unlocked the bedroom door. I found Jenny and the girls out in the living room. They were piled on her and each other, pressing close for comfort.

Jenny's eyes widened when she spotted me. She smoothed a hand over Taylor's back. They were all asleep except Caitlyn, who watched quietly.

Whispering to Jenny, I picked Cassie up in my arms. "I need you to do me a favor."

"What?" Jenny whispered back.

"I can't explain much right now, but I need you to drive my truck a few blocks up the road and wait for me."

Jenny shifted until the girls were lying on the couch. She picked

Taylor up, ready to follow me outside. Caitlyn waited on the couch with Gabby.

"We'll be right back," I told her and headed out to my truck. We settled the girls into the back seat before going inside for the other two. Once we had them secured, I quietly shut the door and waited for Jenny to get into the front seat.

There was an understanding in her eyes. She knew what I was about to do. I didn't see any judgment, only sadness. She laid a hand on my forearm. "We'll be waiting."

I leaned in and kissed her. It wasn't a light meeting of mouths. It was forceful and desperate. I poured all my twisted emotions into the kiss, letting Jenny hang onto them for a while before I went to do what I needed to. I couldn't afford to have the volatile feelings bouncing around inside of me while I did this.

When I pulled away, she brought her hand to my cheek. Neither of us said anything else as I grasped her wrist, kissing her knuckles, and tucked her hand safely inside the truck as I closed the door as quietly as I could. We were lucky the nurse hadn't woken up yet and I didn't want her catching me at the wrong moment.

I watched as the taillights disappeared down the street. Taking a deep breath of the cooling night air, I went back inside. Detouring to Gabby's room, I opened the door a crack. The nurse was still asleep.

There was no time to waste. The nurse had brought one of those dry erase boards and written pertinent information on it, including what time checks were to be done. This was so Wendy could see it and become used to her new schedule. The nurse would be coming by in about thirty minutes.

According to Ming, it wouldn't take very long. I promised Wendy I would stay by her side through it, and I would. I would have a few seconds, maybe a minute tops before the machines went haywire after her pulse dropped off.

CHAPTER 16

Priest

I made my way back to Wendy's room and shut the door behind me, though I didn't lock it this time. Going over to the window, I opened it. Prepping my escape route beforehand would hopefully ensure a clean getaway.

Looking out through the window, I searched the dark streets for anyone who would spot me. According to Ming, there should be nothing that would raise suspicions and it wasn't likely there would be an autopsy, but you never knew. The streets were empty. It was time.

Turning around, I sat down on the bed by Wendy's side. Her eyes opened and she watched me as I picked up the syringe and waited for her to be ready.

She nodded and fear flickered over her face as she looked down at the needle. "I'm still scared, Grant."

Sighing, I pulled her forward and enveloped her in my arms. Her body was frail in my hold, so I was careful. "This is going to stop your heart. It's fast," I explained. "Then you'll get to rest."

A shudder rolled through her body and she pulled away from my hug. She laid back and nodded. "I'm ready."

I leaned forward and brushed a kiss over her forehead. There was a time, in my past, that I loved this woman. Now I just wanted to end this so that I could console my children. It was a soul eating task, taking her life, and even though I hadn't done it yet, I knew it was going to have consequences. I also knew that the consequences of letting her suffer were far worse. I had to help her. "I'll be here. You won't be alone."

* * *

SLIPPING BACKWARD into the darkness of the night, I watched the nurse rush in and try to stop what I'd set in motion. I watched, and waited, until finally the machines flat-lined and the nurse made the call to the doctor. I was beside the window, in the shadow of the house, listening as she relayed to whoever the on-call doctor was that her patient had suffered a heart attack.

I left before she finished. I'd heard enough that indicated she hadn't noticed that someone had helped Wendy end her life. Jogging up the street, I kept a look out for the truck. I found Jenny two blocks over, waiting for me with the lights off.

Approaching slowly, so I didn't startle her, I tapped on the window. She rolled it down and I gave a short nod at her questioning look. "Scoot over," I said, my voice gruff. I was holding myself together by a fucking thread.

Jenny seemed to realize it, because she didn't ask me any questions. She just slid into the passenger seat so I could hop behind the wheel. My pulse relaxed slightly as something soft brushed over my arm. I looked down to see her hand resting gently on my forearm. I placed my right hand on top of hers and gave it a light squeeze, silently thanking her. The lights flooded the street in front of us as I turned them on and put the truck into drive.

We made the trip back to the clubhouse in silence. Lockout must have shut down the party early because he and Riptide came out to help carry my daughters upstairs and no one else was around. Thank fuck the girls slept through it all. There would be time in the morning —once I got the official call—to help them mourn.

Tonight was for me.

Hush met us at my door. "You want us to take them? That way you can have some time?"

They all knew. Lockout would have told them. Something of this magnitude, you couldn't keep it a secret, not from those that would keep you grounded. I didn't mind. My brothers—and Jenny—were how I was going to get through living with the guilt.

I shook my head. "Thanks, Hush, but some other time. I don't want them to wake up and not have me there."

"I understand, Brother," he said, laying a hand on my shoulder and squeezing. "Let us know how we can help." With that he went back to his own apartment.

We carried my girls into their rooms and I tucked them into bed. When I stepped back out into the living room, Lockout was still there. Riptide had left and my bedroom door was open so I knew Jenny had gone in there to give us privacy. She'd been tossed into the deep end in all of this and was handling it amazingly. It was like she was made for me. For this life. I'd do my damndest to convince her of that once I wasn't stuck treading water, barely keeping my head above the surface.

"Take the time you need," Lockout told me as I walked up. "But I'm going to need to know the details. That way I can help make sure you're protected."

I nodded. "I'll go over it with you in the morning, but I stayed long enough that I know the nurse didn't suspect anything. Ming said they'd likely only do an autopsy if requested, which I'm sure as hell not doing. I should be in the clear."

Lockout mimicked Hush's earlier move and put his hand on my shoulder. "I'm sorry." He didn't bother to add anything else. He knew it wouldn't do any good.

I watched as he left, shutting my front door behind him. Sighing, I glanced over at my girls' doors. I almost wanted to wake them. To tell them. It would be easier for me to make it through the night if I was taking care of them instead of being left to mull over what I'd done. Anything would be better than having time alone.

In the end, I let them sleep. I wasn't willing to bring their pain and grief any earlier than I had to. Especially just to keep myself occupied. I'd cut my own heart out if it would allow me to take on their coming pain. I'd bear that burden for them every day of my life, if I could. The girls had a great night with their mother; that is, as great as could be expected. They saw her lucid and loving. They got a chance to say goodbye before Wendy could get worse. I wasn't going to ruin that right now.

Movement caught my eye and I saw Jenny leaning against the door frame, watching me. There was understanding and worry mixing together in her gaze, but she was letting me work through this at my own pace.

Walking over to her, I pulled her against my body and stooped so I could bury my face in her mass of curls. The guilt was pounding against the barrier I'd erected while I'd done what was necessary. Here, alone with her, there was no need for the defense any longer and it dropped.

A shudder ran through my body as the realization that I'd ended Wendy's life slammed into me. Jenny's hand smoothed over my back as she rubbed it. I focused on that. The feel of her hand as she dipped it low so she could run it up underneath my shirt. The feel of our skin touching calmed me.

I'd been taking deep, fast breaths, but the feel of her in my arms soothed me. I squeezed her harder, holding her as close as our bodies would allow.

"Priest," she murmured.

Easing my grip on her so I didn't hurt her, I grunted in response. It was all I could give at the moment. My emotions were taking a beating thanks to the guilt that was rampaging through my chest. I wasn't exactly an emotional person. Most people would claim I was cold—except for with my family—but there was no calling forward that hard shell I'd perfected throughout my years in the military. Not right now. That shell was built out of necessity, and it was there when I needed it.

"Let's go lay down," she whispered to me. "We can talk if you want. Or we can just lay there."

Letting her out of my hold, I allowed her to pull me over to the bed. I was on autopilot, tugging my boots off, then removing my clothes down to my boxer briefs. I left them on and climbed onto the bed. It was almost like an out of body experience. I was doing everything necessary, but I was numb to everything but the sucking black hole of torment.

She was true to her word. She didn't make me talk. As soon as she climbed on the bed, I pulled her to me. Settling her body, back to my chest, against mine, I let go of the last sliver of control and just let myself float.

I felt her turn in my arms. Felt her fingers tracing over me, offering silent comfort while I let the feelings overwhelm me. I deserved to feel every one of them. It didn't matter that I'd helped Wendy. That I'd done as she asked. That she was ready to let go and needed me to assist her in taking that last step. I'd killed the mother of my children.

Closing my eyes, I tried to block out the truth. But the darkness amplified everything ten-fold. A beautiful melody cut a path through the aching in my heart. It was as though it cut a swath of light through the oily pitch that was coating my soul. Opening my eyes, I looked down at the woman in my arms.

She was humming. I didn't recognize the song, but I didn't need to. Her eyes met mine and she gave me a soft smile as she continued. Between that, her touch, and having her wrapped up in my arms, the emotions began to ease. They didn't leave entirely, but they faded a little into the background.

"Don't stop." My voice was raw. A good representation of how I was feeling on the inside.

She kept humming, stroking her hand over my head. I closed my eyes again and this time, sleep was the only thing that dragged me under.

* * *

A SHRILL SOUND jerked me awake the next morning. Swearing, I untangled Jenny's limbs from mine and rolled off the bed. I bent and grabbed my jeans, yanking my phone out of the pocket. I really needed to start leaving it on the fucking bed side table.

"Yeah?"

"Is this Grant Mitchell?" The voice asked after a brief hesitation. They probably hadn't expected someone to bark at them in greeting.

"Yeah." My muscles tensed. I knew before she even spoke that this would be the hospital.

"Mr. Mitchell, my name is Dr. Thompson. I was overseeing your wife's care."

"Ex-wife," I told her. Then something clicked and I knew I needed to play the part so I continued, "What do you mean 'was', Dr. Thompson?"

Silence again. If nothing else, I was keeping her on her toes. "I'm so sorry to inform you, Mr. Mitchell, that your ex-wife passed away last night."

I closed my eyes. I wasn't an actor, but I had to keep up appearances. Digging down deep, I dragged up the feelings that had been strangling me last night. It did the trick and my voice sounded ragged as I responded. "No. What happened? She was fine when we visited her."

"She had a heart attack. Her body was tired and it must have put a strain on her heart, trying to keep everything going. Again, I'm so sorry for your loss."

"Thank you." The words came out hollow. I listened as she explained everything that would happen now. There'd be arrangements to be made. A funeral to put on, but all I could think about was having to wake up my girls and tell them. The reality of last night was coming back to me.

"Do you have any questions for me?" she asked.

"No. I don't think so. Thank you, Doctor."

"The hospital will contact you later to get the name of the funeral home you'd like to use."

I hung up the phone after she said goodbye. I'd been staring at the wall and I allowed myself an extra minute. When I finally turned around, I found Jenny there.

She'd sat up and was watching me. Her hair was a glorious tangle of curls falling like a dark waterfall over her shoulders. The sheets were pooled down around her sexy hips.

Heat sparked inside of me. It wasn't an appropriate reaction after hearing what the doctor had just told me, but suddenly I just wanted to get lost in her.

She must have read the hungry expression on my face, because she flicked back the sheets, baring her legs. My mouth went dry as she spread her legs open, sensually. She was still wearing a bra and panties, but they just accented her beautifully flawless skin.

I wanted to run my lips over every inch of her. "Taz," I groaned. Before I knew I was moving, I was covering her body with my own. Her open arms welcomed me. She wrapped her silky legs around my waist and I let my fingers grip her thigh. My other hand went to her face, cupping it in my palm.

She probably wouldn't ever know how much she'd helped me last night. That what she was doing for me right now was chasing away the demons. As bad as I was at letting emotions in, I was even worse at discussing them. But I promised myself that I'd never let her want for anything. Whatever she needed for the rest of her life, it would be my goal to provide it for her.

My mouth covered hers, my deep groan vibrating between us. She tasted so sweet. Her lips parted, allowing my tongue inside to play with hers. I wasn't sure how she seemed to instinctively know that I needed this—needed her—but I was grateful.

Though I planned to lose myself in the pleasure her body could give me, I fully intended to bring her along for the ride. She was stretched out below me like a fucking goddess, rocking her hips up against my body. Melting my control with every movement.

Her chocolatey brown eyes were soft and understanding. "We have time," she whispered as I stared down at her. "Make love to me, Priest. Let's forget for a few minutes."

She couldn't be any more perfect.

CHAPTER 17

Jenny

It'd been a week since Priest and the girls lost Wendy. I'd been there for every step and we were all exhausted. Helping him and his family was helping me work through my own loss. I still missed Grams, but I'd gained so much by coming back to Tucson. Seeing how he helped his girls through it put things into perspective for me.

Priest was doing his best to hold it all together, but anyone could see he was overwhelmed. He was dealing with his own guilt—I still hadn't gotten him to open up about that—as well as with his daughters' broken hearts. I knew he blamed himself for the way they felt.

I'd been trying to give him time to process, but if he didn't talk to someone about everything he was going to implode. He insisted on having me nearby as much as possible and I fell asleep in his arms each night. Still, it felt like he was pulling away. Like he didn't want to burden me with his grief.

It was such a contradiction. His possessive nature wouldn't let me go. And to some small degree, he used me to anchor himself, that much was obvious. But for as much as he kept me physically near, by not opening up to me, it was like we were both alone.

I wasn't sure how to assure him that I could handle it. That I wanted to be there for him, to be his island in the storm. I knew without a doubt he would do that for me. I saw first hand in Austin the lengths he would go to for his family. He needed to know I would do the same.

"Jenny."

Looking up, I smiled at my supervisor as she poked her head into my office. "Hey, Rebecca."

"Hi," she gave me a warm smile and stepped into the room. "I just wanted to check in. See how you're doing?"

"Oh, I'm great," I chirped, putting a little extra pep in the words. I wasn't about to tell her what was going on in my personal life. We weren't that close. Not to mention the conflict of interest with dating the man who was trying to get custody of Caitlyn.

"Good! I know it's been an adjustment coming back and getting into the flow of things here." She came over and set a file on my desk. "By the way, here's the Mitchell file."

My stomach knotted up as I stared down at it. Trepidation rose as I waited to hear the outcome.

"We've decided, based off the Aunt's request, to grant custody of Caitlyn to Grant Mitchell. Despite his…friends, he has three children and not one indication of being a negligent father."

The breath whooshed out of me and I had to fight back the urge to scream in excitement. This was the good news Priest needed right now. "That's great, Rebecca. Caitlyn has really taken to him and his daughters. This is good for all of them."

She nodded and we chatted for a few more minutes. As soon as she left I let out a little squeal. I buried myself in work for the rest of the day, looking forward to getting out of here so I could tell Priest the good news in person.

The clock finally hit five and I rushed out of the office and straight over to the clubhouse. Usually, I texted Priest first to make sure it was okay that I dropped by, but I was too excited to wait.

As soon as I pulled into their lot, Smokehouse walked up. He smiled at me and walked up to my car as I was texting Priest. "Hey there, Taz."

"Hi Smokehouse. Is Priest here?"

One of his brows quirked up.

"I didn't wait to be invited over," I told him sheepishly. "I have some good news-"

"Taz," he said, stopping me. "You're his old lady. You don't have to wait to be invited to stop by the clubhouse. Only time we'll keep you waiting is if we're in church. Come on, Beautiful. I'll walk you in."

"Thanks," I replied, cheeks pinkening. He wasn't flirting with me, per say. That was just Smokehouse. If it had two legs and was female, he flirted. Still, I frowned over at him when he wrapped his arm around my shoulders.

His chuckle was deep and rumbled within his chest. "Don't worry, Taz. Just giving Priest a run for his money."

I wasn't sure what that meant exactly, but he'd already tossed open the front door to the clubhouse. My brows pinched together as I saw Priest sitting there talking to a couple of the sweet butts. The only one I knew was Pixie.

He glanced over and glowered at Smokehouse. Standing, he walked over and pulled me away from Smokehouse's side. "Hey," he said, tone soft despite the dark look he shot his MC brother.

"Hi." It came out a bit more breathless than I'd intended, but this man set off a storm of butterflies in my belly every time I saw him. "I have great news."

He folded his arms over his chest and stared down at me, his face a neutral mask. He was waiting patiently, reserving judgment on whether the news was going to be good or not. I understood it. He'd had a shitty couple of weeks.

"My bosses got back to me today. They're letting you adopt Caitlyn!" My face hurt, that was how big my smile was. When the look on his face didn't shift my grin faltered. "Um… Is everything alright?"

"Yeah. Sorry." He scrubbed his hands over his face and suddenly looked exhausted. "That *is* great news. Thanks for letting me know, Taz. I needed that today."

I blinked in confusion. He was saying all the right words, but he still looked...cautious. He wasn't smiling at me, or hugging me. Heck he wasn't even touching me. Other than to pull me away from Smokehouse he hadn't touched me once since I walked in. "Is everything okay?" I asked again.

"Yeah. It's fine. I just have a lot on my mind right now."

I reached forward to touch his arm, to give him comfort, and he shifted out of the way. My eyes widened and then it was all I could do to keep from crying.

"Okay," I said, my voice trembling a little. "Well, I'll leave you to let Caitlyn know. She'll be really excited." I turned and walked out the door, ignoring him as he called my name.

I only made it a few steps before something massive clamped onto my arm and spun me around. His grip was firm, but it didn't hurt. "Christ, Taz. I'm sorry. Seriously, I just have a lot on my mind. We're about to have church and there's been a break in The Silverbells mystery..."

Nodding, I swallowed hard. I refused to cry in front of him. I knew he'd been having a rough time and he was trying to juggle everything. I also knew that was when he tended to pull back and shut people out. It's why he'd dumped me before. I was just worried that it was going to happen again. The last thing he needed was me pouring my worries onto his already full plate, however. As much as I needed to, I knew that doing so would make things worse, at least right now. "I understand, Priest. Really. I'll see you later."

With a curse under his breath, he dropped my arm and let me walk away from him. A tear tracked down my face. I was trying to pull myself together, but it was hard to imagine getting everything I ever wanted and then having it ripped away from me. This time I only made it as far as my car.

"Hey there."

I glanced over and paused. "Hi, Riptide." It was impossible to walk around this compound without running into at least a few of these guys. Even when I wanted to make a clean getaway they were here.

He frowned then looked over toward the clubhouse and swore when he saw Priest standing there. I followed his gaze and watched Priest turn and stomp inside.

Riptide's warm blue eyes landed on me again. "Everything alright?"

"Yeah." Even I heard the shakiness in my reply. Steeling my nerves, I nodded. "Everything is fine." Now I sounded like Priest.

He searched my face for a minute then narrowed his eyes. "Want me to kick his ass for you?"

A laugh popped out before I could stop it. "You don't even know why you'd be fighting him."

"Ah, but there *is* a reason," he pointed out.

I looked down and shrugged. "It's nothing."

"You're a shitty liar."

My eyes snapped up and I glared at him.

"There she is," he said with a grin. "I prefer seeing you with a bit of fire in your eyes rather than sadness." He pointed toward the clubhouse with his thumb. "Don't mind him. We guys are clueless assholes half the time."

"What are you the rest of the time?" I asked in a sugary sweet tone.

It was his turn to laugh. "I like you. He chose well." He scratched his stubbled chin. "Horny assholes," he answered.

I smiled and shook my head. "You would be easier to figure out if that were the case."

"Oh we're easy enough most of the time. He's just had a bit of a rough patch."

Guilt pierced my heart. "I know that. I'm doing my best to help him through it."

"Sometimes there's no helping. There's just being there. Don't worry," he set his heavy hand on my shoulder in comfort, "he'll pull his head out of his ass."

"I hope so," I whispered.

"If he doesn't, we'll do it for him," he promised. "It's what we're here for. Meanwhile, if you need to talk, you come to me or Lock. We're here for the old ladies as much as for our brothers."

Patting his hand, I smiled. "Thanks, Riptide."

He removed his hand from my shoulder and nodded. "My pleasure. Drive safe."

I got into my car and headed home. It was past time to have a movie night with my mom. I'd been so caught up in everything we hadn't seen each other much over the last week.

As soon as I walked in the house, my mom popped out from around a corner. "Honey!"

I lifted a hand to my chest, trying to ease my galloping heart. "Jeez, Mom. Don't scare me like that."

"Sorry," she laughed. "I was just about to make some cookies. Do you have time to join me?"

"Do I ever," I replied and followed her into the kitchen. "I thought you'd still be at work." I made a straight line for the cookie dough and helped myself to a spoonful. The sweetness exploded on my tongue and I groaned in delight.

"Took a sick day," she told me.

I moved over and laid the back of my hand on her forehead. "Are you not feeling well?"

She laughed and shooed my hand away. "I'm fine. I just needed a mental health day."

Frowning, I folded my arms over my chest, giving her my best 'Mom glare'. "The question still stands."

"I'm fine," she insisted. "You always were a mother hen, even as a kid." She said it in a warm way, so I didn't take offense.

"Need to talk?"

She studied me. "You seem to have forgotten that I'm the mom here. You look like you've been crying. Seems to me that maybe *you* need that talk." That was Mom speak for, 'tell me everything or no cookies for you'.

"Why don't we both share?" I suggested, picking up a tray of cookie dough and depositing it inside the oven.

"Good idea. I'll get more junk food." Mom and I had a special arrangement at times like this. It was what she and Grams had always done together and now it was our tradition as well. Cookies took time to bake, so you had to have snacks on hand while you were waiting for more snacks.

"I'll get the movie," I told her with a grin. There was no need to ask what she wanted to watch. We always started each movie marathon off with our favorite.

We settled in on the couch and I laid my head on her shoulder. I was so grateful to have her. Even though not having Grams join us was like a missing piece to the puzzle, I knew I could always come to her for comfort.

We arranged the popcorn and snacks over our laps. It would take us a good thirty minutes or so before we'd end up pausing the show and start to talk. We had a rhythm. It was familiar and eased my mind. She'd know how to soothe the worry and hurt Priest had caused. He was the only one who could banish it fully, but for now, Mom would help me push it to the back of my mind. And just maybe give me some insight on how to deal with him.

CHAPTER 18

Priest

I cursed again as I watched Riptide walk up to Jenny and start speaking with her. It hadn't been my intention to hurt her feelings, I was just out of sorts right now. I'd planned to go to church, then go a few rounds in the ring with one of the guys before I spoke to her today. Then she showed up.

She was right about her news. It was fucking amazing that she'd managed to help me get custody of Caitlyn. I'd be forever grateful to her. I just couldn't drum up any enthusiasm at the moment. My insides felt like they were being twisted up through an emotional wringer and the only way for me to deal with that was to numb myself to everything. It was a bad day for me and I wasn't good company for anyone.

The girls were with Wendy's parents and were staying with them for a week. They'd taken Caitlyn as well, claiming they wanted to get to know their newest granddaughter. Her parents were good people. I think after our divorce I'd missed them more than my ex-wife. It was good for them as well, they lost a daughter. By having the girls there, they could heal better themselves.

"What the hell was that?"

I groaned inwardly. The accent let me know exactly who was standing behind me in the doorway. I turned and followed Hush inside.

"Nothing."

"Didn't look like nothin'. Looked like you said somethin' stupid and hurt her feelin's." Hush scowled at me.

"It's none of your business, Hush. I'll make it up to her later." When I wasn't feeling so fucking numb.

Hush's laugh was incredulous. "You poked and prodded at me when I needed it, Boy. Don't think I'm not goin' to do the same. It may not make you feel better, but it's my way of gettin' back at you." He gave me a feral smile as though he was going to enjoy every minute of it.

"Want to spar while you nag at me like an old woman?"

His eyes narrowed and I gave him a humorless grin. "Yeah. We'll go a few rounds," he grunted.

We started walking back toward the meeting room. Butcher came down the stairs as we passed. "You two are sparring?"

"That's right. You want in?" I asked.

"Hell yeah."

We walked into the meeting room and saw Smokehouse sitting there. Everyone started talking all at once.

Lockout had sent Smokehouse out to Wyoming to help out another chapter a few weeks ago. He'd just gotten back in earlier today and we hadn't had a chance to catch up with him yet.

"Took you long enough getting back home, asshole," I told him as I took the seat next to him.

"Thanks. I was beginning to think they'd never let me go," he said with a grin.

"Bullshit," Hush replied. "You found a woman up there," he joked.

Smokehouse grinned. "A woman? Like, just one? Ha!"

Everyone groaned and started giving him shit. We all quieted down when Lockout and Riptide walked in. I settled in, eager to see what it was they'd found out.

Dash was seated across the table from me and he winked at me. The bastard had been secretive about what he and Riptide had found. He just kept saying Lockout wanted to go over it at church.

At least this meeting was keeping me occupied and Hush off my ass about what happened before with Jenny. I stared down at the table as Lockout started speaking.

"Dash and Rip managed to track down Caitlyn's father."

My eyes shot up and I found Lockout watching me closely. "Who is he?"

"It's weird," Riptide answered. "It took a lot of digging to even get a name on this guy. We tried backtracking from Caitlyn's birth certificate, but that record was mysteriously lost. We tried following the mother's name to her marriage certificate, but that was lost, too. Notice the strange pattern? Anyway, long story short we eventually found a paper trail through credit cards and found the father's name. Once we finally got that we started searching and realized that he dropped off the grid the same time Caitlyn and her mom did."

My muscles tensed at hearing that. "What does that mean?"

"We're actually thinking that maybe he has something to do with The Silverbells, but they haven't gotten the full story yet," Lockout answered.

"Tracking this guy down has proven to be more difficult than expected. Which means he has something to hide," Riptide said. "I'm going to figure out what it is."

"You think he was the one who lured them out there?" Hush asked after we all processed what Riptide was telling us.

"Not sure yet," Riptide answered. "But that's the current theory. Either lured, or he took them and forced them to go with him. Stole Sherry's car and drove them out to that area."

"It's a clue to go off, either way," Dash added. "Maybe it'll get us some answers about what's happening out there."

"Fucking finally," Butcher muttered. Toxic elbowed him under the table. "What?" Butcher complained. "This is taking forever and I just want to know what's going on and who I can kill."

"Really?" Toxic asked, one eyebrow raised in suspicion.

"Well, I don't really care what's going on," he admitted. "Just want to know who to kill."

Everyone chuckled at that. Typical Butcher. No finesse. He was more of a smash and grab type guy. He also had more of a heart than he let on and it wasn't hard to see that he actually liked Caitlyn. He'd never admit it, but he was pretty good with my kids. It was only babies who freaked him out.

"So what's the plan?" I asked.

"The guys are going to go check out Chet Holden's last known address. See if there is anything there to find."

"Figures," I said. "Chet. Even without knowing what he did to Caitlyn and her mom, he sounds like a douche. No one names their kid Chet unless they intend to raise a douche," I muttered.

The others nodded in agreement.

"Put me on this, too," I told Lockout.

His eyes narrowed, not because of my request, but because they all knew I was struggling after Wendy. "Not sure that's a good idea, Brother. You're a little close to this one."

Grinding my back teeth together so I didn't do something stupid, I tried to keep control of my temper. The fact that I felt close to losing it—especially on my friend and president—was a testament to the inner turmoil I felt. I was known for my calm composure, in battle and otherwise. The last few days I've been feeling more and more like a loose cannon.

My God, is this how Butcher feels every day?

"Lock." I met his gaze. "I need to be a part of this. Caitlyn is my daughter."

"That's part of the reason it might be better if you stayed here," he said. He leaned forward, elbows on the wooden table in front of us. "But fine. You can go. Don't make me fucking regret it, Priest."

The relief was so sharp I didn't even argue. I listened to them plan the mission. By the time they were done I had my errant emotions under control once more.

"Anything else?" Lockout asked.

"Taz stopped by earlier," I told him. Ignoring the dark looks I was getting from both Hush and Riptide, I continued. "CPS is granting me custody of Caitlyn."

Everyone started talking all at once again. They were all relieved and excited about the news.

"There's still more I'll have to do to officially adopt her, but the biggest hurdle is over with."

I received a bunch of slaps on the back and grinned because despite how hard they connected they were all happy for me. It was finally starting to sink in. I only wished I'd been able to react when Jenny had told me the news. The numbness was fading a bit, thanks to knowing we were finally moving forward with Caitlyn and The Silverbells.

Lockout released us and I glanced at my phone. No messages. I typed out a quick text to Jenny, letting her know I had club business that would keep me out late tonight, but that I'd call her in the morning. I frowned when, after a few minutes, she hadn't replied.

"Still want to get in a couple rounds before tonight?" Hush asked, walking up.

"Yeah. I need it." I followed him and Butcher to the gym. Some of the other guys came with us, eager to watch us fight.

Hellfire was already in the gym lifting when we got there. He arched a brow. "Sparring?"

"That's right," Butcher answered. "You looking to get in on it?"

"Fuck yeah." He dropped the barbell he was holding and the weights crashed to the ground. "You're mine today, Butcher."

"Aw, Hell," he said, fluttering his lashes. "I knew you wanted me."

Hellfire snorted while Hush and I laughed at Butcher's shit talking. Hellfire was huge—even bigger than me—but Butcher was fast and fucking mean. Worse, he took hits like Rocky Balboa, they just seemed to fuel him. It would be a fun fight to watch. Not that we hadn't seen every combination between our brothers that could be made, but it was still fun to watch them pit themselves against each other.

"We're first," I called out, ripping my shirt off over my head. I needed the sting of my knuckles hitting flesh. The blood from being pummeled myself. The feelings slinking around inside of me needed an outlet. Between this and our mission later tonight, I knew I was going to feel a fuck ton lighter by tomorrow.

* * *

I SAT ON MY BIKE, watching the building in front of us. The apartment building was quiet—most of the residents were asleep for the night—but we still waited for about twenty minutes, monitoring the people coming and going. There weren't many.

"Let's go," Riptide whispered.

Me and Butcher got off our bikes, looking around as we walked up the stairs that led us to the apartment Chet Holden had been renting. According to Riptide, he'd stopped paying rent the same day that Sherry and Caitlyn had gone missing in the desert. It was too much of a coincidence for me.

We were lucky; although he had stopped paying the rent, Tucson wouldn't allow you to evict someone for at least ninety days after they stopped payments. We were still inside that window. So if he left anything behind, it should be here.

Butcher and I crowded around Riptide as he picked the lock on the door. It was only the three of us. We didn't need someone spotting us and calling the cops because a bunch of bikers were milling around their apartment complex.

"You sure no one's in there?" Butcher asked, keeping his voice low.

"Not according to the company's database. They aren't allowed to touch a tenant's shit until they are officially evicted. Should all still be in there."

Riptide opened the door and we all stepped inside, shutting the door behind us. I turned the lock then looked around and shook my head. "Light packer."

"Looks like it was a layover spot for him," Butcher said. "Like he wasn't planning on staying."

We split up and started searching through Chet's meager possessions. It didn't take us long to realize we weren't going to find anything here.

"Son of a bitch," I muttered.

Riptide started to say something when we heard someone talking outside the door. His eyes widened and we all looked at each other.

"Hide," I hissed.

We shoved each other along until we ended up in the bathroom. The tub had a shower curtain and I groaned, but pointed at it. By the time the front door opened we were all squeezed into the tub—shoulder to shoulder—barely breathing as we waited to see who'd just dropped in on us.

Butcher elbowed me to make more room and I glared over at him. Sure we could have just killed whoever walked in, but that wasn't our style. What if one of the residents had seen us coming inside and had gotten security? Then we'd be killing innocent people.

No. We needed to figure out who this was. We had to make sure we didn't hurt anyone who didn't deserve it.

"I don't know why you insist on coming back here each week, Chet." A man's voice floated down the hall.

Looking over, I met Riptide's gaze. We both grinned. Butcher looked like he was ready to jump out and torture the men who were walking through the apartment.

"Just grabbing what I need, John. I'll only be a few minutes."

I jerked my chin to catch Riptide's attention. "Should we grab them?" I asked. My voice was so low I barely breathed the words out.

Riptide considered that, then shook his head. He took something out of his bag he'd carried in. I frowned at the tiny thing between his fingers and gave him a questioning look.

"Tracker," he whispered.

Butcher rubbed his hands together eagerly. "We can get all these fuckers at once."

He said it a bit too loudly and I buried my elbow in his ribs. He grunted softly in pain. We all froze and waited to see if the men had heard him.

They were too busy out in the living room to notice us. I motioned to the tracker. "I'll do it," I mouthed at him.

Riptide handed it over and I reached forward and slowly—as quietly as I could—pulled the shower curtain back. I hesitated—listening—as soon as I'd made enough room to get out of the tub.

I stepped out and listened again. The guys were moving back and forth from the bedroom to the living room. I'd stepped behind the door so I wouldn't be seen. I had to make this quick. Poking my head out of the bathroom, I caught sight of movement in the living room.

"What the hell's so important that you keep coming back for it?" Chet's friend asked.

"Don't worry, John. This is the last time. It's all coming with us tonight."

"Good. You should have grabbed it the first time around."

I moved silently down the hallway and into the master bedroom. There were bags on the bed that hadn't been there when we'd first searched the place. Moving over, I carefully unzipped one of the bags and shoved my hand with the tracker inside. I rummaged around until I felt the bottom and dropped the tracker there.

"Good. Because Ethan isn't going to sanction many more of these trips. I'm shocked he even let you come back for anything. You know we're supposed to leave it all behind when we join. No earthly possessions beyond what he provides."

"Yes, but some of these things were requested by him. More importantly, it's not your place to question, only obey."

What in the fuck are these guys talking about?

The voices were coming closer. I swore under my breath and looked around. The closet was open and it was easy to see Chet was taking shit from there and shoving it in the duffle bags. If I hid there, I'd be caught. My eyes dropped to the bed and I sighed.

Dropping to the floor, I worked on squeezing myself underneath the bed. It was a tight fit as I wasn't a small man, but I'd just managed to shove myself back against the wall when the guys came into the room.

Christ it's like I'm in high school all over again.

"I know the rules, but Ethan granted me a favor. This is what I asked for," Chet said.

"Seems like a waste to me," the other guy muttered.

I heard rustling as they picked up the bags. It was too bad they didn't stick around so I could listen in more, but they headed out almost immediately. I was about to crawl out from under the bed when I heard John speak.

"Hey, I have to take a piss before we carry all this down."

Groaning softly, I held still. Hopefully he wouldn't notice the shadows of Riptide and Butcher still hiding in the tub. I waited, holding my breath as I heard the bathroom door shut.

The minutes passed slowly, and it seemed like he was in there for a long time, but finally the door opened again and I let out a sigh of relief. The sound of them loading up all the bags floated back into the bedroom.

As soon as the front door shut I crawled out from my hiding spot. I froze, on my hands and knees as Riptide and Butcher burst out of the bathroom, both gagging.

"Jesus fucking Christ! What did that guy eat?" Butcher gasped.

Riptide had a disgusted look on his face. I gave them a confused look. "That guy just dumped a fucking load that would do an outdoor shitter proud. Fucker said he was going to piss, fucking liar."

The fact that they were grossed out was saying something since all of us had used the outhouses overseas during our deployments. Fuck, we'd even been around when the Privates had dumped jet fuel into the toilets and burned off all the shit inside. These men were no strangers to nasty shit and yet they still looked green in the face.

"Let's get out of here," I told them, shaking my head. I did myself a favor and held my breath as I passed by the bathroom.

We made our way out of the apartment and I pulled my phone out of my pocket to check it. I frowned when I realized Jenny had never texted me back. I could see that it'd been read, but she hadn't responded. Damn it. I was going to have some fucking explaining to do tomorrow.

Shoving thoughts of her to the back of my mind, I got on my bike. If we were lucky, coming here tonight would finally give us an idea of what was going on.

One thing was for sure. Caitlyn's dad was alive and he was a part of all of this. Whatever *this* was. I couldn't wait to fucking find out and put the whole thing to rest.

CHAPTER 19

Jenny

Groaning, I stretched out, easing sore muscles. The night had dragged on into the late hours as Mom and I had talked, ate, and watched multiple movies. I'd ended up falling asleep on the couch and Mom had dropped a blanket over me before she'd gone to bed.

Rubbing the back of my neck, I gasped. My neck was stiff and sore. I'd never been able to sleep on a couch comfortably. I needed my soft bed and even softer pillows or I ended up with a stiff neck.

Knocking on the door came again and I realized that was what had woken me up in the first place. Grabbing my phone, I checked the time, and muttered under my breath when I realized it was seven a.m.

It was Saturday and the start of my weekend. I'd been looking forward to sleeping in. Though maybe I owed whoever was at the door a debt of gratitude. If I'd slept on the couch a few more hours my neck would be completely messed up instead of only slightly.

I opened the door and froze, hand still massaging the strained muscles. "Priest."

Here we were again, him at my door, and me being shocked to see him. I blinked in confusion at him. "What are you doing here?" Again.

His hands were shoved inside the pockets of his jeans, but his eyes narrowed on my hand. "What's wrong with your neck?"

That had me continuing to blink. I wasn't awake enough for this. "You came here to ask me that?" I dropped my hand, and even though my muscles protested, I refused to raise it again. "It's early," I told him, hearing the cold note in my words.

A muscle flexed in his jaw. "Sorry about that. I couldn't sleep."

My brows shot up. "Why's that?"

"My place is too quiet," he muttered. "The girls are with their grandparents... And you weren't there."

I refused to apologize, though the words were right there on the tip of my tongue. It wasn't *my* fault I hadn't slept at his place last night. I knew he was hurting, but he needed to learn that he couldn't take it out on me.

He shifted as the awkward silence stretched between us. "Taz. I'm sorry for how I behaved yesterday. This is all hitting me harder than I thought it would and I don't know how to process it."

My heart softened. This was what I wanted. It was such a simple confession, or at least the words were simple. For him to say it though, and to say it to me? That was huge. I stepped back and opened the door further so he could step through. I wasn't going to make him bare his soul on the front porch. "You hungry?" I asked, extending the olive branch.

"Starving."

Leading him into the kitchen, I started preparing omelets while he leaned against the counter nearby. "I don't expect you to talk to me about everything," I told him, cracking an egg into a bowl. "I know there's going to be times where you can't tell me stuff, because of the club. But I don't want you to shut me out, or take it out on me."

He opened his mouth, but I pointed an egg at him and he shut it. His lips twitched as he studied my face.

"You shut me out yesterday. If you're having a rough day and can't talk, just let me know. I'll give you your space. I'm not unreasonable, but it hurts my feelings when you treat me how you did yesterday. You say you want me around, to be a part of your life. Act like it."

"I know that," he said, stepping forward and taking the egg from me with the same care that he might take a knife from a madman. He set it inside the carton before he wrapped me up in his arms.

Sighing, I leaned into his body. He was all muscles and heat and it felt so good to be held by him. "You need to talk things out eventually, Priest," I told him, tone soft. "Otherwise it will eat you alive. It doesn't have to be me you speak to, but it needs to be someone."

"I want it to be you," he replied.

"I want that, too." Dammit, there it was again. That spark of hope that he always ignited.

"Not here," he said, pulling away and casting a look down the hall.

My smile was understanding. "Whenever and wherever you're comfortable, but my mother would never tattle to the cops," I teased. "She's a cashier, not a CIA Agent."

He chuckled. "Old habits die hard. A lot of the habits I've had from the military and from the club bleed over into my everyday life."

"I can live with that," I told him, going back to cracking eggs.

He settled back against the counter, again a puzzled look on his face. "Why is that?"

"Huh?"

"You didn't grow up the way I did," he said, looking around at the house, "clearly. Did you grow up around an MC?"

"No," I answered with a laugh. "The guys in Austin were my first run in with bikers."

"Then why are you okay with all of this?"

I turned toward him. I knew what he meant. It was the same thing I'd asked my friends in Austin. None of them had ever dated bikers before and had—for the most part—grown up as law-abiding citizens. I told him my own version of what Ming had said when I'd asked.

"Knowing you has opened my eyes to other ways of life. I was raised to follow the law, but sometimes it's important to know when to buck authority. I still plan on continuing on the way I always have, but I don't mind if you do what you have to do." I stepped closer to him and laid my hands on his chest. "Even if the law doesn't see you as a good man, I do. I know what lengths you'll go to for your family. I know you'd protect me with your life." His expression was grim, eyes flashing at the thought of me being in danger. "That's all I need to know, Priest."

"You put your job in jeopardy to help me with Caitlyn."

I shrugged. "So maybe I'm not as law-abiding as I thought, but that little girl has been through so much I knew I needed to help her. You may not know it yet, but I'll go to extreme lengths to keep my family safe, too. I'd do anything for you guys."

It was scary how quickly I'd slipped into the mindset, but I knew it was the truth. It didn't matter what society thought of Priest or his club. I loved them and I'd protect them in any way I was capable. If that made me a bad person, then so be it. I knew these men. I knew they had good hearts. That was all I cared about.

He dragged me against his chest again and his lips covered mine. I moaned into his mouth, letting the desire arc through me at his touch. It would have been all too easy to forget about breakfast and nibble on him, but someone clearing their throat had us breaking apart like a pair of teenagers.

I gave my mom a guilty grin. "Morning."

"Good morning to you, too," she said with a smirk on her face.

"Uh, Mom, this is Priest. Priest this is my mom, Joy."

"It's nice to meet you," Priest said, letting go of me reluctantly so he could shake her hand.

I didn't miss the way Mom wrapped her robe tighter around herself and eyed him like he was candy. I didn't blame her in the least. It made me realize that I needed to speak to her about dating again. She deserved to have her own man to cause her trouble. Then it wouldn't be only me complaining during our movie nights.

We chatted during breakfast and I was happy to see that Priest and my mom were getting along. Once we finished and had shoved our plates away, she gave me a crafty smile.

"I'll clean up here," she said, her face the picture of innocence. "You kids go have a good time."

I knew her games by now. She was making us leave so we could talk more. She was hoping we'd have enough privacy that Priest would grovel a bit. I didn't really want him to grovel, we were past that, I just wanted him to open up and share with me. Though it was a monumental task to get a man to speak out loud about his feelings, I wanted him to so he would feel better. And maybe so I'd feel closer to him.

"It was nice meeting you," Priest told her again. He wasted no time grabbing my hand and pulling me back to my room. I was still in my pajama shorts and shirt, so I appreciated him letting me get dressed first.

As soon as the door shut behind us he pinned me up against it. I gasped as his short beard scratched against my neck while his lips brushed over my skin. It created a delicious feeling that had goosebumps rising on my arms.

"Priest," I hissed. "What are you doing?"

"She interrupted us before I got to finish that kiss," he complained, his breath heating my skin.

"We're not doing this here," I told him with a laugh. My hands caught his wrists as his palms settled on my hips.

"We've already done this here," he pointed out before he licked a path down my neck to my collarbone.

"Not while my *mom* was here!"

He grunted and dipped his head. He used his teeth to tear the buttons free on my shirt and groaned when he saw that I wasn't wearing a bra underneath.

My head crashed back into the door when he took one aching tip into his mouth and sucked. I let go of his wrists and bit down on the meaty part of my fist. I would die if I had to be silent while he fucked me. It wasn't possible. We had to get out of here.

My teeth loosened and I balled my fist tighter before punching him in the gut.

Priest let out a startled grunt and looked down at me in confused amusement. It'd worked though, he'd let me go.

I danced out of his grasp and across the room. When he started to stalk after me, I pointed at him. "No. Stay there. We're not having sex with my mother here." Folding my arms over my chest, I glared at him.

He chuckled and went over to sprawl out on my bed. It didn't matter how good he looked, I wasn't going to be tempted. *Well, maybe a little tempted.* The thought of crawling onto his lap while he opened his jeans and slid my shorts to the side had wetness pooling between my thighs.

Shaking the thoughts from my mind, I hurried over to my closet. I hesitated before undressing, glancing over my shoulder at him. His intense eyes were watching every move I made. It was embarrassing to undress in front of him. It didn't matter that he'd already seen me naked—not to mention touched and kissed most of me—that was in the heat of the moment.

Still, the look in his eyes told me I could either get dressed, or he'd drag me out of here in my pajamas. Or worse, that he'd give into the desire sparking between us and I'd end up on my back trying to hold in my screams. That wasn't an option, so I finished unbuttoning my shirt and shucked both it and the shorts.

It only took me a few moments to get dressed, but when I turned around I saw that his jeans were fitting a bit tighter in the front. I gave him a sultry smile. "Ready to go?"

"Fuck yeah, I am."

I wasn't sure if he meant leave, or he was ready to 'go'. Both probably. I watched as he adjusted himself behind his jeans and bit back a smile. It felt so damn good to have a man like him be so attracted to me. There'd be times we'd fight—it was inevitable—but if he wanted to get rid of me, he'd have to scrape me off like a barnacle from a ship's hull. I wasn't going anywhere. He had everything I'd always wanted, both himself and a family.

I let him lead me out of the house and over to his bike, calling goodbye to my mom as we went. The ride back to the clubhouse would have been comfortable this early in the morning except the heat pouring off the two of us was supercharging the air around the bike. It felt like I was burning up.

CHAPTER 20

Priest

It was early, so most of the guys were still sleeping as I led Jenny through the clubhouse and up to my apartment. Thanks to most of our club activities, we were creatures of the night. We liked to stay up late and sleep in when we were able to. Weekends started around eleven a.m. on Saturday mornings and not a moment sooner.

I shut the door behind me and had Jenny in my arms in an instant. Her laugh rang through the room as I walked her backward toward my bedroom.

"I thought you brought me here to talk?" she asked.

Shaking my head, I lowered it so that I could kiss her, plunging my tongue between her lips and stopping her questions. This was taking too long. I reached down and gripped the back of her thighs, lifting her easily until those sexy legs wrapped around my waist.

She let out the cutest protests. Something about being too heavy. I broke off the kiss and gave her an amused smirk. "I lift twice your weight every day down in our gym."

Her eyes widened, then narrowed. "You still owe me a talk," she insisted now that her mouth was free.

I nodded and gave her a charming grin. "Alright, but after."

She didn't need to ask after what. I turned so that I hit the bed first and she held onto me, falling forward as we landed. Her hair surrounded me like a cloud and I inhaled her delicious scent. She always smelled like peaches and cream and it had quickly become my favorite.

"After," she agreed, then a devilish glint appeared in her eyes. "You made me another promise a while ago."

My brows pinched together as I tried to think of what it was. Her hands pushed up underneath my shirt and she ran her palms up over my abs.

"You promised I'd have my turn." A grin formed on her face as she started unbuckling my belt.

"Shit," I growled. "If you insist." I gave her my own smile, but it was more a baring of teeth because I knew this was going to be tortuous. Fucking amazing, but torture all the same.

I'd been so intent on her and tasting every inch of her since we'd gotten together that I hadn't allowed her the chance to explore. Looked like today was my lucky day.

Sitting up, I stripped off my cut and my shirt, watching as her nimble fingers undid my belt and the button and zipper of my jeans. She slipped down to my feet and unlaced my boots. I toed them off, then lifted my hips so she could drag the last of my clothes off.

Curling my arms beneath my head, I laid back. Her eyes roamed over my body and my dick jerked when her gaze landed there. My arms pillowed my head, but kept it high enough that I was able to watch what she was going to do to me.

"I can't wait to see those sexy lips stretched out over my cock."

Her wide chocolate eyes met mine and I couldn't help but chuckle. I liked to talk dirty in bed and she always seemed so shocked at what I said. I fucking loved it. Loved the way her blush traveled up from her chest and eventually turned her cheeks the same shade.

"Go on, Baby. Suck it," I urged her.

She wrapped her fist around my length and I groaned. Even just having her hand on me felt good. I gathered up her long silky hair and held it back so it wouldn't be in her way, or mine.

With hungry eyes I watched as her lips parted and pulled me into her mouth. I groaned again as wet heat encircled my cock. She kissed and licked her way from the tip to my pelvis, where she nipped my hip, before finally settling in and giving me what I needed.

My chest heaved, my abs flexing as she sucked on me. "Fuck, you look so good with my dick in your mouth."

Her gorgeous eyes lifted and met mine while she slid down my length and it nearly blew my heart out of my chest. It was hammering against my ribs.

She started stroking her hand in time with her mouth and all the slick friction was making my muscles bunch tighter and tighter. This felt too fucking good to stop, but I wasn't about to come in her mouth. Not this time. I wanted to fuck her.

"Come here," I told her.

She glanced up again and met my gaze. Fuck, I don't think she realized what that did to me when she looked at me like that while she sucked my cock.

"Turn," I managed to force the word out even as pleasure gripped me. It was clear she hadn't sucked a lot of dick—something that made me immensely happy—but what she lacked in coordination she more than made up for in enthusiasm. She had me on the verge of coming in her mouth with very little effort.

I reached down and dragged her up my body, enjoying the wet slurping noise she made when I forced her mouth to release my dick. Manhandling her, I flipped her around until she was lying on top of me with her pussy and ass laid before me like a banquet.

She gasped when I leaned forward and licked her wet folds. "Priest!"

"Get back to work, Baby," I told her, smacking her ass. I grinned as it jiggled there in front of my face. Forcing my heels into the mattress, I had to hunch a bit in order to be able to reach her while she went back to swallowing down my cock. "Fuck yeah, that feels so good. You're such a good fucking girl."

That was all I got out before I began eating her out. It wasn't easy to speak with a mouth full of pussy and hers was delicious and sopping wet for me.

She started moaning while sliding her mouth up and down my length and I realized this had been a terrible idea. I wanted to bury myself deep inside her body and feel her clamping down on me. And since that was what I wanted, I pulled her off me for a second time, then dropped her down over my hips. She was straddling me, looking at me in surprise.

"Go ahead," I said, palming her tits. "Ride me."

She lifted her body and seated herself all the way down on my cock in one smooth stroke. Her ass was pressed against my thighs and I couldn't keep my hands to myself.

At first I fisted her hips, helping her set a nice quick rhythm, but then I let them wander. Her breasts were bouncing in front of my face, so I gripped the back of her neck, forcing her down lower so I could nip and lick at her nipples.

She planted her hands on my shoulders and kept grinding as I teased her taut peaks, but eventually I let her rise back up. She looked fucking perfect. Her head thrown back, blissful expression on her face, her dark curly hair trailing down her back and tickling my thighs.

It was a sensation overload. Her pussy was wet and gripped me so firmly I felt every flutter and squeeze. I could tell by her erratic rhythm that she was getting close. I brought my hand up and used my thumb to start circling her clit. Her gasp was like music and she brought her head forward to look down at me. Her lids were only half open and her lips were parted. That pink tongue of hers darted out to brush over her full lower lip and it reminded me of what it'd felt like brushing along the underside of my cock.

"Come for me, Taz," I encouraged her. She was right there, teetering on the edge. I reached back and slapped her ass.

She cried out and I felt her walls contract around me as the orgasm swept her up in its wake. She'd stopped moving, so I grabbed her around the waist and rolled us until she was tucked underneath my body.

I powered into her, prolonging her pleasure and increasing my own. My mouth covered hers and I drank in her cries and whimpers as I fucked her. Her pussy clamped down on me and I groaned against her lips as I thrust as far inside her as I could before I came.

She had my fucking muscles locked up like a vise as my orgasm roared through me, devastating every functioning part of my body. I wanted to do this every day for the rest of my fucking life. The way she made me feel couldn't compare to anything else.

Eventually, I was able to move again and, though I didn't want to, I pulled out of her and rolled until I was on my back. She was tucked up against my side, our legs tangled together and I closed my eyes. This was what I'd been missing last night. The reason I hadn't been able to sleep. Not the sex, though that was mind blowing. Having her next to me, our bodies pressed together. I just needed her, here, with me.

* * *

Jenny groaned deep in her throat and even though I'd just finished fucking her into an almost mindless state, my dick hardened at the sound. I was straddling her, rubbing my hands over her neck.

She'd finally let it slip that her neck was bothering her and this was an easy way to start making up for yesterday's shit attitude. I dug my fingers into her neck, finding a knot under the skin and rubbing my thumb back and forth over it.

She hissed at the pain from the movement and I paused. "Don't stop," she pleaded.

My cock twitched because it wasn't long ago she was begging, using the same words, but for a different reason. Having her around was making me as horny as an eighteen-year-old. I couldn't seem to keep my hands off her, and sure as fuck didn't plan to.

"Please, Priest. If it doesn't hurt, it doesn't feel good."

It was my turn to groan. "You're killing me, woman."

Her head shifted and she shot me a puzzled look, but she must have read the hunger on my face because she blushed. I loved the way her pinkening skin made the freckles on her nose stand out.

A knock sounded on the door before I had a chance to give her exactly what she was asking for, and more. She laughed at me as I grumbled and rolled off the bed, pulled on my jeans, and walked through the living room.

Yanking open the door, I glowered at Ricochet. "What's up, Kid?"

Ricochet was, by far, the youngest of us. He'd been medically discharged from the Marines not too long after he'd gotten deployed. Poor kid had lived through a tough situation. So even though he was here, knocking on my door, and interrupting my time with my woman, I softened my voice as much as I could.

He shoved his hands into the pockets of his jeans. "Sorry, Priest. I wanted to ask you a favor…" His eyes strayed past me and I knew without looking that Jenny had come out into the living room.

Turning my head, I took in her disheveled appearance. Her hair was a clear sign that I'd just fucked her, but on top of that her soft smile and glowing cheeks added to the look. "Give me a minute," I growled at her.

Stepping out into the hall, I shut the door. It wasn't that I didn't want her to hear our conversation. Lockout left it up to us how much we wanted to tell our old ladies about club life, as long as they didn't make trouble for us. I knew I could trust Jenny to keep our secrets, and I planned to keep her in the loop.

This was more instinctual. Ricochet was my MC brother, but I didn't like him seeing her while she was freshly fucked and still wet. That was for me and me alone. Possessiveness rose up inside of me so quickly, I had to clench my fists to keep from starting something with the kid in front of me.

He seemed to pick up on my mood, because he backed up a step and averted his eyes. "Sorry for interrupting, Priest," he said again.

"It's fine." My tone was dark, but I was working on pulling myself back under control. The last few months had thrown me off my rhythm. This wasn't me. I was the guy who handled his emotions and locked them down under layers of rigid discipline and restraint. I wasn't the guy to snap at a brother simply because he interrupted naked time.

Shaking my hands out, I blew out a breath. "Sorry, Ricochet. What did you need help with?"

"I wanted to see if you could talk Lock into putting me in on this whole thing with Chet Holden."

My brows shot up. The kid had been discharged from the military for a reason. We only spoke about it if he brought it up because it was a delicate situation, but the last time Lockout had agreed to let Ricochet go on a mission—to help the Austin Chapter—he'd withdrawn from us for months afterward. It wasn't that he couldn't handle himself under pressure, quite the opposite. He was as proficient a killer as any I'd served with. It was just that once the fighting was over, he would close in on himself.

He was battling demons and we all wanted to help him tackle them. He wouldn't let us. That realization struck me like a sledgehammer. This was what Jenny was talking about. She wanted to help me, but I was acting like Ricochet and keeping her at a distance.

Rubbing my hand over my face, I tried to reconcile that knowledge with how to fix it and focus on the kid standing in front of me. At twenty-four years old he was too fucking young for the shadows I saw lurking there in his gaze. "You sure that's what you want? No one would blame you if you sat this one out."

He shook his head, scowling at the floor. He hated it when we tried to coddle him. I understood it, but it was fucking hard not to. He'd come to us at eighteen years old, wanting to build a family here at home. He would leave to sign up for the Marines, then returned to us after his deployment.

At forty, I wasn't that much older than him, but it felt like it sometimes. Now was one of those moments. These guys—all of them—were family. I'd do anything to protect them.

"Yeah," he said, sounding a little angry. "I'm sure, Priest."

"Alright, I'll talk to Lock and Rip later about it."

"Thanks," he said, giving me a nod and walking back toward his room.

I stood out in the hallway for a few minutes, trying to finish pulling myself together. It was time for Jenny and I to have a talk. Hard rock music poured through the air only a few minutes after Ricochet shut his door.

Blowing out a breath, I walked back into my apartment. Jenny was standing there, waiting for me. Grabbing her by the hand, I led her over to the couch. I didn't dare bring her back to the bedroom because then we wouldn't end up talking. We'd be too busy fucking. As much as I wanted that, I owed this to her.

We sat down on the couch and I rubbed the back of my neck, trying to figure out where to start with her. "I'm sorry that I was shutting you out. I tend to do that when shit gets to be too much."

"I noticed," she told me, a smile spreading over her face.

"I don't fucking deserve you. You're so damn…good. And understanding."

She laughed and shook her head. "Wait until you see what I'm like when you don't come try to fix things with me," she warned.

A grin tugged at my lips. "Not sure I want to be at the mercy of your anger, Taz. You'd rip my life apart."

The smile fell off her lips and she watched me solemnly. I didn't miss the spark of hope there. "You stood by me over the last few weeks. Helped me console my kids. Didn't judge me for what happened with Wendy."

She reached forward and placed her hand on my thigh. I had my jeans on, but not my shirt. Gripping her hand, I held it in mine, needing to feel her skin against mine.

"I've been through some shit in my life, but no woman has ever stood by me like that."

Her eyes softened and the smile was back. She looked so fucking beautiful sitting there the next words popped out of my mouth. I'd planned to find a fancy way of telling her, but in that moment, I couldn't hold back. My heart was beating hard against my chest and I just needed her to know.

"I love you, Taz."

Her eyes widened and her lips formed a surprised little 'o', then she beamed at me. "I love you, too, Priest." There was silence for a moment and then she laughed.

My brows shot up. "Something funny?" I growled playfully at her.

"No, sorry, it's just… I've been waiting for this." She shrugged her shoulders and squeezed my hand. "I can't believe the moment is finally here, that's all."

Leaning forward, I kissed her. To know that she'd been waiting for a man to tell her that he loved her and that she'd chosen to give her heart to me? It was powerful. I vowed, in that moment, to always protect her.

"I'll do my best to not push you away when shit gets real. I'll leave the final decision up to you, but I plan to keep you in the loop on what's happening with the club."

She looked surprised. "Is that typical? The girls made it seem like your club wasn't like the Austin Chapter. That you didn't let old ladies have any decisions in club business."

"We don't," I clarified. "Not out of disrespect-"

"No, I get it. It's *your* club. I'm only a part of it because of you. Honestly, I'm fine with that."

"Good," I said with a smile. "But it's my decision if I want you to know what we're up to. Some guys don't tell their old ladies anything. Gives them plausible deniability if the cops ever come sniffing around."

"I hadn't even thought of that," she replied.

"But you already know a good portion of it, thanks to getting you involved with helping me get custody of Caitlyn. Besides, I think it'd work better with us if I tell you everything." Thinking of Ricochet, I amended, "Everything relevant to what I'm involved with. Some things here aren't mine to tell."

"I'd like that, and I understand." she said eagerly. "At least this way I can help in any way possible."

Raising my free hand, I brushed it over her hair, enjoying the way her soft curls felt under my palm. I settled back against the couch and pulled her into my arms. It would take a while to open up and tell her all the shit I got up to back in my Army days, the club business, and the way I've been feeling the last few months. But she was mine, and we had all the time in the world.

CHAPTER 21

Jenny

I'd been right. Priest opening up—not to mention telling me he loved me—had made me feel more connected to him. We'd spent the week together, with minimal distractions, enjoying our time with each other. And that in itself was amazing. So much of our relationship had been built around danger and, well, drama, it was nice to just do ordinary life things together.

He worked full-time for the MC, I found out, doing pretty much whatever was necessary. It helped Lockout and Riptide by taking a lot off their plates. He was the Road Captain for the club and oversaw the prospects when the others were busy. He made sure the weapons the club had were cleaned and maintained. All sorts of odds and ends.

He was pretty young to be retired, but working for the club—and raising his daughters—kept him busy. He told me he had a good retirement with the Army, so he wasn't hurting for money. I looked down at the bowl of cereal I was eating. We'd come downstairs this morning to eat with his brothers and it felt nice to be slowly getting to know them as well.

Something occurred to me as I watched him step outside. His daughter's grandparents were dropping them off and he'd gone out to get them. I didn't want to impose, so I stayed put. I was still trying to figure out the best way of being a part of their family without intruding.

"I forgot to ask Priest," I said, startling Butcher and Toxic as I spoke in the silence of the room. The other guys had all left to go get ready for work. "Did he get his nickname from the club? Or the Army?"

Toxic and Butcher eyed each other for a minute before Toxic spoke. "Army. He was a sniper."

"He told me that," I said, encouraging him to continue with a smile.

"He was a sniper," Butcher said, drawing each word out as if saying the same thing a second time was going to clue me in to what they were saying. I gave them a blank look and Butcher looked up at the ceiling as though he wasn't sure how to say it any clearer.

"You know how a Priest is a direct line to God, right?" Toxic asked.

"Or so they say," Butcher muttered.

I ignored him and focused on Toxic. He was actually being helpful at the moment. "Yeah."

"Well, so was Priest. Once he got a target he sent them straight up," Toxic explained.

"More than likely it was straight down," Butcher commented.

My eyes widened as the realization hit. He was a straight line to God because he killed them without them even knowing he was there. "Oh." I nibbled my lip as I thought that over. It wasn't like I didn't know that Priest was dangerous. I'd known that the first time I'd seen him. Having the confirmation that he had killed, and so effectively, was disconcerting and a small part of me found it sexy. There was something to be said for having a lethal man as your own.

All of these guys were dangerous. They were well trained and didn't hold back. Instead of making me feel uneasy, it made me feel safe. Not that a lot of trouble happened in my life—I was sort of boring—but if it ever did, I had a bunch of men who would do whatever it took to protect me, starting with Priest.

"So, what do your names mean?" I finally asked them after we sat in silence for a few moments while I processed.

Toxic laughed and shook his head. "Maybe one day we'll tell you." As one unit, they both stood up. Butcher tousled my curls as he walked past, leaving me there alone. Or so I thought.

"Don't mind those guys," Lockout said, walking into the room.

"I like them," I told him with a grin.

He returned it and poured coffee into his mug. "Really? That's rare. I mean, good, because we like you." He looked out the window toward the parking lot. "You're good for him."

Delight made my heart sing. I wanted to be good for him. I wanted to be the best old lady he could ask for, and maybe one day the best wife. Long gone was my worry about hardly knowing him. The more we learned about each other, the more I fell in love with him.

"Thank you, Lockout. From everything he's been telling me you guys are good for him, too."

"We're family," he said with a shrug. "You're a part of that now, too."

"Any pointers on making sure he doesn't shut down?"

Lockout chuckled. "Exactly what you did. Call him on his bullshit and make him realize what he's doing. Hold him accountable to himself. Once that happens he usually straightens out pretty quickly. His time with the Ranger Battalion was tough on him. It is for most of those guys, but his was worse. He had a family before most of the Rangers would. Combine that with multiple deployments as a sniper? He learned how to shut down his emotions to the point where we weren't sure he had them anymore." He gave me a sardonic smile. "He tried as hard as he could to burn them away once he lost Wendy and the girls."

"He told me she took them away from him for a while." I shook my head. "I couldn't imagine how hard that was for him."

"Especially since it happened right as he got home from a deployment. He lost his spotter on that deployment. They were only a week away from coming home and a convoy got pinned down by insurgents." He was watching me closely as he told me the story. Tears welled in my eyes. My heart hurt for Priest.

"He and his spotter, Tango, were laid up on a rooftop nearby. They'd been there for three days laying in wait for a local warlord. When the convoy got hit they broke cover and started to assist. Thing is, they were all alone up there. A few of the attackers peeled off of the convoy and headed for them on the roof. Priest made it back. Tango didn't."

Lockout turned and dumped his coffee out into the sink, as though the liquid were no longer appealing. I understood, my mouth was dry as I listened to his story, horrified about what could have happened. What did happen.

He washed out the cup then left it in the bottom of the sink. Turning back toward me, he leaned back against the counter and folded his arms over his chest. "It was a fucking miracle we didn't lose Priest, too."

"Was Tango a part of the MC?"

"No, but over there, every military member belongs to the rest of us. Our guys aren't just brothers because of the MC, but because of the military as well."

I nodded in understanding. "That must have been awful for him," I whispered.

"He carried Tango back to the safe zone where he could get picked up, but he'd already died on the trek back. It was a huge blow to him. To all of us."

"I'm so sorry." He hadn't told me any of that when we'd talked yesterday. I couldn't really blame him. There'd been enough to talk about and he had every right to keep some things to himself. I raised a brow at Lockout. "Why are you telling me this?"

"When he got back he found Wendy and the kids gone. He folded up inside himself and we almost didn't get him back. There's going to be times when he pisses you off. I'm hoping that by telling you this you'll understand why he acts the way he does. He shut down hard after that, and I swear to Christ, I don't think I saw him smile again until he met you. There's going to be times you need to give him a break."

I didn't have a chance to respond because Priest and his daughters barrelled into the kitchen. Lockout gave me a wink as he said hi to the girls and left.

"What was that?" Priest asked suspiciously.

"Nothing," I replied, pasting an innocent look on my face. He wasn't convinced, but the girls saved me.

"Jenny!" They all ran forward and I gave them each hugs. It was so nice to see them with smiles on their faces. Even Caitlyn, still silent, was smiling so big she was practically screaming for joy.

"How was your time with your grandparents?" I asked. I listened to their excited chatter with a smile. It was a brief reprieve from their grief. I knew it would come in waves and even though they were flying high now, the low times weren't over.

"Priest." We all glanced over as Lockout walked back in. "Need you for a minute."

Priest looked over at me and I waved him away. "Go. I've got them."

I ushered the girls upstairs so they could unpack. Bringing the laundry basket from room to room, I loaded up their dirty clothes and left them giggling together to go throw a load in the washer. It was nice that Priest had a washer and dryer up here in one of the closets. I wouldn't have enjoyed having to run downstairs to the laundry room every time. With four kids and two adults I'd be forever running up and down the stairs. Not to mention what I would find left in the common laundry room.

After getting the washer going, I knocked on Gabby's door. Caitlyn was already in Cassie and Taylor's room and I could hear them giggling together.

"Hey," I said, smiling as I poked my head in.

She looked up and gave me a small smile. I went inside. "Mind if I sit?" I asked and pointed to the bed.

She shrugged her shoulders. She was nine and almost getting to those pre-teen years. That was as much of an invitation as I was going to get. I sat down and studied her. She'd been smiling downstairs, but it was as though being here, alone, brought her back to reality. The sadness was radiating off her.

"Are you okay?"

She nodded and brushed her hair back from her face, looking over at me. She met my eyes defiantly. She was her father's daughter.

"It's okay to be sad, Gabby."

She let out an aggravated sigh and turned away, giving me her back. I knew this maneuver, I did it to my mother still to this day.

That hadn't been the right thing to say. "I hope you know you can come to me if you need to talk."

She turned her head so I could see her roll her eyes. Ouch. *This is my mother's payback for my teenage years.* I could only hope that one day I'd have the relationship with Gabby that my mom and I had now. That was the hope anyway.

"I'll keep that in mind," she replied.

"I care about you. We can be friends-"

She turned around again and a sly smile crossed her face. "Are you and Dad dating?"

"Yes," I told her. It took me biting my tongue to not ask if that was okay. It didn't matter if she didn't like it. We were the adults.

"Does that mean you're having sex?"

I choked on a horrified sound. "What?"

"Billy Lamount said that when his mom started dating again she started having sex with guys." She was watching me closely, judging my reactions.

My face was a calm mask, but inside I was freaking out. I wasn't equipped for this. *Nine-year-olds shouldn't be talking about sex!*

"Um, maybe she was, but that's Billy's mom's business. Just like it's your dad's and my business what we do together."

Respect flickered in her eyes. I'd managed to shut down that avenue of conversation. Thank God. I patted her shoulder and stood up. "Anytime Gabby, you can come to me with anything."

She nodded and I left her alone. I'd have to talk to Priest. She was exactly like him, buttoning up her feelings. If she stayed buttoned up like this, it would make it so much harder for her as she got older. Who better to talk to her about it than him?

Going into the kitchen, I started cleaning. Priest had mentioned spending the day together as a family, so I got to work while we waited for him.

CHAPTER 22

Priest

Lockout, Riptide, Dash, Hush, and Seek were all back inside the meeting room. Dash looked over in excitement as I walked in.

"Yo! We finally got a lock on the tracker's location!"

Riptide gave Dash a bitter look. "That was my fucking line, Dash."

"Sorry, Rip," Dash said, looking not the least bit ashamed.

"Where did Chet go?" I asked. I'd put that tracker in his bag a week ago, but he'd been bouncing around the city for days on end and we'd been waiting for him to settle in one place before looking into it.

"The Silverbells," Seek told me, a wide grin on her face. "He stopped out in the middle of the desert two days ago. Rip thinks he's there to stay for a while."

"In the middle of the desert?" I asked.

"Seek!" Riptide said at the same time as I asked my question. "You're both stealing my thunder here."

Seek gave him a toothy smile. "Yeah, well you guys won't let me go out and help investigate, so that's what you get."

Riptide grumbled and scowled at her.

"Can we fucking focus?" I asked. "What would Chet be doing out in the desert? Camping?"

"That's what we're going to find out," Hush answered. "But given how close it is to where Caitlyn's mother was murdered, I doubt he's up to anything good."

"I'm in." I remembered Ricochet's request and met Lockout's gaze. "We should bring Ricochet in on this one."

His brows pinched together. "I don't think that's a good idea, Priest."

"He asked me if I'd speak to you and Rip. He wants in, Lock."

He was quiet for a few moments. "You think he's ready? It took him a while to get over what happened in Austin."

"Maybe. Maybe not, but if he says he wants in we should probably listen. He knows he needs to do something, and he wants to be helpful."

"He needs the distraction," Hush interjected. "Let him come along. We're just doin' some recon."

"Just recon," Lockout insisted. "I don't want you assholes busting in on whatever is going on out there. We got lucky with Seek and Cait, we don't know anything yet. Go. Check it out. Get your asses home."

"Will do," I said with a grin. This was a welcome distraction with everything going on with me right now, too. I knew exactly how Ricochet felt. In more ways than one. What had happened to the kid over on his deployment could eat at you if you let it. Not to mention his reaction and how it kept affecting him. I'd been waiting for him to come to me. To talk things out with someone. Instead, it seemed as though he was dedicated to internalizing all his agony. Yeah…I knew how he felt because we were too fucking similar.

"Meanwhile," Lockout said, interrupting my thoughts, "I'll go check out the spots here in the city where Chet was staying. See if I can figure out what he was up to. Why he kept moving from place to place the way he did. With him out of the city I'll draw less suspicion poking around."

I noticed Riptide elbow Dash and bit back a grin. Riptide knew better than to tell his president anything, especially in front of everyone, so he often used Dash to circumvent that. Dash's old lady preferred the man to take less dangerous jobs within the club—much to his annoyance—and Lockout and Riptide always tried to appease them both.

"Mind if I tag along, Prez?" Dash asked. "The old lady will shit a brick if she hears that I was out fucking around in the desert. Especially after the whole Dex thing." His son had gotten lost out in the desert at the beginning of summer. It was how we'd first met Seek. Her and her dogs were the ones to find him. Dash's tone was sheepish, but all of us—including Lockout—knew what he was up to.

Lockout gave Riptide a hard look, but he nodded. "Happy to have you along, Brother," he told Dash. He pointed at Riptide. "Take however many of the guys you need."

It was the weekend and most of the guys weren't working today, so we'd end up taking a good amount of reinforcements. After what'd happened out at The Silverbells the last time, we weren't about to be taken by surprise. Who knew what we'd walk in on.

"I need to let Jenny know-"

"I'll tell her," Seek said, interrupting me. "I'm going to need a bottle of wine to soothe the blow to my pride not allowing me to go with you will cause," she grumped. She leaned over and brushed her lips over Hush's.

"Only one?" Hush asked.

Seek flipped him off with a laugh. "If Jenny can't babysit, then I'll take care of the girls while you guys are gone."

I'd already talked to Jenny yesterday about her moving in with us, but she insisted on taking it slowly, for the girls' sake. That didn't mean I wasn't having the adult version of a sleepover as much as possible.

"If you're watching the girls you'll need more than one bottle of wine." It was nice seeing her being able to laugh and joke about the fact that we were taking over her investigation into The Silverbells. We all understood her anger at first, but she was too important to Hush to put at risk. He'd almost lost her once and he wouldn't be able to handle that, not after losing his first wife.

Just the thought of Jenny dying made me want to storm up to the apartment and duct tape her and the girls to something sturdy inside the apartment. If they didn't leave it without me there, they wouldn't get into any trouble.

I knew that was a bit over the top, and wouldn't be received well, so I followed my brothers over to the armory area and unlocked the door. There were too many kids—not to mention Butcher—around not to lock the guns up. It wasn't that Butcher was dangerous with guns per se, it was the opposite. I would come home to find the girls putting precision holes in the wall or shooting clay birds off of the roof. He'd end up training them to be crack shots before they even knew how to drive.

Handing out rifles, I grabbed one for myself and strapped my pistol holster to my belt before loading my Glock into it.

We didn't know what we were going to be heading into. It was best to bring a little bit of everything.

"Prez, mind if I tag along with you for this one?"

We all glanced over as Hellfire walked up. Riptide had rounded up the rest of the guys we'd need for the two missions we had going.

Lockout's brows shot up. "Always happy to have you along. Something up?"

Hellfire was the first one to offer himself up for the most dangerous jobs. Him requesting to go with Lockout—on what we all suspect would be the tamer of the two missions—was unusual.

In the beginning Lockout had been the same. He went on every one of our runs. He was the first one to enter buildings and went running into danger before any of us. As much as we'd all appreciated that our president wasn't willing to ask something of us that he wouldn't do, we'd finally had a talk with him. Riptide, Hush, and I had sat down with him and told him that the club needed him. It was our jobs to face that danger for him. If one of us went down, the club would recover, but if we lost him? It was fucking unimaginable.

He'd been fucking pissed, but eventually had accepted what we were telling him. We weren't trying to tell him how to run his club. We'd just told him the hard truth. It was why he had us as his main officers. He knew we'd tell it to him straight. He still got involved in way more than we'd prefer, but he'd eased off a lot as well. It was the best compromise we were going to get from him.

"Everything's fine," Hellfire told him. "Just needed to be closer to the city. My mom isn't feeling great and I may need to take her to the hospital."

Lockout's eyes narrowed on him as he tried to figure out whether Hellfire was full of bullshit or not. "If she's sick, you don't need to go."

"Eh, you know Mom. She won't let me take her anywhere unless she's on her deathbed." His eyes found mine and the huge man grimaced. "Sorry, Priest. I didn't-"

"Don't be," I interrupted. Shoving the rising mix of feelings back down, I handed Riptide a rifle.

"I'm in for the city mission," Smokehouse called from behind everyone.

"I don't need fucking babysitters," Lockout snarled at Riptide, though he did so under his breath.

"Hey, don't look at me," Riptide replied with a shrug. "I didn't ask them to go along."

"The fuck you didn't," Lockout muttered. His eyes flashed angrily. "We're going to have to have a talk about the chain of fucking command when we finish this, Rip." With that he walked off, snapping at our three brothers who were going with him to hurry the fuck up.

I let out a low whistle. "You managed to piss him off. Good job."

Riptide shrugged. He'd cut his hair a few weeks ago, so instead of hanging down to his shoulders it was just past his ears. He still looked like the quintessential surfer guy, which was exactly what he was. He'd grown up in the Pacific Northwest and lived for the ocean. The fact that he'd ended up in the damn desert was only because of the relationship he'd built with Lockout during a deployment.

He'd left behind his one true love—the sea—to come here and help build the MC. He was a few years younger than me and Lockout, but no one gave a shit. He'd proved his worth and every one of us—even the older guys—would follow him anywhere. It's why Lockout had made him his VP.

Riptide looked around at the group coming with us. There were six of us counting him. Everyone else had been busy. Six was fine. It was all we needed for a recon mission.

Something bumped my leg and I looked down into a furry face. "Your mom is going to be pissed that you're down here without her," I told Jecht. The Malinois didn't look the least bit worried. He whined low in his throat. "I swear," I said, kneeling to scratch the dog behind the ears, but looking up at Hush, "these dogs can fucking speak English."

"You and me both," Hush replied with a chuckle. "Jecht, back upstairs," he ordered, pointing up the staircase.

The dog whined again, but left, tail drooping as he trotted up the stairs with exaggerated slowness. "Great," Hush muttered. "Now I'm in trouble with Seek and her dogs. At least Auron stayed upstairs."

"Guaranteed he's glued to Caitlyn's side," I said with a grin. Seek's dogs loved my girls and the feeling was very clearly mutual. The day was coming when I was going to have to give in and get them their own dog. Things had been too chaotic before for a puppy, but soon—once things settled—I'd get them one. Especially since we had Seek around to train it. She was amazing with the animals.

"Let's go," Riptide called out. "We need to get in and out of there before dark. I don't want to alert whoever is out there with Chet that we're coming."

The ride out to the area where we'd found Caitlyn more than a month ago was eerie. It was like the desert knew something we didn't. Summer was officially coming to an end, though we'd still have hot weather up until November—just not blistering heat—so the Cicadas were quiet. Their mating season had come and gone and it was weird not to hear the bugs buzzing from the trees.

There wasn't a cloud in the sky, yet I still had an ominous feeling.

The others felt it, too, and we were all silent as we rode out together in one of the trucks.

"Stop here," Riptide told me. He had a handheld antenna outside the window and was holding a radio in his other hand. I knew the contraption was called a telemetry GPS tracker, or some such shit, since that's what he'd called it when he told Lockout he had a way to track Chet. I wasn't sure how the damn thing worked, but we were about to find out.

The hairs prickled on the back of my neck. I turned and looked over my shoulder at Hush, Ricochet, Butcher, and Toxic, who were all smashed together in the backseat. Hush had the same scowl on his face that I was sure was on my own. This had been the exact spot where Sherry Holden's vehicle had been parked that day.

Riptide frowned down at his handheld radio receiver—it was connected to the foot-long antenna by a cable—as it emitted a beeping noise. He hadn't even noticed the significance of having us stop here. Riptide had been a communications Sergeant within a Green Beret special forces team, so he had all the coolest gadgets. I wasn't sure how he kept getting the equipment now that he was out, but it was clear he still had some contacts within his old team. He was a techie to the extreme.

He finally looked up and his eyes met mine when the realization hit. "Well hell. What do ya know?" He shrugged. "This puts us directly in line with Chet." He held up the receiver and grinned at me.

I stared at it blankly as it continued chirping, then lifted a brow. It wasn't like I had any idea what the fucking beeping meant.

Riptide shook his head with a sigh. "Come on, let's go."

We got out and got our gear together, pulling out camelbacks filled with water. We weren't sure how long this was going to take, or how far we'd be hiking and the last thing you wanted was to get stuck out in the Sonoran Desert with no water. That would lead to a miserable death. We left the truck parked under a mesquite tree. The whole point was to be discreet. The truck would be loud and kick up a lot of dust. By walking the last few miles, we could stay out of sight.

"You're bringing that thing with us?" Butcher asked as Riptide started walking, holding the antenna out in front of him.

Riptide rolled his eyes. "If we want to find Chet, it comes with us." He moved the antenna around and I started to notice that every time the beeping grew fainter, he'd sweep the thing around until the signal was strong again, and change our direction.

Pretty fucking cool.

I hadn't realized, until this moment, that the thing I'd dropped into Chet's bag had been a radio transmitter. That's what we were following now. *Makes sense.* Out here there was no cell signal, and your off the shelf commercial tracking devices needed cell service to work. We walked along with Riptide, listening to the beeps echo around the quiet desert surrounding us.

CHAPTER 23

Priest

We paused as we came into the clearing. An ominous feeling swept over me. This is where we'd found the men who'd been burying Sherry Holden. Where we'd buried them instead, only to come back later and find their bodies missing. This was where we'd first seen Caitlyn. I remembered her tear-filled eyes meeting mine and it'd felt like she was screaming inside of my head. She hadn't uttered a word, of course, but that look had been a punch to my gut. She'd come such a long way in a short amount of time, even though she still wouldn't speak…or couldn't. I honestly wasn't sure which it was.

Staring down at the empty hole where we'd buried the men, and later found them missing, I shook my head. "I can't wait to finish this," I muttered. The thought of Chet and whoever he was working with finding Caitlyn had me seeing red. "I'm going to kill them and leave them out here for the coyotes to polish off. Make sure no one ever finds them again."

"There'd be remains," Butcher said. His tone of voice suggested he thought he was being helpful as he told us, "There'd be an arm or leg left around somewhere. And the bones and clothes, of course. Way too much evidence. That's why pigs are a better way to dispose of bodies than wildlife scavengers. They eat all that shit." A surprised look flashed over his face as he realized we were all staring at him. "I assume anyway," he muttered, looking away.

There was no assumption needed. He'd spoken with complete confidence. Which meant he had experience with this. I didn't want him to explain, and the others must have felt the same because no one said anything. Now was not the time.

It's Butcher, there's never a time when you wanted to know what he did.

Everyone in the club knew what Butcher's 'specialty' had been while he'd been in the military. He'd been a part of an elite task force that most of the country's three letter organizations hadn't even known existed. The CIA, FBI, NSA, hell even the brass inside the DOD hadn't had a high enough security clearance to know about his team's exploits. They'd reported directly to some bigwigs in Washington D.C. and had every mission wiped clean after it was completed.

Butcher wasn't one for following the rules—one of the reasons they'd recruited him for that task force—and he'd been more than happy to fill us in on some of the 'fun' he'd had while in.

I honestly wasn't sure if he'd always been a little fucked up in the head or if his time in made him that way. I'd only met him after the attack on my Ranger team. His task force—he'd been in charge of it—had been called in after my spotter had been killed and our operation blown.

He'd found me a few weeks later, sitting in my bunk still trying to reconcile how my partner and best friend had been killed, and told me—in detail—how they'd dispatched each of the men responsible for the loss of my brother.

Somehow the gory retelling had helped and Butcher and I had become friends. With him came Toxic. The two were practically joined at the hip, though Toxic wasn't a part of Butcher's task force.

He'd been one of the pilots assigned to Butcher's team. He was dual certified in both Blackhawks and Apache helicopters and had been the one to either drop off Butcher and his team where needed, or would be hovering overhead providing cover from the air.

Riptide and the others had started walking again, so I caught up to them. Despite the blazing sun burning down on our skin, none of us bitched about the heat as we hiked along. We were all used to it by now and had done far worse in our time overseas.

My muscles relaxed and loosened as we walked for a few hours before buildings started coming into view between the brush.

"What the fuck?" Ricochet asked softly. We stepped behind a cluster of mesquite trees and took a knee. Ricochet faced forward, scanning between the buildings, Butcher scanned behind. The rest of us huddled around Riptide.

Riptide turned off the receiver and instantly the beeping stopped. We waited as he folded the antenna up and put it inside his pack. Shrugging the bag onto his back, he asked, "Am I fucking losing it or are those actual houses?"

"Shacks," I offered up.

"Somewhere in between," Hush said in a quiet voice.

We were in a little alcove just west of The Silverbell Mountains. It was the perfect spot to hide a community. The roads that led to The Silverbell Mine gave them easy enough access, but it was behind a set of hills that kept them out of sight of the mine. There was nothing else out here, making it the perfect location. Only, why would anyone want to live out here? Without electricity. Without running water. No air conditioning. No creature comforts of any kind. I'd had enough of that from my time in the military. The thought of living that way here at home was unfathomable.

As one unit we ducked in and out of brush as we got as close as we could to the buildings. There were sixteen that we could count from here, and it looked like more were being built.

I shot Riptide a questioning look and he shrugged. He didn't know what this place was any more than I did. They were starting to build a huge fence around their compound, as though to keep the world out.

Or maybe their own people in. My muscles tightened as I watched men and women spilling out of all corners of the compound and forming a loose circle in the middle. I was practically vibrating with fury as I saw a man dragging a young girl—maybe ten or eleven—toward everyone. She was digging in her heels, trying to get away from him, and kicking up dust everywhere as she did so.

A hand came down on my shoulder. I glanced over at Riptide. He squeezed my shoulder and shook his head. "We're too fucking outnumbered, Priest," he whispered, though I saw the torment there in his gaze. He pointed to the corners of the compound. Men with rifles surrounded the place. We were outnumbered three to one. All of us knew this scene playing out in front of us couldn't be a good thing, but there wasn't much we'd be able to do.

I stayed put, ducked down behind the fence—out of sight of the guards—but had to grind my back molars together to keep from bellowing at the fucker to take his hands off that kid. She wasn't much older than Gabby.

They came to a stop in the middle of the circle and for a short time no one spoke. Then a man started up.

"My people!" he called out.

My lip curled up in disgust. Who the fuck said shit like that?

"How many times should one person be forgiven?" He looked around as he asked the question, catching the eyes of the adults standing nearby.

All the young kids were hiding behind their parents' legs while the older children were near the back, staring at the dirt in front of them. One glance was all you needed to know those kids were afraid. Which made me instantly dislike the man who was speaking. His words just amplified the feeling.

"How many mistakes can we make without consequence?"

The parents, on the other hand, were fixated on the speaker. The glassy look in their eyes, some bizarre mix of fear and admiration. For the first time in a long time, I was actually afraid. I'd seen that look in people before. *Fanatics.*

"What the hell," Hush muttered. "Who is this freak?"

"Abigail has been warned many times before that she has broken the rules. Still she refuses to obey. To repent. She casts off the beliefs that I have bestowed upon you. She defies the commands of her earthly father, the commands of her god. And for what?" He glared down at the girl. "To this day, she still will not confess. Well, I know her reasons," he said the last sentence a bit quieter, so we had to strain to hear him. Almost as if he were speaking to himself.

He shook his head, his blond hair reflecting in the bright sunlight. A crazed smile formed on his face. It wasn't forced and it was completely out of place with his words and the aggression oozing out of them.

"How many times?" he boomed again.

"Too many times!"

"Once is too many!"

It was mainly the men standing around who started yelling out answers to the man's questions. A few women joined in, but the others just stood quietly, as though they feared opening their mouths. The men easily outnumbered the women and they were getting restless. I began to worry that we were going to see a mob mentality take over when another voice cried out above the low buzzing coming from everyone else.

"As many times as it takes until she can seek forgiveness!" A young woman rushed forward. If I had to guess, I'd say she was in her late twenties. She had light brown hair that fell to her hips and pretty features. A strangled sound from beside me had me glancing over at Riptide. His eyes were fixed on the newcomer and a grin formed on my lips.

A quick glance over showed that Hush hadn't missed our brother's interest either. There was a calculating look in his eyes and I knew that sometime soon in the future, Riptide was going to be regretting his involvement with Lockout's plan to push Hush toward Seek before he was ready. I had after he'd pulled his stunt with Jenny. Though now I was fucking grateful he'd interfered.

"Isn't that what our faith teaches?" she called out again, struggling to be heard over the din of murmurs from the people around her.

"That our earthly father—who knows our hearts better than we ourselves—that his mercy forgives?" Her words were pure desperation as she spoke to the crowd, but her eyes were locked on the leader. She was begging him not to hurt the girl.

"It's a fuckin' cult," Hush muttered.

"What are they doing all the way out here?" Toxic asked.

"These types like to be as far away from civilization as possible," Butcher said in a low voice. "They're fucked up in the head, but the guys in charge need to keep them away from anyone who might talk sense into them."

My brows shot up as I listened. "Sounds like you have experience, Butcher."

"Ran across a few with my task force. Never called themselves cults, of course. But it's what they are." He motioned around at the buildings and the half built fence we were hiding behind. "Looks the part. Explains why they're out here."

"Think they're the reason those hikers went missing?" Ricochet asked.

Butcher grunted and nodded. "Most likely. They probably stumbled across the place by accident. Don't see any other reason for it."

"There's Chet," Riptide said, pointing off to the corner where the man was standing at the back of the circle. Riptide and Butcher had managed to get a look at him as he'd passed the bathroom in the apartment. They'd gotten a very good look—and smell—of his buddy, who was standing next to him.

"Maybe a punishment will help her understand the error of her ways!" That had come from Chet.

The leader had a manic look in his eyes. The woman had tripped him up, messed up his 'righteous indignation'. Chet had just given him an out, a path back to hurting the girl.

My disdain for Caitlyn's father tripled in that moment. He was standing close enough to our hiding spot that I could see the wild glee in his eyes as he tried to casually suggest punishment for a young child. Something told me it wasn't going to be a time-out. No wonder Sherry had taken Caitlyn and left him. It was too bad he'd followed her out to Arizona. How he'd gotten mixed up in something like this was what we were going to have to find out.

My chest rose and fell quickly as my temper flared. I wasn't going to be able to sit by and watch them hurt a kid. It wasn't within my abilities to do so.

"Hank," the leader called out and a thin, wiry man stepped forward. The guy in charge didn't bother to look at him. His attention was on the crowd. "Chet has proposed a solution. Who here agrees?"

The roars of 'aye' made the blood pound in my ears. My muscles were bunching, preparing to take me into the middle of that fucked up trial so I could help the little girl. She was standing there, eyes blank and glassy. I couldn't tell if she was drugged, or had distanced her mind from what was happening. The idea that this had happened before made my gut twist and bile rise to the back of my throat. These people needed a fucking wake-up call in the form of bullets. I'd seen all I needed to in order to know they weren't good people. The fact that we suspected them of either killing or kidnapping hikers out here was honestly just the cherry on top for me. Their main crime was what was happening right now.

"Easy," Butcher uttered near my ear. He and Toxic both put their hands on my arms, trying to restrain me.

"No!" the woman who'd stood up for the girl—the only one—cried out as Hank pulled his hand back.

Ricochet had to all but tackle Riptide as the loud crack of flesh hitting flesh echoed through the still, hot air. Toxic had left me to hold back Hush. They were doing their jobs and thinking with clearer heads than we were right now. We were severely outnumbered and not prepared to take on this community of people. It was possible innocents would end up getting hurt in the fight and we couldn't have that. Not to mention that my whole crew would likely get wiped out. It didn't mean watching what was happening was easy for any of us.

The woman had stepped in front of the little girl and taken the backhanded slap for her.

"If you want to take Abigail's punishment for her, Sloane, then so be it. For I am a merciful God, and I see that punishment is distributed fairly."

Our brothers were doing their best to drag the three of us away from the scene before we blew our cover. I managed to catch sight of the woman—Sloane—curled up on the ground, trying to protect her head while Hank kicked the shit out of her.

I struggled against Butcher, surprised that the smaller man managed to muscle me back out into the desert, away from the fence. This was why we all lifted weights and sparred with each other on a regular basis. You never knew what you'd end up coming up against in our line of work. You never knew when you'd have to bodily drag your own brothers away from something that would get us all killed.

"Fuck," Riptide hissed, running a hand through his long, tousled hair.

"We'd better go," Butcher said. He was eyeing our VP like he expected him to go running back in there at any moment.

"How are we supposed to leave them?" Hush growled at Butcher.

"Look, it's not like I necessarily want to leave all those women and kids in the hands of a bunch of abusive assholes, alright?" Butcher snarled at us. "But we have orders. This is a recon mission. We're fucking outnumbered and outgunned. I counted twenty men with rifles. And that's just what I could see, who knows how many more are back there. We have half a dozen pistols and a couple rifles between us. If we go bursting in there, trying to play the fucking heroes, they're going to be burying our bodies out here in the desert next. You want to help these people, or just have a glorious death?"

We were all glaring at each other and panting with rage, but Butcher's hissed argument managed to calm us down…mostly. That was what brought me back down to something resembling calm. When Butcher was the voice of reason it was time to re-evaluate.

"They're not going to kill her." Butcher said with confidence. "I know these types. Smack, kick…other things, but killing is the last step. He needs obedience. He won't get that by indiscriminate killing." He saw my look and continued before I could ask. "Sherry must have done something extreme."

"Or Chet killed her without permission," Hush said, finally calm enough to think clearly.

"Let's go." The words came out hoarse and Riptide looked like it'd taken all his willpower to say them. "We'll sort this out at the clubhouse." Without another word, he turned and started back toward the truck.

Hush grabbed a fallen mesquite tree branch and I watched as he ducked down and ran back toward the fence. No one stopped him this time. We watched as he swept it over the dirt, brushing out our tracks.

I grabbed another branch and helped him. We brushed out all sign we'd been there for up to a mile before we dropped our branches. "What the hell is the plan, Rip?"

"We get back, update Lock, and figure out everything we need to know to take these fuckers down," he said with a grim look on his face.

CHAPTER 24

Jenny

The clubhouse had been quiet today with most of the guys out at work or on the missions Seek had told me about. It was nearly sunset and we were having a movie marathon—well, Seek and I were having a wine drinking marathon—to cheer the girls up. They were transfixed with the show, curled up on one end of the huge sectional. They were bunched up together lying in a tangle of limbs. Seek's two dogs were somewhere in the pile, loving having kids to chill with. I'd gotten to meet Auron and Jecht not long after Priest and I became official and I was over the moon in love with them. There was nothing better than having a combination of kids and dogs in the house. It made my heart feel like it would burst with happiness.

Seek was half asleep, head resting back, watching the movie. I'd only had one glass since I was technically babysitting.

The girls had been thrilled to have a 'sleep over' with auntie Seek and the pups. Things were going as well as they could with them. Their grief came in waves, pulling them to oppressive lows before finally allowing them to claw their way up out of it. At this stage their hard fought peace didn't last long, but I knew eventually they would have longer and longer bouts where the grief was held at bay. At some point, that hurt and sadness would only creep in every once in a while.

They were too young to realize it now, but that blinding agony we suffered when we lost someone we loved was worth feeling. It was the price we paid to know the person, to love and be loved in turn by them. Without it we would have never had them there in our hearts to begin with.

I wasn't responsible for the beautiful sentiment. That honor belonged to my grams. She had the most incredible way of making me feel better, no matter the situation. I only hoped I could help heal these little broken hearts the way she'd helped me over the years. A knock on the door broke me from my musings about family. I stood up, careful not to distract the girls, and went to the door.

Pulling open the door, my brows shot up in surprise. "Sylvia, hi."

Sylvia was one of the older sweet butts. She was closing in on fifty and had never married or had kids of her own, though you could see the affection in her gaze whenever she looked at the children running around the clubhouse. She always spoke up whenever anyone needed a babysitter and she was an honorary member at this point. The guys all loved her to death and it was easy to see why. She was the sweetest lady. I had a feeling she'd gravitated toward the club because she didn't have a family of her own, so she'd made one instead. And though none of the men had fallen in love with her and made her an old lady, we all treated her as though she was. She was a part of the club, a part of the family, and always would be.

"Hi, Taz," she replied, giving me a warm smile. "The guys are back and Priest asked me to come watch the girls. He wants you and Seek to meet them downstairs."

"Okay, thanks, Syl." I turned and found Seek already stumbling to her feet. She giggled and swayed her way across the room toward me.

Wrapping an arm around her shoulders, I helped her downstairs. "Careful," I warned as we navigated the stairs.

She tripped, stubbed her toe, and bent forward to rub at it, almost causing us to topple headfirst down the last five steps. Strong hands managed to catch us just in time.

Another giggle sounded and Seek patted Priest's chest. "Thanks, Muscles. 'Preciate the help."

Priest lips quirked as he stared down at her. "You drunk?"

"Psft, no," she denied, then brushed past him so she could finish going down the stairs.

Priest eyed me for a moment, then turned to help her. Hush was already heading over, shaking his head at his old lady, but there was a grin on his face as he and Priest shared a look.

He turned back to me and held out his hand. I didn't need help with steadying, so I linked our fingers and held his hand as we walked back to the meeting room. We'd just gotten in and settled when Lockout, Dash, Smokehouse, and Hellfire came in and sat down.

I listened quietly, horror rising as Priest and the others relayed what they'd found out near The Silverbell Mountains.

Seek's eyes were hard and cold, her lips pressed into a firm line as they finished telling the story. Her buzz was a thing of the past as anger burned the effects of the alcohol from her system. "I knew it. I knew something fishy was going on out there." Her eyes landed on Hush. "Are they killing the hikers? Or pulling them into the cult?"

"It's hard to say," Riptide said, answering before Hush could. "I'm guessing a little of both."

"They probably keep the women," Butcher added. "And any kids."

"Odds are they end up killin' the men they can't convert," Hush told her.

"Maybe not just the men," Seek pointed out. "Since they killed Sherry."

"That might have been Chet," I said with a shake of my head, thinking about what Hush had brought up out in the desert. "Maybe he wanted his ex-wife out of the picture, so he lured her out there and killed her."

I swallowed hard, but forced myself to say it. "And Caitlyn?"

Lockout's eyes met mine and I saw the anger burning there. We were all pissed off about this entire situation. "He was probably going to kill her too… Which brings me to what we found."

I shifted in my seat, finding it hard to sit still while I had this ball of anger and sadness building up inside of me. Chet had wanted to kill his own daughter. Or maybe have some of his friends from the cult kill her. Priest had told me the entire story of how they'd found Caitlyn and it'd chilled my blood. Now knowing this had all happened to her because of her father? It was inconceivable. What kind of person would do that to their own child?

"He was hotel hopping, checking out all the local hospitals."

Lockout's words brought me back fully into the conversation. My eyes widened. "He's looking for Caitlyn?"

Priest's hand covered mine and he squeezed. He picked my hand up and brought it over into his lap, keeping our fingers tangled together.

Lockout shook his head. "Maybe. We're not sure. We weren't able to get any information out of the people who'd seen him."

"Why would he be checking hospitals almost a month after the shootout?" Toxic asked.

"Maybe they didn't know what had happened and finally figured it out?" Hellfire suggested.

"The bodies were missing from the grave," Riptide added. "Maybe they were waiting to make sure no one was setting a trap for them."

"Which means they're patient," Lockout muttered. "It makes sense, but that's going to make finding out more about them difficult. Whoever is leading them is going to keep them in check."

"When we were in the apartment Chet mentioned that Ethan owed him," Priest pointed out.

"Why?" Ricochet asked.

Shrugging his shoulders, he shook his head. "Don't know, but the one in charge is Ethan."

"They didn't find Sherry and Caitlyn's bodies with the men in the grave when they came back and dug them up. Maybe they thought they escaped," Hush said.

"He's looking for Sherry," I added as the realization struck.

"Caitlyn seems to be like a by-product for him. Sherry is his obsession. He's searching for her. Maybe when the men didn't come back, they thought they had escaped with her. When they found the bodies, that would confirm that Sherry had help."

"And we didn't bury Sherry out there. We used our friend at the morgue to make her disappear. As far as they know, she's still out there," Priest pointed out.

We all thought about that for a minute before Priest spoke up again. "So what do we do?"

I jumped in before anyone else had a chance. "I know it's not your guys' style, but what about calling the police? I mean, it's a cult, beating women and killing people."

The looks I got were anger masking offense. The idea of calling the cops versus just killing the bastards left an unpleasant taste in all their mouths. It was written all over their faces. Despite the non-verbal answer, Lockout decided to explain it to me.

"I spoke with an FBI Agent—ex-agent—Flynn about that." I knew Murphey Flynn—she was the sister of one of the Texas MC's old ladies and now one herself—but I didn't interrupt him. "She pointed out that all we have is a group of weirdo's building houses in the desert. While they are on Federal land, that is in fact the only crime that can be proven. If we bring cops in, they'll just pack up and move. Then we'll have to start hunting them down all over again. And they'll probably end up killing more people in the meantime."

"I hadn't thought of that," I said sheepishly.

"It's okay," Priest said while soothing me with his hand. "None of us did. That's why we called Flynn. But that brings us back to my question. What do we do now?"

"Well, Caitlyn is safe here with us. Chet has no idea she's here. The cult has no idea we know about them," Lockout answered. "So, we're going to find out everything we can about them and then we're going to dismantle that fucking organization brick by brick."

"Umm…" I piped up. "Depending on how smart these guys are, they can find Caitlyn. CPS processed her, by her birth name. We did everything legal, by the book. If he gets it in his head to check with the system, it will bring him straight here."

"I can put a notification into the system at work. It will send me an email if anyone contacts CPS or goes through our systems to look for her," I continued.

"Perfect. That just gives us yet another head's up in case Chet somehow gets too close," Priest said.

Lockout studied me for a long minute before saying anything. The whole table was quiet, no one dared chime in. They were waiting for him. "No one is going to touch that little girl. We will solve this before they get the chance."

A glance around the table was all I needed to see that everyone was wearing the same determined, eager expression I was. I wanted that cult gone and Caitlyn safe. They'd mentioned that there were women and children out there, who may not be there by choice. We'd help as many as we could, but the guys were going to take out the rest. Considering they may have killed people to keep their awful community a secret, I didn't feel guilty about that idea in the slightest.

* * *

"Taz?"

I smiled over at Taylor as she and her three sisters approached me. "Yeah, Sweetie?" The girls had taken to calling me by my nickname as well and I didn't mind. Given how horrible the past month was, they could have treated me like an evil stepmother. Instead, they've treated me like part of the family. Well, most of them did.

It'd been a little over a week since we'd found out about the cult. Riptide and Dash were doing their best trying to track down information about the cult. They'd even called over to Texas and enlisted the help of Rat and his wife Ari. So far they'd all come up with nothing but giant goose eggs.

How could these guys be hiding so effectively? We hadn't been able to figure out pseudonyms they were living under or even where they were going to get their food and water. Of course, as Rat pointed out, you don't exactly post your cult activities to social media. While the mystery of disappearing hikers was mostly solved, who the cult members were was another story. Even if they tracked missing persons reports from across the country, without pictures of the people there it would be pointless. And that's assuming that missing persons reports were even filed on them. If they joined willingly, then they could vanish without a trace.

Lockout had decided after a few days that the guys needed to start staking the compound out. It was dangerous. If they found out we were on to them, we lost the element of surprise. Luckily the MC was used to this kind of thing and they'd managed to stay off the cult's radar so far. If they could gather faces or names, that would give our techies something to work with.

No one had left the compound in over a week, but they'd have to restore their food and water supplies soon enough. Priest was going out on the day shift to keep an eye on them. He let the others take nights. He knew he needed to be here for his girls in the late hours. It was when missing their mom hit them the hardest.

Taylor gave Gabby a pleading look. The younger girls had taken to me right away. They just saw an adult who obviously loved them and clung to that. Gabby was a bit tougher. She was old enough to have doubts plague her about my intentions. I'd already spoken with her a few times about the fact that I didn't want to take her mom's place, and I think—despite herself—she was starting to welcome me in as well. It was a struggle. Though I understood it, it was hard because I just wanted us all to be a family.

"We have a favor to ask," Gabby said, taking over.

I faced them, giving the girls my full attention. "Okay, I'm listening."

"We want to go to Mom's house."

I wasn't sure what to say at first. They'd been handling Wendy's death as well as could be expected, but this took me by surprise. Priest had talked about selling the house later on, but for now he still owned it. It was sitting, fully furnished, though no one was living in it.

"May I ask why?"

Gabby swallowed, her eyes misting over, and I had to blink to hold back my own tears. It pained me to see them hurting. "We just want to spend a little time where…" She didn't seem to know how to explain.

She didn't need to. I understood it. Hanging out in Grams' house after she was gone had given me comfort. I nibbled my lower lip as I considered their request. Any other time, I'd pack them up and bring them over, but with everything we'd learned about Caitlyn's father and the cult—granted it wasn't much—I wasn't sure if it was safe.

"I'll ask your father," I promised them.

They nodded and went back into the living room to continue reading. School had started up for them, but Priest hadn't made them go yet. He'd talked to the school and gotten permission for them to take time off and considering what they'd gone through, the school had agreed. But they'd be going back in another week or so and I'd been working with the younger girls on things that would help them with the upcoming year.

Pulling out my phone, I texted Priest, asking him to call me. I smiled when the phone immediately rang in my hand. "Hey."

"Hey, Gorgeous. Everything okay?"

"Yeah, I'm so sorry to bug you while you're busy." He was out with Hush and the others watching the compound, which was why I hadn't called him. The last thing I wanted was to distract him or have someone hear his phone ring if he forgot to silence it. "The girls want to spend some time at the Oro Valley house."

There was silence on the other line for a long enough period that I pulled the phone away and looked down at it. Still connected. I brought it back to my ear.

"Okay. The key is on the ring hanging on the hook above the microwave."

"You think it's safe?"

"It should be. If Chet had any idea where Caitlyn was, you would know. You handled her case, any inquiries should go through your office. If anything he'd come looking at the clubhouse. But I'll send you a few phone numbers of the guys who are going to be around just in case you need something. Maybe take Seek with you."

"She got called out for a rescue job." It would still be hot for a few more months, but Seek had explained that things started slowing down for her now and wouldn't pick back up full time until next summer. She'd have a few rescues over the winter months versus a couple a week during the hottest parts of summer. She'd only grinned when I asked her how she managed her bills with such an unsteady schedule, and said, "I get paid really well by the state for each rescue and it's more than enough to live comfortably. Besides, then I get a bunch of time off and I train with my dogs."

"Okay, well, that's fine. I don't think it'll be an issue. Are they okay?" The worry in his voice floated over the connection.

"I think so. They miss her. They miss you, but they understand that you're working."

He sighed. "I can't tell you how much I appreciate you taking the time off to give me a hand with them."

I was using more of my annual leave with work. I was grateful that they were so understanding of my recent absence, but I needed to be here for the girls and for Priest. There was no way I was going to go to work only to be distracted and miserable while there when I wanted to be here. Priest had been shocked, but thankful when I'd offered to watch the girls while he dealt with The Silverbells situation.

"It's my pleasure," I told him. "It's giving us a chance to get to know each other."

I heard someone nearby say something to him, though it was too soft for me to make out much.

"Well, still, I appreciate it. Look, I have to go. Let me know if you need anything, but I'll be home around eight. Love you."

"Love you, too." I hung up and walked into the living room. "Why don't we have dinner over at your mom's place?"

Four faces lit up with smiles and three of them started talking excitedly. Grinning, I started to gather the food I'd need to take with me so I could cook it over there. That way the girls got to spend a decent amount of time at the house.

CHAPTER 25

Jenny

It didn't take long to get over to the house. I smiled sadly as I watched the girls go directly to Wendy's room and snuggle in together on her bed. I left them to go get dinner started.

Pouring myself a small glass of wine, I began dicing the vegetables. Thinking back over the last few months since I'd moved back to Tucson, I shook my head. It'd been a whirlwind, even for me. I wasn't complaining. I had new friends, the other old ladies and I were trying to get together at least once a week to hang out. Unlike Seek, I hadn't gotten into any fights with the sweet butts, I was relieved about that. I didn't want to cause any problems and I pretty much wanted everyone to like me.

Then there were the little girls in that back room. I was completely head over heels for them and it seemed like they cared for me, too. Even Gabby was warming up to me day by day.

Arms wrapped around me from behind, making me jump, but as I turned my heart melted. Kneeling down, I wrapped Caitlyn up in my hug. "Thank you, sweet girl," I murmured.

She smiled at me before scampering off to the living room. Walking out, I checked on them. All their eyes were dry and they were putting on a movie to watch. It eased my mind about bringing them here. I hadn't wanted to keep them away, but I didn't want to make things worse. It was a delicate juggling act and this time it'd seemed to work in my favor.

I set the table as the food cooked, finishing the one glass of wine I allowed myself. There was no forgetting that even though I'd gained friends and these kids, Priest was the biggest prize. Even though he'd hurt me before, he'd more than made up for that. He'd helped heal my own broken heart. It wasn't like us getting together meant that I didn't miss Grams. Priest had just managed to fix up the cracks a bit by replacing that aching loss with love.

If someone had told me a few months ago that I'd end up coming back to Tucson and find myself with the man of my dreams—right down to the kids he had and all—I'd have told you that was crazy. Especially, if they had said Priest was the one I'd end up with. I thought for sure he was gone for good once he'd ghosted me.

"Dinner time!" I called out, as I went about setting the food on the table. I began dishing up for the younger girls and smiled as they all filed in through the door that separated the dining room and the living room.

It was unusual for a house here in Tucson to have a layout like this one. Most of them had open floor plans where the kitchens, dining rooms, and living rooms all bled into one another without doors separating the rooms. It wasn't the case for this home. I didn't care for it. I preferred to be able to keep an eye on the girls while I was cooking. That's how the apartment back at the clubhouse was, all open. It gave the illusion of more space.

Priest had asked me to move in with him right away, but honestly I didn't think the girls were quite ready for that. Enough had been thrown at them already, so I'd asked for more time. It was the right call judging by the way Gabby was relaxing around me. It didn't hurt that I'd been watching them each day while Priest was out working with the club. I wasn't going anywhere, and Priest knew that. We could do this at a slow pace and make it easy for the girls.

I watched as the girls chatted and dug into the dinner I'd made. I could see the shadow of melancholy in their eyes, but they had smiles on their faces.

"Are you girls ready to start school?"

I saw the worry creep over Caitlyn's face. We didn't have much of a choice. CPS was going to be checking in on her and her new family for the next six months to a year to make sure she was in the best possible environment for her. Sending her to school was going to be a requirement. I knew kids could be mean to anyone who wasn't like themselves, but thankfully she had her new sisters. They'd watch out for her.

"Yeah, I can't wait," Gabby said with a grin. That got her started talking about her friends that she was looking forward to seeing. With everything that'd happened this summer there hadn't been any sleep overs or anything like that and they'd already missed the first weeks of school.

I frowned as I thought about that. How were the other parents going to feel about sleepovers at the clubhouse? Not to mention, where would we put all the kids? The apartment was great, but they were already cramped with the five of them. Add in me, then eventually the friends that would want to come hang out and it made me realize we'd need more space.

That was a worry for another time. I'd mostly listened during dinner, just enjoying hearing them chitter at each other. It impressed me how much these girls loved each other. With four of them in close contact continuously I'd have thought there'd be some fighting, but they'd banded together and were taking care of each other.

We'd found Gabby sleeping in Cassie's bed this morning. Auron and Jecht had been sleeping with the other girls. A grin spread over my face. Seek had given up on trying to keep the dogs in her and Hush's apartment. Each night they scratched at the door until she let them out and then Priest let them in. They understood that those kids needed comfort and they were happy to provide it.

"Why don't you go finish your movie while I clean up," I suggested as the girls finished up.

"I can help you…if you want," Gabby offered. Her eyes strayed toward the door to the living room though.

There was plenty of time later to get them on a routine of doing chores. For now, I just wanted them to take the time they needed to settle in and heal.

"Thank you, Gabby. I appreciate that, but I've got it. Go enjoy the movie."

She gave me a shy smile and all but ran toward the other room. Chuckling, I started clearing the table. I ran hot soapy water into the kitchen sink and let my mind wander.

The scream split the air, echoing throughout the house. The glass in my hand slipped from my fingers and crashed to the floor, shattering into a million pieces. I wasn't even aware of thinking, instinct had me running into the living room. As soon as I burst through the door it was as though time slowed. I saw the figure bashing at the glass window. The pane gave in and shattered glass flew everywhere. Without thinking, I pulled my phone out, hit Lockout's number and dropped it on the floor. I needed to focus because the scene that was in front of me had fear and rage gripping at me.

I saw the girls, huddled in the corner of the room, staring in terror at the man as he crawled through the broken glass and into the house. The pounding of my blood in my ears kept me from hearing what the man yelled at them. I didn't stop, never slowed, instead I raced across the room.

The only thought running through my mind was to save them. Nothing else registered. He hadn't even had time to turn toward me, that's how quickly everything happened. Still, I didn't stop. I lowered my shoulder.

As soon as I made contact, time settled back to where it should be, and we both went flying. My shoulder hit him in the side, just below his own shoulder and I heard something crack. I could only hope it was his ribs and not my collarbone. I couldn't feel a damn thing with all the adrenaline pumping through my body. All I knew was I'd hit him hard. An NFL linebacker would have been proud of that tackle.

There wasn't time to let satisfaction fully settle because he slammed into the wall and only half a second later I hit him a second time. He screamed. The sound reverberated through my mind, but I knew I couldn't let the pain sparking inside of my body slow me down. I was going to be battered and bruised tomorrow. Fear kept me moving. I didn't know who this man was, or why he was here, but he was going to be damn sorry that he'd just broken into this house and threatened and scared my girls.

I wrapped my limbs around him—clinging like an octopus—trying to keep him down so the girls would have time to hide.

"Run," I gasped. "Hide!"

The man started fighting my hold. I wasn't a black belt. I didn't know what I was doing. Sheer desperation kept me holding on. I heard Priest's voice in the back of my head. *Whatever you do, don't stop. Just keep fighting.*

Sports weren't my thing, and honestly, I'd never been in a fight in my life. The only dangerous situation I'd even been in had been with Julie back in Texas. The case manager we'd worked for had been working with some bad people, trying to take one of the MC members' kids. Not through legal channels either. We'd ended up in the middle of it, but all I had done was lead the bad guys away so Julie could escape with the babies. I hadn't done any fighting.

My lack of skill didn't mean I wasn't going to do everything within my power to keep this creep from attaining whatever his end goal here was tonight.

I pummeled him with my fists whenever I could, stalling so the girls could run. I grabbed and pulled and somewhere in the fray a piece of his ear wound up in my mouth. The girls scampered toward the back hallway and I was glad. Who knew if there were more men waiting outside? I didn't want them running around outside at night. Darkness had fallen an hour or so ago.

It was going to be easier for this man to find them here in the house, so I needed to make sure he left. Raking my nails down his face, I smiled grimly as I felt wetness drip down my hand.

I'd always heard that any kind of push back usually scared off burglars. I hoped that was true because I was beginning to tire. "Get the hell out of my house!" I screamed directly into his ear.

He was squirming below me, trying to stand, but having a hard time because of my combined weight and whatever damage I'd managed to do to him during the tackle.

I was just about to roll off him and get out of the way when he jerked his arm back. Pain exploded behind my eyes as his elbow rammed into my forehead. Gasping in pain, I released him and stumbled away, holding my head. Now I knew why the cartoons always depicted stars floating over characters' heads when they got knocked out. I was reeling. The world was rotating on its axis as I tried to stay standing. Touching my hand to my forehead, I couldn't tell if the blood on my fingers was from him or from me.

Knowing I needed to keep fighting until he was out the door, I turned. My eyes widened because he was standing right there in front of me.

"You stupid bitch." He didn't yell. In fact his voice was tight, like he was in pain too.

Good.

I tried to duck as he brought his hand back, but everything was too fuzzy. I was too damn dizzy. The slap of his palm hitting my cheek had stinging pain blazing over my skin and the force behind it sent me to the floor.

His feet shuffled and I tried to curl into a protective ball as he kicked me. Over and over the blows came until I wasn't able to gasp anymore. I was hardly able to breathe. Finally, they stopped. His shoes left my line of sight.

My cheek pressed against the carpet and I fought to gain control of my body. My limbs wouldn't work no matter how hard I internally screamed at them to move. He hadn't gone toward the front door. He'd gone after the girls.

It felt like hours passed before I was able to haul myself up off the floor. Everything ached, and I was pretty sure I was sporting a matching set of broken ribs just like the intruder. Holding my side, I considered my options. There were knives in the kitchen, but if he got it away from me, I was dead and maybe so were the girls.

I didn't have a gun on me and I doubted Priest had left any in the vacant house. My eyes landed on the door that led out to the garage and an idea popped into my mind. I limped over toward the garage as quickly as I could.

Screams broke the silence of the house once more, just as my hand closed over what I'd been looking for. I hurried back into the house. Ignoring the protesting of my body, I fought to reach my girls in time.

CHAPTER 26

Priest

I stepped into the apartment and frowned. Jenny had called hours ago and asked to bring the girls to the house. I would have thought they'd have been back before me. We had still been hiking back to the truck when she called.

Heading back downstairs, I caught Lockout's attention. "Did you talk to Taz and the girls before they headed over to the Oro Valley house?"

"She popped her head in my office real quick and let me know they were going." Realization lit his eyes. "They aren't back yet?"

"I'm sure it's fine. One or more of the girls probably just fell asleep after dinner." Worry coiled in my gut. I hoped that was all it was.

Pulling my phone out, I was about to call her when the phone rang. Irritated, I connected the call. "Yeah?"

"Umm, is this Grant Mitchell?"

"Yeah, who's this?"

"This is Abe Holland."

The lawyer I'd hired to help with gaining custody of Caitlyn. I'd been too distracted to recognize his voice. "Yeah, sorry. What's up?"

"I just wanted to let you know I finished filing all the paperwork with the court this afternoon. You should be getting a call about an official court date soon. I also spoke with CPS and other than some home visits to make sure everything is working out satisfactorily you shouldn't have any trouble officially adopting Caitlyn."

"Thanks man. I appreciate that." I listened as he rambled on about a few other things.

What he said next had the blood icing inside my veins. "If you happen to have a change of address or any contact information, you'll want to file some paperwork with the court and the CPS office. It's really simple to do-"

"Wait." He paused as I interrupted him. "The paperwork you filed today. What was the address on it?" He listed off my Oro Valley house and my eyes closed. We'd covered our bases with CPS, but it never occurred to any of us that the documents that get filed with the court would be online for everyone to see. "Okay, thanks. I'll have to call you back tomorrow to finish going over all this."

My hoarse voice must have notified the others standing nearby because they crowded closer as I hung up on the lawyer. Before I had a chance to open my mouth, Lockout's cell phone rang.

Relief washed over his features as he answered and switched it to speaker phone. The expression vanished and every muscle in my body tensed as I heard my little girls screaming.

"Taz!" I shouted. There was nothing. No answer, but something thumped loudly.

That was all I needed. I was out the door before I'd even realized I'd started moving. Time passed in a series of flashes as we raced over toward my house. I didn't ask my brothers to come, didn't need to. I knew they would be following me. The bike vibrated below me. I saw Lockout pull up beside me as we pushed the limits on our bikes.

Nothing was going to stop me. Not red lights, stop signs, or the flash of red and blue lights that pulled in behind us. Gritting my teeth, I tried to push for more speed but my bike was maxed out. We were flying down the road and I didn't give a single fuck that the Oro Valley Police were hot on our heels.

The house came into view and we all rolled to a stop. I was off my bike before I had a chance to put the kickstand down. Letting it fall to the concrete, I ran across the driveway.

I was only steps away from the front door when someone tackled me from behind. Fury exploded within me and I fought back. "My fucking kids are in trouble, you piece of shit!" I bellowed right in the cop's face.

We were rolling around on the ground. I knew better than to punch him—though it took every ounce of willpower not to—but I wasn't about to let him prone me out beneath him and cuff me.

"Let me go! Now!"

I glanced over and saw my brothers being detained by the cops before they could even get off their bikes. Lockout met my gaze and nodded. That was all I needed. The cop on top of me had rolled me onto my stomach, so I jerked my head backward. The feel of his nose breaking against my skull was a small consolation. Lockout would settle the situation outside.

Darting to my feet, I rushed into the house. I didn't yell for them. If Chet was still here—because who else would have come after them—I didn't want him to know I was inside. Pulling my gun out, I ran back and found them in Wendy's room.

Jenny was standing between Chet and my girls, a shovel gripped in her hands. There was blood on the end of it. Her eyes widened when she saw me and there was a small amount of relief mixed in with the fear. Her face was pale and there was a stream of blood running down her face from the split skin between her eyebrows. Seeing her hurt and bleeding made my own blood boil.

"Get away from my family," I growled at Chet. I had my gun trained on him, but there was no way I could shoot. Not in front of my girls. Not in front of Caitlyn. I would try to spare them seeing that. Not to mention, at this distance, if I missed or if the round went through him, I'd hit one of my girls.

Chet had turned to face me and an evil grin split his face. There was blood trickling across his right eye from where Jenny must have hit him with the shovel. He was a maniac. "I don't think you're going to take the chance of shooting and missing," he taunted. The man wasn't completely stupid and it meant I was going to have to disarm him another way.

"Let them go."

"Fuck you! That's my daughter. I'll do whatever the fuck I want with her." Spit flew from his mouth as he hissed at me.

"You're a fucking idiot if you think I'm going to let you hurt her," I told him, my rage settling down and allowing the calm demeanor I adopted whenever I had to kill to take over.

"You can take the woman and the other kids," Chet said. "I won't stop you, but Caitlyn is mine."

My gaze met wide brown eyes. Tears were flowing down Caitlyn's face. She started to stand and Gabby grabbed a hold of her, forcing her down next to her. None of us were going to give that little girl up to this asshole.

I tilted my head as I holstered my gun. I stepped forward as I spoke. "I can take the woman and other kids?" I repeated back to him. "As in, you'll allow me? Motherfucker, you don't understand. They're mine. Including Caitlyn. You won't do to her what you did to Sherry."

The color leached out of Chet's face as he stepped back. This wasn't playing out the way he thought it would. Despite putting my gun away, he was even more terrified now, as he should be. "How do you know about-" He shook his head as though to clear it. "Sherry's dead?"

"You killed her," I insisted. I brought my hand up, pointing right at him as emphasis.

"I thought I had," he muttered. He was trying to back his way to the door. I started to sidestep, trying to put myself between him and the girls. We were halfway there when he started blubbering. "She wasn't there." His eyes narrowed and I saw a spark of madness there. "Caitlyn's all that's left of her."

I knew then that he wasn't going to let his daughter go. Every day that he lived, her life would be in danger. Chet's gun hand had dropped as he realized his wife was dead. I couldn't be sure whether he was sorry about that or happy.

Everything happened quickly. I ran forward intent on getting my hands on Chet. He turned and raised the gun. I didn't care if he ended up shooting me, as long as he wasn't going after my family. My hands were outstretched, ready to grab the weapon from him. We both watched with wide eyes as the head of the shovel smacked directly into his skull.

The wet thud preceded Chet dropping to the floor like a sack of potatoes. Jenny raised the shovel over her head and was about to bring it down on Chet's head again.

"Freeze!"

I slammed into her, preventing her from braining the dickhead on the ground a second time. She let out a groan of pain when I did, but there wasn't time to check where she was injured. Wrapping her in my arms, I covered her body in case the cops behind us got trigger-happy. They weren't going to shoot a group of little girls, but Jenny and I both had weapons on us.

My body stilled, and I kept Jenny pinned against my chest. "Just hold still," I whispered to her. "Everything will be okay."

"Drop your weapons!"

I took the shovel from her and, slowly and rather dramatically, squatted down, setting the shovel and my gun on the ground before I stood up again.

"Move away from them."

Pushing her backward a few steps, I turned and faced them, arms up, with her safely behind my body.

"Step to the side," the cop ordered. There were three of them inside the crowded room. "Keep your hands up." Two of their guns were pointed at us as one of them checked Chet's pulse.

"He broke in here and tried to hurt us," Jenny told them. Her voice shook and her voice was tight with unshed tears. "Grant came here to protect us."

Uncertainty filled their eyes as they listened to her. They glanced over at the girls. "We have to take you in to figure all this out," the lead cop told her. "Both of you turn around, slowly."

"Listen to them," I told her and did as he asked. "We're not in danger anymore. Just listen to the cops and we'll get this fucking mess all sorted out."

"Down on your knees."

We both knelt on the ground. I glanced over and it broke my heart to see my girls crying. "Stay there," I told them. "We'll be just fine, okay? Just listen to the policemen alright? I'm going to talk to them and then we'll be heading home together. They won't hurt you." What I wanted to do was drop kick the asshole who was about to put cuffs on me, but even I had to concede to my own advice. Tonight was just another in a long list of traumatic nights for my girls. Watching their father get shot by the police was the last thing they needed.

Gabby nodded and held onto Caitlyn tighter as the little girl struggled in her hold. Caitlyn looked frantic.

I met her gaze. "We're okay. I promise. Everything will be okay."

"Lay down on your stomachs. Put your arms out like an airplane," the cop instructed.

"That might be hard," Jenny told them. "That guy over there kicked me in my ribs and they hurt pretty bad."

"Get the EMT's" the cop directing us told another. "Fine," Put one arm out like an airplane and keep the other by your side. You'd better not go for a weapon," he warned her.

Anger and worry flooded me as I listened to him speaking to her, barking at her was more like it. I wanted to run my hands over her, check that she was okay for myself.

As soon as we assumed the positions the officers came in and I grunted when one knelt his weight onto my back as he jerked my hands behind me. The cuffs clicked tightly over my wrists. I turned my head and found Jenny watching me. I schooled my features into a cold mask. She didn't need to see me pissed off that they were arresting us when fucking Chet had tried to kill my family.

The cops helped us stand up and walked us toward the door. "Wait," I called out. "Those are my kids."

"CPS will be called."

"No," Jenny said, shaking her head as the second cop finished searching her. Satisfied that she didn't pose a threat, he helped her up, being careful of her ribs.

"Both of you are being detained until we figure out what happened here," the officer told her, helping her to her feet. He was being kind to her so I kept my mouth shut. I wasn't happy to see his hands on her, but they weren't about to uncuff me so I could help her.

"Their Aunt Kit can pick them up from the police station," she told them. "She'll meet us there if you let me call her."

EMS pushed their way into the room and loaded up Chet's body onto a gurney. We all watched as they wheeled him out.

"Is he…dead?" Jenny asked.

"Yeah, he is," the cop answered. He looked down at her and saw the fear on her face. "If what he says is true," he says, motioning to me, "then it will be self-defense. But we have to look into it."

"What's the number?" the second cop asked Jenny, holding up a phone.

She rattled off the clubhouse phone number. We listened as the cop talked to Kit and relief made my knees almost buckle as I heard him tell her that we'd meet her at the station.

Another EMT came in and poked and prodded at Jenny. I was worried about her. Each time he put pressure on her ribs she winced. "They're just bruised," he told her. "I'll wrap a bandage around them and it'll make things more comfortable for you. I'll clean that up, too," he said, pointing at the cut between her brows.

"Let's go," the officer said to me.

"Go with the police," I told the girls. "You'll be safe with them." The cop holding onto my arm shoved me out of the house and into a cop car. None of my brothers were around so I assumed they'd already taken them in.

Laying my head back against the seat, I shut my eyes. I was holding onto my control by a thread. It wouldn't help any of us if I lost my shit in the back of a police cruiser. Seeing my girls and my old lady's scared expressions as they'd walked me out had made me want to fight back. Instead, I'd had to swallow down my anger and go peacefully.

It didn't take long for the uniformed cops to take me to the police station and book me. They shoved me into a holding cell near my MC brothers.

"Are they okay?" Lockout asked, worry coating the words.

"Mostly. Chet went after Taz before I got there. Bruised her ribs. She got him back though. Bashed his skull in with a shovel. He's dead."

Butcher chuckled from where he sat on the other side of the cage. "I knew I liked your old lady."

"What happened to you?" I asked Lockout, who was sporting a split lip and a black eye.

"Had to give you a chance to get your ass in the house," he said with a shrug.

"Lucky you didn't get fuckin' shot fightin' back like that," Hush muttered. "Especially with the rest of us already sportin' handcuffs."

"Where's Riptide?" I asked, looking around.

"Hospital. He wasn't cuffed up yet either so he helped Lock."

Dread swirled around inside me as I heard that. "Is he-"

"He got tased," Toxic told me. "He's fine, but he hit his head on the ground pretty fucking badly, so they took him in to get checked out."

I leaned my head back against the wall. "Fuck. I shouldn't have told her she could take the girls to the house."

"This isn't your fault, Priest," Lockout snapped. "None of us knew he'd end up looking through the fucking court files to find Caitlyn. We thought if anything he'd start with CPS. Not go around them entirely."

"Who knew the asshole was smart enough to think of that?" Toxic asked.

Guilt still pricked at me as we settled in to wait. If this caused me to lose custody of Caitlyn—or my other daughters—it was going to fucking destroy me.

CHAPTER 27

Priest

There wasn't a clock back here with us, so I didn't know how much time had passed. All I could do was wait here to see what was going to happen. It was making me antsy and I shoved to my feet and began pacing the cell I was in. I was worried about Jenny and my girls. I couldn't help any of them right now and it grated at me.

The rest of our brothers were out in the desert, watching the compound, and we wouldn't hear from them until sunrise. Hopefully things wouldn't take that long. It had the potential to be a long fucking night.

Nobody was talking, an unusual thing for this group. There wasn't anything to say. Chet was dead, and Jenny and my girls were safe. That was the important part. Now that the immediate threat was over, it was time to face the consequences.

Would I lose custody of my girls over this? Would I—we—get charges filed? Had I cost my brothers their freedom? No one asked out loud. No one tried to reassure me, nor did they blame me. We weren't the type to offer platitudes nor to cast the blame. Still, the longer this took the worse the foreboding became.

My brothers watched me with worried eyes, but didn't comment. We were all helpless in this moment and that wasn't something any of us liked.

A cop walked past and Lockout stood up, going over to the bars. "I want my phone call," he told the officer.

The guy paused, then shrugged. "Soon as the Lieutenant says so, you can have it." He kept going while we all swore.

More time passed before another officer finally stepped up to the cell. "You get one call between the lot of you."

My eyes narrowed, but we all looked to Lockout. He stepped forward and the cop let him out of the cell. He brought him toward the back of the room and cuffed him to a bench there and handed him a cell phone.

Lockout waited until the officer stepped a ways away before he punched in a number on the screen. His expression was grim as it met mine. He straightened up when whoever he was calling answered.

"Static. It's Lockout." I leaned against the bars and waited, listening in. "Gonna need your help, old friend."

Lockout ran the man through what had happened tonight, giving him the names of those of us locked up and Jenny's. "Get here as fast as you can." He paused for a moment and sighed. It was a relieved sound and it eased the tension curling around me. "Thanks."

Disconnecting the call, he motioned for the cop and handed the phone over. The officer put him back in the cell and left us alone.

"Who was that?" I asked as soon as we were alone again.

"Friend from my time in," he replied.

"I don't know a Static," I pointed out.

"Me neither," Hush added.

"Tried to get him to join the MC while we were forming it and he wasn't in a place to be able to. I've kept in touch with him over the years, but he hasn't been ready. None of you have met him," he said, sitting down on the bench near Toxic.

"How's he going to be able to help us?" I asked.

Lockout gave me a feral smile. "You'll see."

Rolling my eyes at his cryptic ass, I stood up and pounded on the bars. The cop came back into our area and glared at me. "I want to check on my kids…and my girlfriend."

"Kids were picked up by your sister," he said. "Girlfriend is still in interrogation." He gave me a toothy smile and left, ignoring the curses I threw his way.

Riptide had made up IDs for all our old ladies and Kit so that if anything ever happened to any of us they'd be able to get information on us. He'd made Jenny a set just last week, which is why she knew she'd be able to call Kit and have her pick up the girls. She'd brought along the driver's license and paperwork that 'proved' she was Kit Mitchell. At least my girls weren't stuck here in the police station and they hadn't been taken away by CPS. Yet.

I knew the girls must be terrified, but as long as they were safe, I could focus on the rest of us getting out of here. Not that I was in any position to help. I paced around the cell, waiting for something—anything—to happen.

When it finally did it felt like we'd been waiting for hours. I knew it probably hadn't been more than one, but time moved differently when you were stressed the fuck out.

A tall man in a suit walked in next to the cop. He gave Lockout a wolfish smile and a wink before turning to the officer. "I need a few minutes alone with my clients."

"Yeah, alright," the officer grumbled and walked out the way he'd come.

"Took you long enough, Static."

"It's damn near midnight, Lock. Took me a few minutes to get my shit together." His blue eyes swept over us as he raked a hand through his light brown hair. "What the hell did you get into?"

We stayed quiet while Lockout went more in depth on what had happened. Static nodded as he listened. "Alright, well, I'm going to handle Jenny first since they've got her in interrogation. Hopefully she hasn't said anything. They're holding you assholes on resisting arrest and assault on a police officer." His eyebrow raised at that and he looked over at Lockout.

My president shrugged. "Had to buy some time."

Static shook his head. "This is going to take a while, so settle in," he warned.

* * *

"Priest!"

My head jerked up from where it'd been resting on my chest at the sound of Jenny's voice. The lone bench in the place had put my ass to sleep hours ago as I dozed.

She rushed over to the cell and grasped the bars, her worried eyes roving over me. Once she realized I was fine she looked over at the others. "I'm so sorry," she said softly.

"Hey," I walked up to the bars and put my hands over hers, "there's nothing to be sorry for." I shot the cop accompanying her a dark look before lowering my voice. "You couldn't have known that asshole would have figured out to go to the Oro Valley house. If we're going to play the blame game then it's my fault. I told you to take them."

She shook her head, tears filling her eyes. "No, it's not your fault."

I lifted my hand and brushed her tears away. "Then it's not yours either. No more guilt."

"Okay," she replied with a wobbly smile. "I talked to Kit. She got the girls calmed down and they're asleep. She told them that you had a wrestling match with the police, and that they were being sore losers."

Relief nearly made my knees buckle. I laughed at the thought of that, and it wasn't far from the truth. I sucked it up and shoved my emotions down so I could concentrate. "Good. What about you?"

"Mr. Henderson showed up and I ran the police through everything that happened… Well, everything from the time the man busted through the window and attacked us." Her eyes strayed over to the cop.

Good. She hadn't told them she knew who Chet was or what we knew about him. The coroner would run his prints or dental records soon enough and figure out who Chet was. Whether they ever put together that he was Caitlyn's father didn't really matter. It was obvious, thanks to the broken window, that Chet had illegally entered my home and that Jenny had feared for her and the girls' lives. There's no way they'd charge her for his death. It'd been self-defense.

"Mr. Henderson?" I asked.

"The lawyer?" She gave me a puzzled look. There hadn't been time for Static to properly introduce himself.

I noticed her hand go to her ribs and I reached through the bars, gently placing my hand over hers. "How are these?"

"Just bruised like the medic said. He wrapped them and gave me some painkillers. They only hurt occasionally."

The door behind the officer opened and everyone perked up as the Chief of Police walked in, Seek on his heels. My grin was sharp and filled with amusement when I saw her.

"...can't believe you didn't call me Tyler. I should have been the first one you notified as soon as you knew you had my boyfriend in lockup."

"Come on now Jamie. You know I couldn't do that. Not until we finished the investigation-"

"Bullshit. How many people have I saved on your watch, not to mention one or two of your officers?" When he didn't answer, she huffed in irritation. "Is it over now?" she snapped, cutting the Chief off. "Are you letting them out?"

Static walked in behind them. The Chief sighed and rubbed a hand over his face. He stopped in front of our cells and let his gaze run over all of us. It was soft when it landed on Jenny, but hardened for the rest of us. "Considering what we found out about Chet Holden and the fact that you were trying to get to your family and stop him..." he said, looking at me. "We're going to be dropping all charges on you men." He looked over at Jenny. "You've been released pending the completion of the investigation. We'll have to finish up the reports and put everything through the proper channels, but it's shaping up to be a clear case of self-defense, so I'll give you a call and let you know once everything is finished. Don't see a reason to keep you in custody while we do that—might take a few days—but don't leave the city until I give you the all clear. Got it?"

Jenny nodded and the Chief motioned for his officer. "Release them all and get them out of my station." He glanced over at Seek. "Happy now?"

She gave him a wide smile. "Yes, sir, I am."

"Now she calls me sir," he muttered as he walked away shaking his head. "You're lucky you're the best damn Search and Rescue contractor in the state, Jamie," he called out before the door slammed shut.

On the way out of the cells we could see the dirty looks from the cops we'd fought with. I wasn't sure if they were pissed we were being released, or ashamed because we were trying to stop a kidnapping and they interfered. One of them, a tall officer with a black eye, grabbed Lockout by the forearm as he passed. We all stopped dead in our tracks, round two was on the verge of erupting.

"One day, I want a rematch," he growled. Lockout narrowed his eyes on the officer. But the man let go and slapped Lockout on the back and walked off, laughing. Lockout burst out laughing as well, and with that the tension released and we all let it out.

It took another hour to get us all out and get our belongings back to us. Static gave us a ride back to my house so we could pick up our bikes. I checked mine over and noticed some scratches from when I dumped it, but that didn't matter. I'd get her fixed back up easily enough. Butcher and Toxic offered to stay behind to board up my window. I was happy enough to take them up on it. I just wanted to get home to my kids, then wrap Jenny up in my arms.

We waited as Lockout spoke with Static, then rode home. We came into the clubhouse and I saw the girls asleep on the couches in the living area. As soon as the door shut Caitlyn woke up. Her eyes widened and she bolted toward us.

"Daddy!"

We all froze as Caitlyn choked out the word. It was followed by sobs as she tossed herself into my arms when I knelt down to catch her. I squeezed her tight to my chest as emotion clogged up my throat.

"Everything's alright, Love," I crooned, rocking her in my arms as she cried. It'd been a shock to hear her speak, but I could only hope that she wouldn't shut down again after this. The poor girl had been through hell and back over the last few months. All my girls had.

Looking over my shoulder, I found Jenny and Kit standing there, tears streaming down their faces as they watched me comfort my daughter.

I picked her up in my arms and headed upstairs with her. There'd be plenty of time later to ask her all the questions that were burning in the back of my throat. I settled her into bed and grinned when Auron hopped up beside her. He curled his furry body around her as I tucked her in. "Get some sleep."

"What if he comes back?" she asked me quietly.

I swear my heart fucking grew a whole size hearing her speak. "He won't be back." I considered whether to tell her the truth or not. I didn't want to freak her out, but the fear hovering there in her eyes answered the question for me. "He's dead, Cait."

Her tense little muscles relaxed hearing that and I knew I'd made the right call. "Get some sleep, okay? We'll talk in the morning."

She nodded and closed her eyes. I only had to sit with her for a few minutes until her breathing evened out. She was exhausted. I went downstairs and gathered up each of my daughters and put them into their beds.

Most everyone had wandered off to their own rooms, but Jenny, Seek, and Hush were out in the hall waiting for me. There would be time in the morning to thank my brothers and Kit for everything they'd done for me and my family.

I stepped into the hall and gripped Jenny's arm. My gaze met Hush's. "Can you stay with them for about an hour?"

"Of course," he replied. "Damn dogs practically live over here anyway." Seek laughed and pulled Hush inside my apartment.

CHAPTER 28

Jenny

I frowned as Priest pulled me down the stairs and back out into the heat of the night. The nights were only starting to cool down a little now that summer was over. I was ready for the cooler temperatures that winter would bring.

"Priest," I called out as he dragged me back out to his bike. "Where are we going?"

In answer, he pulled me in and wrapped his arms around me gently. He was breathing heavily and I craned my head back to try to catch a look at his face. He had it buried in the crook of my neck, making it impossible to read his expression.

"Give me a minute," he breathed against my skin.

I was happy to wrap my arms around him and sink into his embrace. It'd been a hell of a night. Everything had hit me while I'd sat in that confession room. I'd cried long enough that my head had been killing me by the time I was done. I wouldn't change what had happened tonight, but the guilt was tearing me up inside. I'd killed a man. How was I going to live with that?

Priest pulled back and cupped my face in his hands. "Thank you."

I blinked and shook my head. "Don't thank me for what I did." The last word came out on a choked sob.

His fingers tightened until they were digging into my skin. "You saved my daughters' lives. All four of them, Taz."

My chest tightened and I tried to hold back the tears that were threatening to fall. "I put them in danger," I cried out.

His grip gentled and he pulled me back against him as I lost the battle with my grief. Tears tracked down my face, wetting his t-shirt and cut. "None of us realized he'd be able to find her. We thought we'd covered all the bases. This was going to happen, if not tonight, then tomorrow, or the next day. All that matters is that when push came to shove you stood up for them. Stood between them and danger."

"I wouldn't ever let anything happen to them," I told him, voice muffled against his chest. "I love them."

"I know you do. And I love you."

Sobs wracked my body. "I…love you…too."

"Why all the tears, Baby?"

"I killed him," I whispered in a horrified tone. "The feel of the shovel hitting his head… Seeing him drop like that…"

He rocked me back and forth as he tightened his hug around me. "What would have happened if you hadn't hit him?"

"He was going to shoot you." There was a chance that Priest might have been able to disarm him, but in the moment I'd been so scared for his life I'd just reacted. "I couldn't stand by and do nothing." I hiccupped my way through the sentence.

"Taking a life is hard," he soothed. "Trust me, I understand that. The only thing that helps is remembering your reasons for doing so. You knew if he shot me he'd be coming after you next."

I shook my head. "I didn't care about myself-"

"I know. But if he got through you…"

"The girls," I whispered, more tears welling in my eyes. I leaned back and looked up into his face. "I couldn't let him get the girls."

He leaned down and kissed the butterfly bandage that was covering the wound on my forehead. "He'd have killed Gabby, Taylor, and Cassie. He'd have taken Cait and would have eventually killed her. Who knows what horrors she'd live through until then." His eyes darkened as he spoke. It couldn't have been easy for him to vocalize the grim future his daughters might have had, but he was doing it so he could help me.

My heart hurt with how much I loved him. It ached and I yearned to get so close to him that I burrowed into him. I wanted to be so close nothing could break us apart. It wasn't a rational feeling, but my emotions were so overwhelming in the moment it's what I needed. I knew how to gain that closeness.

Pushing up onto my toes, I kissed him. He shook his head. "I don't want to hurt you anymore than you were tonight." His hand gently went to my ribs.

"I can hardly feel them," I insisted. "The pain meds the medic gave me helped a lot, so did bandaging them." I poked at my ribs while holding his gaze. "Promise. Please Priest. Even if it hurts…I need you."

Indecision played across his features, but finally he kissed me. A real kiss this time. All thoughts of Chet and his body fled my mind, replaced with Priest. He was all I wanted to think about. He seemed to understand what I needed because he crushed me against his body and kissed me as though his life depended on it.

It was clear to me that we both needed the closeness and the release. I moaned against his lips. We were outside and though the lights from the property didn't brighten this end of the parking lot much, they still had members who patrolled the compound at night.

"Wait. We should go back inside," I whispered. "Someone's going to see us."

"Let them," he growled. He turned me away from him, my back pressed against him while his hands roamed over my body.

"I thought you guys weren't allowed to have sex outside the club-house?" I asked, remembering back to something Butcher had said.

He chuckled. "That's only a rule for Butcher. Though, Butcher doesn't know that. No one wants to see the shit he gets up to when fucking."

"Priest," I gasped as his hand snuck under my shirt and palmed my breast over my bra. The idea of someone seeing us was kind of sexy, only not when I knew I'd have to face them again. The idea of seeing someone who saw me in that position was horrifying.

He grumbled, but let go of my hip to dig into the pocket of his jeans. I looked back over my shoulder as he lifted his phone to his ear. "Hey. Take a break for the next half hour." He listened to whoever he was speaking with, but his eyes were on me. He looked down at me with a glittering, wild gaze and it made goosebumps pop up on my skin. "Yeah, I'll handle it until then." He disconnected the call and shoved the phone into his back pocket. "There. No one will be out here patrolling."

"Thank-" My grateful answer ended in a squeak when he flicked open the button on my jean shorts and shoved his hand inside.

His fingers curled as he cupped my pussy, making me gasp. "I need you, Taz."

I moaned as he used the heel of his hand to rub my clit. All I could do was nod. I knew exactly what he meant. Desire was gripping me hard and all the emotions I'd been feeling had to go somewhere. We could help each other with that release.

He bent me forward over his bike and my forehead dropped down onto the leather seat. I flinched when I remembered the broken skin there. I probably looked like a freak with a butterfly bandage on my forehead and a wrapping around my ribs. The pain meds made it so I didn't really feel much of either injury, but I hoped I hadn't just started up the bleeding again.

All thoughts fled from my mind as he gently removed my bra—leaving the wrapping below it on—being careful not to jostle my ribs. I gasped when he bent and ripped my shorts and panties down my legs. There were no injuries to my legs, so he didn't bother to be careful while removing them. I stepped out of one side, but he didn't bother pulling them all the way off, just left them lying there.

Raising my head, I tried to turn to see what he was doing, but his huge hands on my hips pinned me against the bike. He held me still effortlessly as he swiped his tongue over my core.

My mouth dropped open as pleasure sparked through my veins. He was eating my pussy from behind. I groaned low in my throat as he shoved his face against me and started licking me. I should be embarrassed because he basically had his face buried against my ass so he could lap at me, but it felt too good to worry about it. My hands clenched down on the seat on either side of my head as I laid my cheek down on it. I stared at the chrome handlebars as he made my entire world shake…or maybe that was just my legs.

One hand left my hip, but the last thing I wanted was to run away, so I stayed where he'd put me. Panting hard, I tried to hold off the orgasm that was building too quickly.

His hand encircled the back of my thigh as his tongue disappeared off my clit. I whimpered at the loss. "Fuck, Taz. Even out here I can see how wet you are." His other hand left my hip and his finger trailed up my inner thigh. "You're mine," he growled, cupping my pussy again.

"Yes," I gasped out, unable to say anything else.

"Good. The thought of anyone else seeing this pretty pussy makes me want to rip them apart."

I shook my head. There was no one else I wanted. Only him.

"Do you like getting eaten out in the middle of our parking lot? Stretched over my bike like a good little girl?"

I moaned and arched back toward him, trying to tell him nonverbally how much I needed him. My brain was so scrambled with desire I could barely speak. "Please," I whimpered.

"Please what? What does my old lady want?"

"Fuck me!"

"Soon, Baby. But first I want another taste. And I want to finger fuck you. You're waving that enticing pussy all over the place and I'm going to get my fill." His voice was low and raspy and I could tell he was as turned on as I was.

I was grateful I had his bike to lean against, because he buried his face and tongue against me again and it was all I could do to keep my knees from buckling. It didn't take him long to have me built right back up and trembling on the verge of an orgasm. As much as I needed it, I wasn't sure I was ready. Everything that'd happened throughout the night had me over sensitized and feeling raw. Coming now was going to burst the dam that was holding it all in.

"Wait, Priest."

He pulled back a little and bit my ass cheek, making me squirm. "No waiting. Give into it, Taz. Let go." He moved forward again and his tongue started flicking my clit. One of his long fingers slid inside of me and stars exploded behind my eyes.

I tried to muffle the sounds of pleasure that were spilling from my lips, but he kept pushing me higher, stretching out my orgasm until my cries filled the still night air.

With one last lick he stood up and I heard the jingling of his belt. I was a melted pile of goo, bracing myself on his bike. I couldn't have moved if I'd wanted to and I certainly didn't want to. There was no more embarrassment or worry about being discovered. After that scream all of Tucson knew I was getting railed out here.

"You want me to fuck you, Taz?"

"Yes," I moaned, arching my back and shoving my ass up in invitation.

"Tell me."

"I want you to fuck me. Please, Priest."

My eyes fluttered as he rubbed the head of his dick over my opening. I was already greedily wanting to come again. It didn't matter that the last orgasm had opened up the dam, releasing every pent up emotion that existed within me. Now I wanted him to shatter me so I could let go of them and allow them to escape out of me.

"You're so fucking wet, Baby." We both groaned as he pushed forward and his dick slid inside of me. "You grip my cock so fucking tightly. Goddamn, you're perfect."

He grunted as he pulled out to the tip then slammed back inside my body. My mouth opened on a silent cry. I'd felt that thrust in my ribs, but I wasn't about to stop him. It was more of an ache than sharp pain, so inside my head I cheered him on. This was how I needed it, how we both needed it. Hard, fast, and dirty. His hips pounded against my ass and the bike rocked below me as we absorbed his thrusts.

The friction he was creating had heat roaring through my system. His hands slid up my sides and forward so he could cup my breasts as he slammed inside of me. His fingers pinched my nipples and I cried out as they tingled and hardened further.

"Again," I moaned into the leather seat.

He leaned over me, his body blanketing mine. Whispering in my ear, he asked, "You want me to pinch those pretty nipples again? Is that what you're asking for, Baby?"

I nodded, eyes closing as the new angle caused him to stroke somewhere deep inside of me. I bit my lip to hold back the sudden need to beg him. It was all building up and pulling me down. His cock was rubbing so perfectly against me it was threatening to crack me open and I wasn't sure I'd be fixable.

One hand stayed on my breast while the other stroked down my body. His fingers settled on my clit and I panted in anticipation. I needed it. I feared it. But I trusted him and I knew he would glue me back together afterward.

"That's such a good girl. Come for me. Now," he growled the last word as he rubbed my clit. His fingers twisted my nipple and the pain merged with the pleasure coming from his dick dragging in and out of me and I obeyed.

I sucked in a deep breath as my body broke apart. He shot me straight into the stars above. His fingers kept rubbing, causing my pussy to clamp down rhythmically on him. I was only vaguely aware of him groaning as his hands went back to my hips. He raised over me and lifted my right leg up onto the bike. He arranged my body, opening me so he could slam inside of me over and over as he chased his own release.

Finally, he seated himself as deep inside my body as he could and came. His cum filled me and I let out a soft sigh of pleasure. My mind was drifting, finally silent for the first time since I'd seen Chet breaking through the window.

His forehead dropped down onto my back, between my shoulder

blades, as he enjoyed his own orgasm. Eventually, he pulled out of me, adjusted our clothing and picked me up in his strong arms.

I was relaxed in his hold—though I could feel the steady ache of my ribs as they let me know I'd done too much—as he walked across the lot toward the clubhouse. My body was sated and my mind was silent, so I ignored the thrumming of my ribs and drifted off. He had his arms around me and I felt love and trust wrapping around me like a soft blanket. I stirred as he tucked me back against him in bed. His lips brushed over the back of my head.

"Sleep, Baby."

Again, I obeyed, more than happy to rest in his arms.

CHAPTER 29

Priest

I dragged my eyes open after only a few hours of sleep. Lockout had sent a text last night saying we'd have church early this morning. He wanted to get everyone together before the day crew went out to watch over the cult compound.

Sliding out of bed, I leaned over and kissed Jenny's forehead before I pulled on my clothes. I checked in on each of the girls and kissed them as well before heading downstairs.

The officers and enforcers were gathered in the meeting room. The rest of the members were out in the living area, waiting to hear what our decision would be on how to move forward with the cult.

I sat down and looked over at Riptide. "Damn, man. When they said you hit the ground I didn't realize it was with your face."

Hush choked back a laugh. Butcher and Toxic didn't bother to hold back and their laughter rolled through the room.

Riptide was sporting a shiner and a busted up cheek. His eyes narrowed on me. "That's the fucking thanks I get for helping your ass?"

I sobered at the reminder of why he wasn't looking his usual pretty boy surfer self. Before I could answer, Toxic had to double down. "I think your face is proof that you weren't much help."

"Fuck off." He gave Toxic the finger, but smiled while doing it.

"Seriously, thanks, Rip. I appreciate it."

He sighed. "No. You don't have to thank me. I'd do anything for those girls and your old lady. Fuck. There isn't much I wouldn't do for you, you fucking asshole."

Everyone chuckled at that. Lockout walked into the room and sat down. "What's funny?"

"I just wanted to thank all of you for everything you did for my family last night," I said to the room, ignoring his question.

"They're our family, too," Lockout said.

The others nodded and that was the end of it. It was just another reminder why I chose this group of men as my family. We'd do anything for each other, even fight a bunch of cops and get tossed into a cell for most of the night.

A knock on the door drew my attention. My brows shot up when Static walked in. He grinned at Lockout and walked over to him, handing him a file folder. "Once you take a look at that, give me a call."

Lockout frowned and opened the folder as Static went to leave. "What the fuck?"

Static tossed a grin over his shoulder. "Told you you'd want to see what I had."

"How did you get this?" Lockout asked, handing the folder over to Riptide.

"Lady came in last night and bitched out the Chief. Gave me a chance to sneak into his office and copy a few things."

"That was my old lady," Hush said, pride ringing in his voice.

"Hell of a lady." Static gave him a wink then walked out.

"What's in the file?" I asked.

Riptide shook his head as he read. "It's all the background they have on Chet. No wonder they ended up wrapping up the investigation early. Chet was in deep shit."

"What kind of shit?" Hellfire asked.

Riptide handed me the folder and I started skimming through it. Whistling between my teeth, I looked over at Lockout. "No wonder Chet abandoned his life to live out in the middle of the desert with a bunch of crackpots."

"Will someone just explain," Butcher snarled in frustration.

"Chet is wanted for embezzlement," Riptide told him. "Guess he was some hedge fund guy and he ended up skimming money off the top from the company he worked for. Apparently he fell into drugs, bad. Coke, heroin, and psychedelics. Probably skimming money to pay for the habit. It all came down when he had a mental breakdown. Broke out of police custody and skipped town. That was right around the time Sherry and Cait moved out here."

"How come none of this came up when we searched for him?" I asked

"Because he did it under a different name. Holden wasn't Chet's real last name. It's Chet Young. According to these records he's suspected of several scams under a half dozen different names. Normally he just takes a chunk of money and runs. This last time though, he just lost his mind. He's never done anything illegal under his real name. Hell, he's never done *anything* under his real name, not even get married. He did that under the name Holden. In the last decade he hasn't so much as gotten a credit card under the name Chet Young. We didn't find anything for Chet Holden except for that apartment and when Rat searched police records under that name, nothing came up, not even his marriage certificate. The man's history is a rat maze of names and crimes."

"But when the cops got his prints in the morgue they found his real identity, Chet Young," Lockout continued. "They had his wallet, according to the report, and figured out he was using a fake ID and then started digging into him and found all the aliases he'd used in the past. Once they had his real name and a photo, it all went quickly from there."

"So anytime he did something illegal he shed that identity and started a new one," I mused.

"Exactly. It wasn't until he started snorting his way through life that it all came apart. Then Sherry left him and he lost it."

"So he decided to follow her since he had to get the hell out of dodge anyway," Hush concluded.

"I found something last night, too," Riptide added.

Lockout frowned. "You didn't get home from the hospital until after one a.m. How did you have time to find anything?"

Riptide shrugged. "Couldn't sleep."

"This have anythin' to do with the woman we saw out at the compound?" Hush asked with a sly look.

We'd been keeping a close eye on that place and we hadn't seen the woman since the day she'd taken the beating for the little girl. I hoped like hell they hadn't killed her. Something about her had piqued Riptide's interest and he wasn't going to forgive himself if she ended up in a shallow grave because we hadn't intervened.

"You want to know what I found, or not?" Riptide asked, scowling at Hush.

Hush shrugged and waited, knowing our friend wouldn't keep the information to himself.

Riptide tipped back onto the back legs of the chair, a habit for him, and gave us all a grim smile. "In order to get those court documents so quickly Chet had to go down to the courthouse. They eventually put all that shit online and you can look cases up by people's names, no problem. But since the paperwork had only been filed yesterday morning, he must have been told he had to go in person to access it. They make you fill out some paperwork when you go to the courthouse."

I leaned forward, elbows on the table, wondering why he looked so fucking smug. We already knew Chet's name and the last address he'd stayed at and still our best techies—Riptide included—hadn't been able to find anything on the weasel.

"Imagine my surprise when Chet Holden didn't request the information."

We all glanced around in confusion. Ricochet voiced the question we were all wondering. "Who did then?"

"Derek Holden."

Smokehouse grinned and slapped a hand on the table. "That can't be a coincidence."

"Exactly what I thought, so I hacked into the courthouse security footage. It wasn't Chet who went to the courthouse. Did a bit more digging and found out that Derek Holden is Chet's cousin."

I flipped through the file folder in front of me and a grim smile covered my face. "Care to guess where else Derek worked?"

"No shit?" Toxic asked. "He worked for the same company as Chet?"

"Gladen International," I said in confirmation. "Says here he went missing right around the same time as his cousin. Cops suspect he had something to do with the embezzlement."

"Found a bunch of emails between the two once I had Derek's name," Riptide continued. "Turns out Derek was in charge of setting up the offshore account and making sure the money was squeaky clean before the cousins planned to use it. He was in Tennessee working on that up until a week ago. The plan was to have him come here and join the cult. It was the perfect hiding hole for them."

"They could disappear off the grid for a while and by the time they resurfaced the heat would have died down," Butcher said, shaking his head. "Not a bad plan."

"But he couldn't let Sherry go," Ricochet added. "Little did he know that would end up getting us involved and himself killed."

"Were you able to find out anything else about the cult?" I asked.

Riptide shook his head. "They didn't talk about that over email. In fact, they never directly mention it. They just talked in circles, but if you know about the cult it wasn't too hard to figure out."

"Back to square one there," Hellfire muttered, crossing his arms over his chest.

"Actually... I have an idea," Riptide said, his eyes straying to Lockout.

Lock's jaw tightened and he looked pissed off, though a bit resigned. Whatever Rip was about to say he already knew about it.

"What's that?" Hush prompted.

"One of us joins the cult."

I snorted. "There's no way they're going to just let some random person waltz up to their compound and ask to join. And we have no clue how they're finding their people. Pretending to be a hiker out in the desert is likely to end in a death sentence for one of us."

"Probably not one of the women," Butcher offered. When every eye glared his way, he shrugged. "I was just saying. I didn't mean we were sending one of them out there, fuck." He closed his mouth and scowled at us.

"How does this idea work, Rip?" Smokehouse asked, getting us back on track.

"I'll take Derek Holden's place."

Silence fell over the room and we all looked over at Lockout. The dark look on our president's face told us he wasn't fond of this plan, but honestly we didn't have a lot of choice. We hadn't been able to dig up anything on this cult and infiltrating it was going to give us the answers we needed.

"That's fucking dangerous," Butcher muttered. "These types of people aren't the kind you want to fuck with."

"You'll be alone," I added. "Derek wouldn't just be showing up with friends in tow."

Riptide nodded. "It'd just be me."

"Why you?" Hush asked.

"First, it was my idea. Second," he motioned to the file and I looked down. His point didn't need to be spoken out loud. He looked similar enough that if anyone had been given a picture of Derek Holden they wouldn't question it. Especially not with Riptide's longish hair. He'd cut it recently, but it still hung down past his ears. It was a surfer thing, he'd told me once before. He liked having it long and had only ever cut it short because of military regulations.

"We'll give it a few days," Lockout told everyone. "Think it over. We're voting on this, so if majority says no, we find another way."

Riptide looked pissed, but he knew better than to challenge Lockout on the decision. Instead, he looked around the table. "I can do this. I need to do this."

"Is it because of that girl?" Hush asked him, pinning him with a dark look. "You don't owe her your life, Rip. And that's what could fuckin' happen out there. If somethin' happens to you, we won't be there to back you up."

"I know. And no it's not her. Or not just her," he amended. "We need to shut this shit down for good." He cast us all a beseeching look. "Let me do this."

"Two days," Lockout told us. "That will give us time to get Derek Holden in police custody and ensure we have enough time to think it over. Plus, we need time to go over the recordings and notes from the recon team."

He ended the meeting and we all filed out of the room. A hand closed over my shoulder and I glanced back at Riptide. We stood aside and let the rest of our brothers move down the hall.

"I have something for you," he told me with a shit-eating grin. He handed over a USB.

"What's this?" I scowled down at it.

"The little film you made for me last night." When I frowned in confusion, he chuckled. "You always forget…I have cameras all over this compound, Priest. That way if our patrols miss anything, I'll still see it."

Realization dawned with those words and I glared at him. My hardened gaze didn't stop the words from escaping his mouth, though.

"You need to tan that ass. It was like a fucking beacon on the video while you were thrusting away." He laughed and took off down the hall before I could get hands on him. He knew better than to mention anything about my old lady, not that he'd make fun of her in any way, but I knew I'd be hearing about this for some time to come.

God damn it.

CHAPTER 30

Jenny

I wrapped my arm around Caitlyn's shoulders, offering her silent comfort. We'd given her a day to unwind after Chet's attack, but the guys had questions and now that she was speaking it was time for answers. I stayed close to make sure the guys didn't revert to their military selves and inadvertently interrogate the poor girl.

"Just take it slowly, sweet girl," I whispered.

"I'm okay," she insisted. She took a deep breath and met Lockout's eyes. "He killed Mama."

Priest picked up her hand and held it. She was sitting between us on the couch and Lockout was seated on a coffee table in front of her. None of us wanted to push her too far, but there was a determined glint in her eyes. Sadness was there too, of course, but she wanted to help us.

"Ethan caught Mama trying to escape with me-"

"Ethan is the guy in charge?" Priest asked. He'd told me they'd heard his name the night they'd broken into Chet's apartment and on Riptide's surveillance recordings.

"Yeah." Caitlyn and Sherry had only been there a short time, a couple of days at most. Kids lost track of time easily so we weren't sure exactly, but we knew that by the time Sharon called the cops and they finally allowed her to file a missing persons report they'd been there for at least twenty-four hours.

"Da-" She bit her lip and gave Priest an apologetic look. As if almost calling the man who'd sired her Daddy was offensive to her new father. Priest swiped a soothing hand over her back. "Chet was there for a long time, he brought us there. Mama tried to fight him, but he made us stay. Once we were there he told us all the rules. Mama wouldn't listen. Ethan said that she was tainted and beyond being saved. Both of us were. So he told Chet to get rid of us." She whispered the last sentence.

Even without using the word 'kill' the little girl had picked up on Ethan's meaning. I wanted to march out to that compound and strangle the man. I'd already killed one guy—and even though that weighed heavily on my heart—I'd do so again to get rid of the prick who had set Chet loose on his ex-wife and daughter. I thought about that for a second.

What kind of power does he have over these people that he says, "Kill your wife and daughter" and they just do it? No hesitation.

"Why did you and your mom go out to the village?" Lockout asked. He was being as gentle as he could with her. We all were. This had been a traumatic experience for her and we didn't want to make it worse.

"He took us from home," Caitlyn told us. "Made us go with him. He said if we didn't he'd hurt me." Her bottom lip wobbled and I leaned over and squeezed her against my side in a hug.

"You're doing so good, Cait," Priest said encouragingly. "We're almost done. Do you remember anything from the village? Anyone other than Ethan who stood out?"

"There was a nice lady who helped us. She undid our ropes and showed us how to leave."

My stomach sank and I looked back over at Priest. It had to be the woman who'd tried to help Abigail, the other little girl. Riptide had said they'd called her Sloane. At least we knew she hadn't been killed for her part in helping Sherry and Caitlyn disappear. I just hoped she was okay. I knew the guys were coming up with a plan to rescue any of the people who weren't out there willingly.

"Thank you, Caitlyn," Lockout told her, giving her a smile.

She answered it with her own and Priest took her upstairs to hang out with her sisters.

"She's a brave girl," Lockout said, shaking his head. "I've seen full-grown men who haven't dealt with situations like that with half as much grace."

I nodded. "She deserves happiness."

"She hit the jackpot with you and Priest." He patted my knee then stood up and left.

* * *

"Have a good day at school!" I gave each of the girls a hug. We were dropping them off on their first day of school. Already the lady watching over the drop off line was scowling at us because we'd gotten out of the vehicle and had caused the line to come to a screeching halt.

It was their first day back. She could wait on us. Gabby wrapped her arms around me and gave me a fierce hug. Her attitude toward me had already been changing, but since the other night, she'd done a complete one-eighty. She knew now what lengths I was willing to go to for her dad, her sisters, and herself.

Her hug made my heart flip-flop in my chest and I had to swallow back happy tears. This was going to be the beginning for us as a family. It was everything I wanted.

"Bye!" she called happily as she and the others ran up the walk.

I turned and met the scowl of the school employee. "Get in your vehicle. No stopping," she snarled at us.

"Who shit in your cereal?" I snapped back.

Priest was laughing as we got back into the SUV he'd borrowed from the club. "I think the expression is 'who pissed in your Cheerios,'" he told me.

I shrugged. "She got the point." I frowned as he pulled out onto the road, but in the opposite direction from the clubhouse. "Where are we going?"

"You'll see." We fell into a comfortable silence as we drove. He pulled into a parking lot and I gasped in pleasure when I saw we were at the Wildlife Museum.

I'd told him a long time ago—when I was still living in Texas—that this was one of my favorite spots in the city. "We're going in?" It wasn't actually a museum. It was a huge outdoor space that was like a zoo for the local wildlife that could be found in Arizona. I loved walking through and looking at all the animals who lived here.

He chuckled. "Yup. That's why I brought you."

"Don't you have church?" I knew they were making the decision today whether to send Riptide in undercover. Most of the guys were uneasy with the idea of him being in there alone, but Priest had explained that there wasn't much else they could do.

"That's not until tonight. You've got me all day." He wrapped his arm over my shoulders and I snuggled into his side.

We walked along and I enjoyed the calm early morning hours. The animals were active and playful and it was nice not having anything menacing hanging over our heads. I let go and enjoyed the time with him. Since I'd gotten back to Tucson things had been crazy and filled with grief and fear, but everything seemed to be clicking into place.

Soon the cult would be taken care of and we wouldn't have to worry about them anymore. Even more importantly Caitlyn was safe. Chet wouldn't ever bother her again. Our family would protect her.

Priest tugged me to a stop and I turned and my eyes widened as I found him down on one knee behind me. My lungs refused to cooperate and my breath stalled out inside of me.

"Jenny." He hadn't used my name in so long it felt weird to hear him say it. "There was a time that I thought I'd never get married again. That it wasn't worth the pain that came along once it ended."

He smiled as he saw the hope on my face. "You're worth it all. Not that I plan on letting you go anywhere," he told me with a stern look. He dug into the back pocket of his jeans and pulled out a box.

Flicking it open, he looked up at me. "Will you marry me?"

My mouth was still hanging open and I couldn't breathe. I slowly nodded up and down, trying to make my lungs work.

Priest smiled, his head nodding up and down in rhythm with mine. "Is that a yes?"

My eyes misted over and I managed to choke out, "Yes!" He got up and put the beautiful sapphire ring on my finger. I wasn't a diamond kind of woman, never had been. The beautiful hues of sapphires had always called to me and the fact that he'd remembered that—remembered so much of what I'd told him in those early days—made my heart sing.

He wrapped me up in his arms and gave me a kiss that made my head spin. This gorgeous man and his amazing daughters were going to be mine—forever.

A laugh belted out of me when he tossed me over his shoulder and smacked me on the ass. "Let's go see those otters of yours."

I knew in that moment he was going to spend the rest of our lives making me the happiest woman in the world.

SNEAK PEEK

Riptide

Everyone was slowly piling into the meeting room. I was apprehensive, an unusual and almost foreign feeling for me. Covert Operations weren't really a thing for Green Berets. Our main function had been to train other troops. We'd trained our own men and other countries' armies on how to effectively fight. The best way to train those forces was to fight alongside them, but nothing was ever undercover. That kind of work was for the Feds.

Go behind enemy lines, lay up in the woods, hide out in an abandoned building and prepare an ambush? That was too easy. I'd done that more times than I could count. But to actually go into the enemy's lair and pretend to be one of them? That was new for me. And yeah, I was nervous. My life, the lives of my brothers—if the cult found out who I was working with—and the lives of innocents out there on the compound could be at stake if I fucked this up.

I thought about the woman I'd seen only a few weeks ago—Sloane. I hadn't stopped thinking about her since then. I only saw her for a few minutes. She'd been trying to stop the cult mob from beating a kid. She'd taken the punishment instead. At the time I'd tried to run in and save her, but my brothers had pulled me back. I can't recall ever going into a blind rage like that in my life. But when I saw her, that gorgeous long brown hair glinting in the light, eyes so blue they shone from a hundred yards away, and a heart big enough to care about a child that way, I hadn't been able to help myself. To see those men hurt something so perfect had me seeing red. Now I was about to go undercover, into the cult. I would need to contain my anger, or else I would never be able to rescue her.

As if my own imagination wasn't enough to keep me on edge, Butcher, our resident psychopath, was serious and somber. That was never a good sign. I took my seat at the table, directly across from him. He had some expertise in this area, so as much as I appreciated the others being there, I needed to be face to face with him. None of the rest of us had dealt with cults before. At least not in this capacity. He was the one who was going to help me get through this, hopefully alive.

"Alright, everyone, settle down. Sit down and shut up." There was instant silence at Lockout's order. "It's time to vote. Are we sending Riptide in?"

He didn't need to clarify. We'd been thinking about nothing else since he'd announced two days ago that we'd be putting this to a vote. It was time to decide and I sure as hell hoped the others were on the same page.

Everyone was uneasy about this. We never sent our brothers out alone. The guilt was heavy on their faces. They didn't like that I was going into the lion's den without them. Shit, if I could figure out a way to bring one of them along with me, I'd jump on the chance. Unfortunately, Chet only had one cousin that was supposed to be joining him. We'd had no trouble tracking him down and handing him over to the cops. There was a rap sheet on him a mile long that would keep him detained long enough for me to get through this mission.

That meant that my brothers would have to sit back and wait, powerless, until I was able to bring them something actionable on the cult. In that regard, I had it easy, and didn't envy them. I would be too busy trying not to blow my cover to ever get bored and feel powerless.

Before I could answer, Toxic spoke up. "We could still kill the bastard outright. There's no need to send Rip in alone. He would still get his girlfriend and the cult would be done."

I ignored the dig about 'my girlfriend'. Everyone at this table knew the reason I'd volunteered was because of her. Her stunning beauty, her courage, her defiance, she was pulling at me, drawing me in. I needed to figure out what it was so I could go back to my normal life. A life without her haunting my dreams.

"Won't work." Butcher's tone was wooden. "Back when I worked for the secret squirrel agency, more than once we ran across these Jonestown type cults. All over the damn world. For as much as they seem different, they really are all the same. They all have a basic religion they start from, Christian, Muslim, Hindi, whatever. They begin with the accepted religion, but then pervert it into a worship of the cult leader himself."

"That tracks," Dash interrupted. "This guy frequently calls himself the Earth God."

We'd been listening in on the recordings Dash and I had managed to get off the cult. It wasn't much since they rarely held their weird ass meetings out in the open. We hadn't infiltrated the camp, so I hadn't been able to set any surveillance equipment up in any of the buildings.

Butcher shot him a look so stern that Dash almost fell out of his chair. "Don't get ahead of me, I'll get to that."

"Sorry."

"Butcher," I muttered, getting him back on track. My muscles were tense and I was practically vibrating in my seat. I was amped up to ten and itching to go. The sooner I started, the sooner I finished. Everyone just needed to agree first.

"Anyway," Butcher said, focusing back on me, "these guys prey on the weak and disenfranchised. You'd think that they'd go after the dumb and gullible, but that's never how it works. The cultists tend to be smart, capable, and fanatically dangerous. It's like once they have something new to set their sights on they come alive again. In a way that usually isn't good for anyone." He looked over at Toxic. "It's why you can't just outright kill their leader. The consequences are always unpredictable and violent. They might commit mass suicide, killing off the women and children first. They might engage in ritual sacrifice. Or they might attack. Randomly kill dozens or hundreds of civilians that aren't even connected to the cult."

Butcher stopped and rubbed his forehead, as though he needed a minute to shove down whatever memories were battering at him.

I pushed down the thought of her getting killed by the other followers. I couldn't focus on that right now, or I'd drive myself crazy. If killing Ethan would put her in jeopardy, then that option was off the table. No way would I let her get hurt. I looked back at Butcher. I was left with the feeling that, more than once, he'd tried the direct approach by killing a leader, and that it backfired. That he was talking from personal experience. We all stayed silent while he gathered himself.

"We only have one real option here, and that's to send Riptide in. Let him become part of the cult. Identify the members that are there against their will. Once we get them out, then, and only then, can we take on a direct approach. Kill them all."

It still seemed like an extreme approach. Priest spoke up. "Far be it for me to advocate for police assistance, but we're talking about dozens of people here. How is this not mass murder?"

"Mass murder?" Butcher's head snapped up and locked onto Priest. His normal, wild eyes were back, so dark they nearly looked black. "Have you been listening to Dash's recordings of these guys? Have you listened to his 'sermons'? This isn't your run-of-the-mill scam like a pop-up church. Some hillbilly preacher, rolling into town and filling the collection plate before bailing. This is the real deal." He looked back towards me so he could really emphasize his next words. "Ethan is a believer. A true believer. He believes that he is God incarnate, flesh and blood on earth. That's why he calls himself the Earth God. That's not some hippie tree hugging term. No, he believes that he is God, here on earth. And they believe it too. Most of them anyways. Hopefully not all of them."

"What about gettin' the innocents out, then lettin' the cops handle it?" Hush suggested.

We weren't the kind to go to law enforcement with anything. We handled our own shit. So for some of our brothers to consider bringing in the police it spoke to how dangerous all this was. How much they didn't want to have to send me into that place alone. It wasn't my idea of a fucking good time either, but I was the best choice. I came closest to fitting Derek's—Chet's cousin's—description. Hell, our first names even matched. Add to that I was the VP for the club and had more authority to take action than anyone—other than Lockout. It meant I wouldn't need to check in before making decisions. Lockout and I had already talked and he was giving me full approval to do what needed to be done while I was in. If I fucked things up we'd handle them once we took out the cult.

"The cops would get slaughtered. Oh sure, eventually they would call in the FBI and end up taking them down. But it would take years of surveillance before they even attempted to arrest or kill the members. In the meantime, any of the cultists who aren't there by choice would be subjected to this sick fuck's every whim. Besides all that, cops are stupid, and they have rules to follow. How many would die before they figured out what they were dealing with? Remember Jonestown? They killed a U.S. Congressman. The part they leave out is how many CIA and FBI tried to infiltrate the place. Over a dozen agents. All of them were killed. Better that we just take care of it ourselves."

Butcher's outlook made sense. He'd been part of a team that hadn't needed to follow any kind of procedure while he'd been in the military. The rest of us still had to follow those 'rules' so we knew exactly what he was talking about and how those protocols bound our hands so many times in the past. He was right and I saw the resignation on everyone's face. We had to do this ourselves.

I thought of the woman again. The way she took a beating for that child. It left me with a selfish hope that maybe she wasn't one of them. Maybe I could save her. A pang of guilt struck me as I realized that I almost didn't care if no one else there could be saved. So long as I could get her out. That didn't mean I wouldn't try. The more people we saved the better. One, because it would make what I was about to do worth it if we could help them. And two, because that meant less people for us to fight in the end.

"But if they really do think he is their God, wouldn't killing him break them out of their trance? Prove that he isn't their 'Earth God'?" Ricochet insisted.

"You'd think so, but too many times that has proven not to be the case. They're too far gone, too obsessed with him to see it like that. Their minds will collectively create a story around it. He returned to heaven, rejoined the spiritual plane, blah, blah, blah. The end result is the same, mass murder or mass suicide. And the mass suicide is almost never voluntary."

"Time to vote," Lockout said, putting an end to the other options. "All those in favor, raise your hands." He started it off by putting his in the air.

I gave him a grateful look. He didn't want to send me in there any more than the other men did, but I'd pulled him aside yesterday and asked him to do this for me. With him voting in favor the others were more likely to do so as well. He hadn't asked me to explain. He trusted that I knew what I needed and I had to do this.

Looking around, I relaxed a fraction. Every hand at the table was up. No one looked pleased about it, but they'd voted in favor. I was going in.

Lockout stayed quiet for what felt like a whole minute, watching me, before he spoke again. "Last chance. It's not too late to pull the plug on this."

"I'm good." I said definitively. "I've made up my mind. Butcher, run me through this. Tell me everything you know about cults. I don't want to end up buried out in the desert because I don't know what the fuck I'm doing. We know there's no taking him down, not by assassination. I assume that discrediting him and making his worshippers abandon him is out of the question?" I asked, already knowing the answer.

"Not a chance. Chet Holden killed his wife and was going to kill his daughter for this creep." Butcher was watching Priest as he said it.

Priest was squeezing the end of the table so hard I thought that he might snap it. He'd adopted Chet's daughter, Caitlyn. The thought of anyone hurting that girl was enough to send him into a flying rage. But it rammed home Butcher's point. The 'true believers' were beyond our ability to help. All we could do was rescue the children and those kept there against their will.

Butcher focused back on me. "Don't forget that. You aren't smart—or crafty—enough to discredit him, and he'll kill you if you try."

Don't forget about the woman. One way or another, she's coming with you.

"How do I fit in once I'm there?"

"That's going to be the fun part."

I groaned inwardly. Butcher's idea of fun wasn't what the rest of us would consider a good time. It always turned out to be horrible in one way or another.

"You're the new guy, everyone will be suspicious of you. Play stupid, apologize for everything. Only ask *him* for forgiveness, though. The other members are going to test you, try to assert dominance over you. Stand your ground to a point, but don't attack them. You may even have to take some punishment at the beginning."

Gritting my teeth, I thought again about the woman, and how they had circled her and kicked her for standing up for the girl. *This is going to be hard.* Not losing my shit over that kind of behavior would take all my willpower. It was one thing to let people beat on me, but to stand back and watch them hit women and children. I sighed and relaxed my hands, which had balled up into fists at the thought.

"Oh, another thing. They'll have a strict set of rules. Guaranteed they'll be bizarrely contradictory. Like, don't touch the children, but women are fair game. Don't rape a married woman, but an unmarried one has no protections. Never mind the contradictions, don't try to make sense out of them. Just don't violate the rules, and never point out the contradiction. They might kill you on sight. Just nod and agree."

Fuck. Me. How the hell was I going to pull this off?

ACKNOWLEDGMENTS

A huge thank you to my partner in crime and Co-Author, Frank Jensen. I couldn't do this without you.

To my amazing beta readers Heather Ashley, Aurora Welkin, and J.L. Avery thank you so much for all of your time and effort you spent helping me make these books the best they can be!

Also a heartfelt thank you to my editor, Ce-Ce Cox of Outside-Eyes Editing and Proofreading! Thank you for catching everything I always seem to miss, especially those pesky commas.

Thank you to the awesome Kari March of Kari March Designs for giving me gorgeous covers each and every time.

To my wonderful and perfect fans! Thank you all for giving an unknown author a shot and for reading my books! I hope you love them and I can't show my gratitude for you enough.

Lastly, to my family, you're the best. Thank you for the love and support.

ABOUT THE AUTHOR

Cathleen and Frank live in SE Oregon where they have a family farm. They split their days between working with their animals and writing. Both left a law enforcement background to pursue their passions and for Cathleen that meant picking back up a long-forgotten hobby with writing. They strive to bring readers steamy, action-packed stories that provide hours of entertainment.

ALSO BY CATHLEEN COLE

The Vikings MC Series

Heart of Steel

The Viking's Princess

All's Fair In Love & Juárez

'Til Encryption Do Us Part

Bass & Trouble

War & Pieces

Heavy Is The Crowne

The Vikings MC-Tucson Chapter

Hush

Priest

Riptide

The Discord Series

Havoc

Inferno

Deviant

Malice

Soldiers of Misfortune

Captured By The Mercenaries

Protected By The Green Berets

Saved By The Marines

Printed in Great Britain
by Amazon